Everything, Except You

Emma Jordan

About the Author

Emma Jordan has been reading and writing since childhood, in between teaching, travelling and raising her family. She doesn't go a day without listening to music, and loves a three minute story.

Emma lives in Devon's Plymouth with her family, and when she's not *front and centre* at gigs she can be found at the beach.

For Eve –

my favourite reader and writer

Prologue

Lucy

'Dr. Rawcliffe, I can't believe what I've just done!'

Startled from my planning reverie, I looked up at the sudden outburst in my office doorway.

'Whatever is the matter, Tallie? Come in, come in.' I reached up to the bookshelf, behind the Austens and Brontes, for the good cookies; dark chocolate and coconut.

The final year student sank down on the sofa and let out a huge sigh. I waited, patiently, offering the Cookie Monster tin.

'I thought I'd secured the perfect research trip.'

'Yes, studying Mark Twain. At Yale.'

'In Connecticut. I'd be living in New England in the actual fall, not autumn! I've totally miscalculated the scholarship. By half!' Tallie reached for a cookie, chomping both miserably and dramatically.

'Do you have your flight booked?' I asked.

'Yes, I'm supposed to fly out in the middle of next August. And then I'll be eating irony and drinking misery! This is why I study literature, and not mathematical equations.'

'What do you remember of the playwriting module?' I asked, pulling up my emails on my computer.

'I remember Arthur Miller.'

'That's good – the Crucible or Death of a Salesman?'

'Oh, seventeenth century witchcraft for sure; I can't handle modernity.'

I smiled inwardly at my own twenty year old self shunning the twentieth century; my almost-thirty year old self still hadn't reconciled with post-war literature or culture, no matter that I'd been teaching it for the last five years. Books would always outweigh technology in my world.

I found the email I was searching for.

'There's a group of secondary school students who need a drama teacher. The position pays twenty pounds an hour, ten hours a week, for the year ahead.'

Tallie held her cookie in her mouth, fingers dancing across her phone. She shot her head up, beaming at the possible income. 'I'd be the perfect drama teacher!' she declared, suddenly rising from the sofa.

'Here's the school. I'll email their faculty head, and let them know you're heading over tomorrow. Just so you know, the kids have a reputation for being tough.' 'Nothing will stand between me and Samuel Longhorn Clemens.' Tallie declared, fiercely. 'You're the best, Dr. Rawcliffe!' She threw her arms around me, and I laughed as the passionate student almost levitated out of the door.

I returned to the scheme of work and first four weeks of lessons, and immersed myself in poetic devices for the rest of the afternoon, only briefly looking up to stretch my muscles and sip my peppermint tea. I needed to complete the planning tonight, so that I could focus on the upcoming conference in Plymouth this weekend, which I was dreading.

There were too many social engagements that I'd have to prepare for over the three days.

The prospect of listening to academics share their work on Victorian Gothic Literature was the main reason I'd agreed to attend. And Moira had made it very clear that in order to become the next, and youngest, Head of Department, I had to meet living people, and make those cross-university connections that would support my application for headship when she retired.

My tummy rumbled and I realised I'd skipped lunch.

I packed the papers into my bag, locked up my office, and walked the five minutes from my building to Sam's. Hidden from traffic, on one of the many squares around London's Bloomsbury area, the inside lights were bright enough to continue work, and the burgers delicious enough that I wouldn't need to cook later. A bowl of cereal, my usual go-to dinner, wouldn't help overcome my nerves at trying to engage with strangers this weekend in quite the same way that a cheeseburger would.

Cain

'Today, you lucky listeners of WPEK radio, we have British singer-songwriter Cain Adams here with us to talk about his upcoming...second...album, and possibly a run of shows in the fall! How about that?!'

 'I love being on the road, and I can't wait to perform for you all again'. I spoke close to the microphone, catching the thumbs up of the DJ and trying to work out if this was the sixth or eleventh slot of the morning.

 'Listeners, don't you just love that accent?! We'll be right back after this commercial from our sponsors.'

 I looked around the glass booth, the giant station lettering watching over the broadcasters, and I could be anywhere. Radio studios all looked the same, and that hyperactivity in a morning was a little too much, even for me.

 But I knew this wasn't really work; music ran through my veins.

 Since writing songs as a teenager, and pounding the floors of Nashville's Broadway begging artists to play my stories, I love every minute of this life, especially when the songs reached number one, and the arena-headlining artists started to seek out my door.

 Yeah, I wish I was writing from my beachfront home in North Cornwall right now, but every month or so I fly out to Nashville when needed. And an album gathers a lot of air miles.

 After years of writing for others, I was finally performing my own songs, and I'd never known energy like night after night of playing to a crowd, hearing them sing my words back to me.

The promotional activity was a necessity, and I was grateful every day for the opportunities that afforded me. To be on the stage, feeling the music run through me, straight to an awaiting audience.

'And we're back, WPEK listeners, with Cain Adams. And, you know what, Cain?'

'Er, what's that?' I asked. Suddenly the host looked at a sheet of paper that had been handed to him.

'Listeners, we have an exclusive for you this morning. I've just heard that Cain's first album, Before you Wake, has just been certified platinum. One million sales, people. Cain, can I ask how you feel right now?'

Edit, edit, edit.

'Wow. That's just incredible news, man, thank you. And thank you to everybody who has bought a CD or downloaded on to their devices. Did you hear I have a second record out soon?'

I managed to talk to the broadcaster for a few more minutes, and then called Sarah aside when the slot ended. Sarah, the woman I couldn't live without.

'What time is lunch?'

'One more press interview and you can devour your steak, son. Then there's a run of phone interviews this afternoon, Eastern, Mountain and Pacific Time.'

I nodded, wrapped my arms around her in thanks, as she dealt with her phone and wandered to my happy place; the present moment. No matter what's happened before, or what's around the corner, enjoy every sense of every minute. That's what Mum taught me, and I lived by those words.

Lunch was served on the bus, buffet style. Seb and Jam - Nashville natives, but essentially the only band I need - dived right on in talking about family and chords and football. We'd only met in Nashville last year, and already we were as close as brothers. I thank that difficult artist every time we play on any stage, for not listening to reason on my production of the track and insisting we turned a ballad into an upbeat pop tune. When I walked out of that studio Seb and Jam were right behind me.

They attended some promotional tours, but the interviewers only wanted to hear from Cain. Didn't matter that Seb was the best bassist ever heard across the US, and Jam has the beats second only to Queen's Roger Taylor.

By midnight I was done.

At least for today, Sarah informed me, as she handed me the week's itinerary. Flight home to England in two days, then a run of gigs, including one on Friday near my home town. That would balance out my energy. Then back in Nashville the following week.

Mr Sarah - Seb - was a lucky man indeed.

I climbed into the tour bus and crashed out on the bed, my arms hanging over the side.

I couldn't face another bland hotel room. At least the bus felt like home.

1

Lucy

Friday, 1st September

Dear Elle

Finally arrived in Plymouth (Devon; I haven't returned to the States already) after almost four hours on the train...honestly can't remember the last time I travelled so long and was still in the UK, and STILL on the south coast.   Hotel has great views of the sea, although there are no immediate beaches nearby, just a long walk to the harbour. Reception said I'd have to either catch a ferry to Cornwall (not as dramatic as it sounds – it's right across a river) or drive for around half an hour. And we both know how rubbish I am at twentieth century things, like driving. Anyway, I'm only here for the three day conference.
 Hope classes are going well.
 Love always, Lucy.

I rummaged in my purse for a first class stamp and secured it on the corner of the postcard to my sister. Checking the time on my watch, the familiar swirl of the unknown doing lengths across my abdomen, I reluctantly left my long-ago-drained pot of tea on the table.

I couldn't put dinner off any longer.

I walked to the hotel's reception desk to hand the card in for posting and exited the hotel. The sun was just starting the descent over the sea, a stunning backdrop to the red and white lighthouse in front of me, and the depths of the pinks, oranges and blues illuminating the sky arrested my feet. The warmth against my cheeks made me wonder when I'd last wandered alongside such a view. Perhaps last summer, when I strolled around the pretty villages of Cape Cod.

I untangled my sunglasses from my hair, lowered them to my nose, and began the slow walk across this new city.

I'd spent most of these last few weeks researching for this conference paper on Emily Bronte and I'd barely seen daylight some days. The nineteenth century Yorkshire family of novelists was a fascinating story, with Emily the centre of my attention, for her introverted character and reasoning voice. Had she not written under a male pseudonym, along with her sisters Anne and Charlotte, the world might never have known the drama of Wuthering Heights, Cathy and Heathcliffe.

Visiting the north again had also meant a brief catch up with Elle, in the neutral city of Leeds, between her social life and A Level revision. Away from Manchester.

I followed Plymouth's coastal curve towards the university area, the sun warming my neck. I'd seen the sun disappear over the River Thames many times, usually as I pottered around the South Bank at the weekend with my bag of English literature papers to mark, or glimpsed the rays bouncing around Trafalgar Square as I headed to The Dinner Club. In early summer I even managed a few bare foot meanderings in the green squares of Bloomsbury, on my short walk home from work.

But this ocean vista was only just over three hours away. I'd heard some colleagues travelled that distance on their daily commute.

It was just a shame my stomach was flickering between shrunk Alice and giant Alice, even though I wanted neither drink nor food right now.

Unable to delay dinner any longer, I reluctantly left the waterfront and continued the walk north across Plymouth's city centre, to the welcome social that had been arranged by the English department.

My nerves wrestled with fight or flight every step I walked.

Sanctuary with the sunset, or small talk with tipsy strangers?

Career or unemployment?

As I snail-paced towards my fate, I spun around when I sensed the light change behind me, apologetic at having to leave before the inky blue of the final curtain call. Next Saturday I would visit the National Gallery for the Impressionists' collection, so my eyes could feast on the lights of Monet.

I wonder if he ever made it to the sunsets of Devon?

The restaurant chosen for tonight's dinner also doubled as a late night bar, and was located just off the university campus.

I hadn't felt such dread since my own A Level days, when my future depended upon the grades to leave the house I grew up in. Actually, with years of solitary study behind me, I'd been confident about my academic destiny. I wish I was sitting an exam right now, instead of trying to make small talk on a Friday night.

Normally, September is my favourite month; new terms signaling the end of long summers, the promise of crisp, golden sycamore and horse chestnut leaves underfoot, unexpected cloudless, cornflower-blue skies. Autumn is the season of the senses, a comfort before the dark deluge of winter and shallow neon nights.

But for the next 52 hours I'd have to put on my social face. I just hope that I don't come across as too bolshie or too Victorian-teacher aloof, to people who could judge me in thirty seconds and affect my promotion to Head of English next year.

One of my panic attacks would almost be a welcome distraction.

Except that I was in a city, my natural habitat.

But my body started to feel light.

I stopped walking, leant back against a cool, tiled wall and gripped my eyes closed.

Find the blue, Rawcliffe, I instructed myself, drawing in Plymouth's waterfront horizon to my mind; forget-me-not blue giving way to cerulean.

Inhale, exhale, inhale, exhale.

Follow the thin blue line.

Sea meets sky.

Keep going.

Back and forth.

The attack settled quickly; I hadn't even hunkered down.

I was merely nervous, not fearful.

If only my coping mechanisms were all that I needed to be Moira's successor.

After a few more minutes of controlled breathing, I pushed myself off the wall and turned the corner to the restaurant.

As I approached the brightly lit building on the hill, I recognised the canvas bags of some conference delegates and I quickly followed the people inside, adjusting my own cloth bag over my shoulder.

I'd much rather deal with the daytime activities, whether that was participating in panel discussions, quizzing experts or analysing post-anything theories, that will take up tomorrow and Sunday. Even after half a decade of supporting students through their own careers, the evening networking – where most of the achievements and contacts are made – is still alien to me. It probably didn't help that I'm not keen on wine, and even less enthusiastic about bottled spirits. Thankfully, a live band was promised later; maybe the amplifiers would drown out conversation.

I remembered Elle's tip for photos and new situations, and pretended I'd smeared Vaseline on my teeth, as I joined the table. Four people sat at the furthest edge of the circle, frantically writing on tablets with a stylus. I said hello, as I pulled out my chair, but they were clearly preoccupied and ignored my smile.

Two women were sat either side of me. One turned and immediately started talking,

'Hi, honey - how are you enjoying the conference so far?' She thrust out her hand to pump mine. 'I'm Gill, I teach communication studies in Chicago

– this here is Debbie-Ann, my technician. We've had a blast today, haven't we, Debbie-Ann?'

Debbie-Ann nodded, sipping her short glass of clear liquid, focusing straight ahead to the entrance.

'Oh, wow, you've travelled far for this conference.' I commented, placing my napkin on my lap and fiddling with a corner of the starched white cotton while I concentrated on my breathing.

'Well, I wasn't about to let a free trip to the UK slide through my fingers.' Gill continued. 'We arrived in London on Wednesday, saw all the sights, and then we came to Plymouth yesterday. I can't believe how pretty this place is.'

Teams of waiting staff brought out the first course and I gratefully tucked into the warming bowl of carrot soup, suddenly hungrier than I'd realised. Gill continued to talk as she sliced her melon, occasionally bringing in Debbie-Ann to the conversation, although sometimes only rhetorically.

By the time dessert arrived, I was feeling quite lightheaded, whether from the rapid conversation or the wine glass that never seemed to empty I couldn't tell. Gill toasted everything – health, happiness, yesterday, tomorrow, academia, vacations. When Debbie-Ann returned from a bar trip with three glasses of cranberry juice I was so grateful I downed mine, and half of the next one that suddenly appeared. I toyed with the lemon tart in front of me, but my appetite was waning as my head throbbed for attention.

   I excused myself from Gill to escape to the toilet, passing through quite a large bar crowd to find the loo. I walked in time to a steady guitar rhythm, and assumed the live music had begun, although I couldn't hear a singer or see the stage. Luckily, I found a clear path to the toilets.

   The bathroom was huge, with a wall of mirrors each way I turned. I felt like I was in an Abstract painting. Women of all ages giggled, reapplied cosmetics and competed to tell louder and, perhaps, over-exaggerated versions of their week, to anyone who would listen. I smiled and checked my own reflection as I listened to their hyperbole. The bare minimum powder I'd applied to even out my face this morning had long gone. But in its place was a rosy and twinkly complexion that I wasn't entirely unhappy with. I reached into my bag for a lip balm, but a hand dived in and clenched warm fingers around my knuckles.

   'Oh, hell, no, girl, you gotta go bright – here, this shade of red is perfect for your gorgeous blonde hair, honey.' Before I could move away, Gill had whipped out her wand and covered my startled lips.

'Th-thank you,' I began, smarting from the sudden contact. I glanced in the mirror, as was expected, and, feeling suddenly too hot, followed Gill out of the room into the dense atmosphere of the bar, now crowded with bodies. Someone had started to sing, and people made their way to a dance floor. Gill dragged me with her and was as enthusiastic a dancer as she was a talker.

Two men, considerably taller than my own five foot three frame, appeared either side of me, hemming me in on the floor. I tried to smile politely, non-threateningly, and walk backwards, away from them, but they came closer. The music was too loud for me to think.

Do they not understand that I have a headache, and need space? Why are they still just smiling at me?

'That's right, all the attention's on you now, honey,' Gill yelled over the music 'told you that shade was your colour! Go see the girls at the mall, tell them G sent you!'

I really needed water.

Head down, I stumbled to find a gap off the floor, and found myself facing the same two men.

Drums throbbed in my head.

One of the men stood back partially, and I struggled to walk past without colliding into him.

Debbie-Ann was buried somewhere deep in the wave of bodies now, enjoying the band.

I found a cranberry juice from earlier on the table, and downed most of the drink. My throat was as dry as my lips, and my head was pounding louder than a student knocking on my door trying to query a final grade.

At a quieter volume from this distance, I could hear the music was quite good.

I'd leave soon, after another dance.

Right here where I stood.

Safe.

Finally, I was by myself.

My favourite place.

It felt good to unwind, after weeks of research.

I closed my eyes and spun on the spot to the beat, smiling; the bass on this song was really very good.

An arm brushed mine and I blinked around to see the men from earlier grinning at me.

They offered me a drink, but a lifetime of aversion to strangers began to thud in time with a resounding thought - time to leave.

I smiled politely, complacently, but shook my head a definite no, and made my way past the table.

The tallest of the men grabbed my elbow and whispered in my ear about how hot I was looking. I certainly felt warmer than I should be. He had a graze on his cheekbone that looked recent.

I grabbed my bag and walked towards the bar. The room whirled as I looked for the exit, which seemed to be in a different place to my arrival.

Needing air, I stumbled through a doorway, out onto a tiny cobbled alley.

My eyes, smarting from the late night chill, darted across the narrow space, but there was no immediate street access.

A bitter taste began to form in my mouth – what was in that juice?

'Hey, girl.' The tall man had followed me out.

I turned around and in a moment he was up against me, my back pressing against a wall.

'Oh, I don't think so.' I said. Rather cockily, perhaps, for the enclosed situation.

'Waaaat?' He drawled, as lazily as a second year undergrad who thinks they understand literature.

'I don't live in London to get mugged in Plymouth.' I admonished. Then I may have hiccupped.

I was undeterred. 'Plus, I'm an academic, so we've been on a pay freeze since before actual Austerity.'

'You think it's your money I'm after?'

I definitely hiccupped. And laughed a bit.

'Listen, I'm old enough to be your Mum in some countries.'

'I like a mature...'

Before I could laugh again, he fell sideways. Another man stood before me, a mess of sandy hair and indigo eyes, wearing one hell of a grin on his face.

'Y'all okay, Darlin'?' He stepped back, and offered a hand for me to step over the knocked out man at my feet.

Suddenly I doubled over, retching and shivering. Bloody adrenaline.

The stranger pulled my hair gently away from my face, his strong, warm fingers rhythmically stroking my temples. In a few minutes the nausea subsided.

But I was still in a dark alley with a stranger.

I looked up at him, through wisps of fallen hair, at the same time he said, 'I'm Cain. They know me in there, let's go back in and get you some water.'

Water sounded good.

I motioned for him to lead the way, and followed him back through the bar, determined to walk straight through the entrance and into a taxi.

But the heat and noise of the bar brought on another bout of stumbling.

Cain lifted me to my feet and guided me through another doorway.

A quick glance around revealed a staff room with a woman retrieving napkins from a shelf.

'Cain.' She acknowledged, at the same time as she pulled out a chair for me, which I sank gratefully into.

He reached for a bottle of water from the shelf, unscrewed the lid and handed it to me, watching as I downed half immediately.

'She okay?' The woman asked him. 'I have ta-get the accident book?'

'I think she'll – sorry, what's your name?'

'Lucy.' I patted my lips with the back of my left hand, and held out my right hand to shake his. His touch was warm, but dry ... and ... assured. I snatched my hand back.

As I downed the rest of the bottle, my eyes glanced across him, still assessing for danger.

He kept a little distance between us. He wore ripped black jeans, a light grey t-shirt that had seen better days and brown boots. Although he was sat down, he seemed to be around six foot tall. There was a natural relaxed air about him.

'Okay, Jo – I think Lucy here will be okay. But there's a couple of guys outside need some attention. Mind if we sit here a while?' He smiled. 'I'll yell if I need to, and I'm sure Lucy will if she feels she needs to.'

'You're okay with Cain – but I'll happily floor him for you, just shout.' The woman yelled, opening the door as she left. Snatches of dance music momentarily filled the room.

'Remember where you're staying?' Cain asked.

'So, I'm not obviously a local, then?' I bit, the adrenal glands calming down; were they clearing the way for a tsunami of panic? I glanced around – I was closer to the door than he was. And I was thinking.

'Your cloth bag has the university logo emblazoned across it, and it's September – the time for new visitors to Plymouth.'

I groaned. 'I know the hotel isn't that far from here, but I can't remember the name. I think I'd know it if I saw it. It was by the sea.'

'Take your time, finish your water, then we'll go and look together, if you'd like?'

I considered his offer, and sipped more water, hoping my banging head would soon subside. The alternative, of asking a taxi driver to drive me around the unknown city, didn't sound appealing.

Was I about to follow a man I'd just met to a hotel I couldn't remember?

The only crumbs I could leave behind a trail of are Jane Eyre quotes:

-I am a free human being with an independent will.

-I would always rather be happy than dignified.

-Reader, I (followed) him.

Ash would know how to make use of my film collection, should anything untoward go on.

'Need a water top up?' Cain asked.

I handed my bottle over and he refilled it from the tap and then returned to his chair.

'Do you work here?' I asked, this time sipping my drink.

'Not really – I hang out here a lot. What brings you to these fair shores?'

'Work. I teach literature in London, so I'm just here for the weekend. Thank you. For what you did back there.'

'Hey, I'm just sorry they even got you outside.'

'Still. Things could have been worse.'

Cain nodded, his deep blue eyes mesmerizing as they bobbed up and down.

It had been a long day.

'Hey,' He leaned forward. 'What else y'all got planned for the weekend?' His accent didn't sound American, but there was that southern drawl again.

'Well, tomorrow we're in sessions all day, then there's another social event tomorrow evening, but I think I'll skip that in favour of films and room service. My presentation is on Sunday morning, and there are a few sessions I'd like to attend, then we have the rest of the day to explore Plymouth, though I'm looking forward to catching an earlier train, and being back home in London, with a pizza, by bed time.'

 'Aww, the South West is stunning – don't let tonight spoil your time here. I could show you around tomorrow afternoon, if you like? We'd be in very public places. And you have to try a pasty and a cream tea while you're in Devon.'

How did I feel about spending a day with someone I barely knew?

I didn't feel any worrying instincts, worryingly; I was technically spending a weekend with strangers anyway.

If Cain showed me around Plymouth, it was sort of still networking, right?

What would Moira say?

What would a Bronte do?

I nodded once, before I changed my mind.
'Ok, but please help me find my hotel first...I'm shattered.'

2

Cain

I sauntered through the city back to Jo's, hands deep in my pockets, wondering what the hell had just happened.

Bob Seger nailed gigging with *Turn the Page*, from his Back in '72 album; the sweat pours out your body like the music that you play. Up there on the stage I'm both a million miles away and right in the moment.

I have the best bloody job in the world.

The crowd responded well tonight at Jo's, despite the lull between tourists and students on this Friday night in early September. I love playing gigs where I can work out which songs bring the crowd on the floor, and which ones send them to the bar.

But then, I'd play to three people if that's all that turned up. After almost a decade of watching other people perform my songs, from their arena show sidelines, my second album is about to launch and I couldn't be bollocsing happier.

Jam kept perfect timing behind me, his beats matching my vocals, as always. To my left, Seb's intuitive bass completed our trio. It may be my name at the top of the set list, but I know I'm nothing without those guys, though they're gonna be pissed that I'm not there to pack up. But I'm in no hurry to rush away just yet.

I'd spotted Lucy towards the end of the set, skirting the edge of the dance floor. I may not have paid her any attention except for the two men who followed her; I don't write number one stories without studying people, and their intentions.

We'd only had two songs to go when she stumbled up some steps, and the taller of the two men stood just a little too close to her. The merest nod to his pal and suddenly they were out of the side door and I was off the stage; I barely heard Jam and Seb fade out the track.

Years of surfing and hauling guitar equipment around have given me a core and agility that few see coming; I've stepped lightly away from trouble, or right into it when needed. As in that cobbled alley.

Like a cannon ball I laid out the first guy, and reverberated against him to knock out the one too close to Lucy, whose back was against the wall. Her tight breathing told me I'd made the right call in following her.

I'm not unsuccessful with women, especially when they find out I play a six string, but I'd never had a woman retch and double over at first meeting.

I held her dark blonde hair back from her face and kept my feet back. When her breathing was under control, I held out my hand for her to step over the laid-out dude.

Right there, when our fingers connected, I got one of those feelings in my gut; I'm not a scientist, but I'm not one to ignore chemistry. She'd dropped my hand and I led the way back inside, heading for Jo's staff room. I felt her lurch again as we entered the room, and I turned to gather her to her feet. When she followed me into the room I realised I'd been scared she'd run off before I at least learned her name.

She'd taken the water bottle I offered, and seemed to relax because Jo was in there, and she vouched for me. I owed that woman a pint at the next free gig I played for her.

I learned Lucy's name, and shook her hand, glad of the opportunity to connect with her skin again.

Her touch was cool and trembling and something else.

When I found out she was visiting from London, and she couldn't remember where here hotel was, I had to help out. Then I found myself inviting her for the obligatory lunch of a pasty and cream tea that any visitor to the South West must indulge in.

When she said yes, to both suggestions, I knew we were taking the scenic route back to her hotel.

We'd stepped outside into the cool air and headed as far away from the direct route to her hotel that I could think of, grateful that she was in a flat shoe. I've carried a fair few women across the Barbican's cobbles, their heels swinging in their hands, as we street-karaoke'd to our destination – normally her place - but I suspected that if I offered to carry Lucy our possibilities would end right there. And they simply couldn't.

Any visitor to Plymouth inevitably ends up at one of the three chain hotels, and we were going to broadly circumnavigate Smeaton's Tower – our famed lighthouse, smack bang in the middle of tourist central – as that was the most likely location for her hotel. The university always wants guests to have the best views of the city.

I talked about anything, even any history I could think of, as we walked towards the Barbican's waterfront, and the sight of the infamous Mayflower Steps; with two flagpoles proudly sharing the special relationship between the UK and the USA, sitting above a cobbled archway that offered a popular photographic spot. I knew I was talking too much, but she seemed happy to listen to my stories of the Pilgrims setting sail to the New World, almost four hundred years ago, and I silently thanked Mum for dragging me around

Plymouth's historical markers as a child. We'd both be surprised at how much I remembered.

The Barbican's streets were full of people, night or day, so I hoped Lucy would feel safe; I knew I would keep her safe, but I was almost painfully aware of the complete stranger I was to her. And that that had to change.

The next fifteen minutes of the walk had been up a more isolated incline, as we rounded the Royal Citadel fortress and made our way towards the Hoe, home of Smeaton's Tower and possibly Lucy's hotel. I continued to talk, this time about sixteenth century escapades from local lad Francis Drake and his Spanish Armada adventures. She smiled, and not in a terrified way, and only yawned once or twice.

When we reached the tower, the way she had stopped suddenly, turning towards the water. Her face looking up into the night sky. She'd inhaled the salty air and closed her eyes.

I swear I nearly kissed her right there.

Instead, I'd jammed my hands into my pockets and watched as the breeze toyed with her mid-length hair.

I guestimated her height would fit perfectly under my arm.

Or rest easily on my shoulder.

Absolutely any time she wanted to.

I already knew her eyes were a delicate blue, the colour of the sky on the first spring day.

'My hotel is definitely around here. Thank you.' She'd smiled and turned to look around her for a familiar path.

'I'll walk you there.' I'd offered, continuing to stand still.

'I'll be okay. I'm used to walking around the centre of London.'

'Yeah, but you know where everything is there. Let's make sure we have the right one.'

'Ok, lead the way.' She'd held out her hands, openly. Her smile actually reaching her eyes. I needed much, much, much more time with this woman.

I'd turned to the central path which connects the lighthouse to the city centre and, unfortunately, found her hotel immediately.

Even more quickly we were inside the crypt-like marble lobby. Give me a crowded tour bus over a bland chain hotel, any time.

'What time shall I pick you up tomorrow?'

'Oh, umm, you really don't have to tour me around – you've told me so much already.'

'Yeah, but I agreed to introduce you to proper Devon food.'

Her smile.

I was going to have to write her down as soon as I had my notebook.

But my feet were immobile.

'I can be back here – presumably, if I don't lose my way again – by around two o'clock. Is that okay?' She'd asked.

'Perfect.' I'd nodded and turned towards the doors, before my feet decided to do the thinking and go after her.

I'd turned to wave as I left the building, just to see her one more time as she walked towards the lift.

A kick drum began an involuntary beat in my chest.

I practically flew back to Jo's, before I started singing through the streets as if I was in a musical.

3

Lucy

My eyelids fluttered open and it took me a
moment or two to remember where I was.

A shaft of sunlight invaded my bed and I turned
over, screwing my eyes closed against the sudden
movement, doing a quick check for nausea.

Nope, no swirls or wobbles.

I was just exhausted.

When I reopened them I found my phone under
the pillow and read that it was the right side of
seven. I still had time to make the first session. I
threw the phone down on the duvet and blinked a
few times. Like a flower in search of energy I
turned to face the sky.

It was the wrong shade of blue.

On that thought, I rolled out of bed.

He wouldn't find his way back to the hotel again.

When he interrupted in the alley, it was just like
that scene in Dirty Dancing where Johnny bowls
into Robbie, knocking him to the floor, defending
Baby's honour. Ash and Luke would love this story
when I relayed it back at The Dinner Club next

Saturday. I've watched so many films from the eighties I've merged them with my life.

And it was thoughtful of Cain to walk me back to the right hotel, although it took a long time - it was well after one when I finally crashed out on the bed. I may be in dire need of an afternoon nap later.

I washed and dressed, collecting my bag from the chair and skipped breakfast in favour of a stroll by the lighthouse – what was it Cain had called it... Smeaton's Tower? He certainly knew a lot about his home town.

Only one or two people strolled along the path between the green and the lighthouse, with dogs or small children. The contrast between the calm early morning here and organized chaos in London had my senses wondering what was going to happen next.

Within twenty minutes I was at my first session, with a plate of raisin pastries and my travel mug of filter coffee on the table in front of me, awaiting insights into Poe's horror stories. I glanced around at the thirty or so delegates and hoped I'd have as many at my session tomorrow. Presenting first thing on a Sunday morning was always a dubious slot.

I was halfway through my fourth session of the morning, when I could feel myself start to fade away. The topic of masculinity in Jane Austen novels was insightful, but the lack of sleep was catching up with me and the mid-morning second round of pastries was wearing off. I just had to wait half an hour before I could walk back to the hotel and take that afternoon nap. I blinked a few times, and forced my pen to write notes about my first year classes next week, if not my shopping list (bread, milk, pizzas), hoping the small action would keep me from snoring.

Finally, we were released from the classrooms and into the sun. I smiled at the people either side of me, politely declined their offer to join them for lunch, mentioning preparing my own session (which was on two USBs and printed out in my bag) and headed straight for the lighthouse, by now a familiar route through the city.

As I walked into the hotel lobby, to my right I saw Cain sat on a sofa, his phone in his hand.

He looked up as I entered. The creases in the corner of his eyes ever so casually stopped my feet from walking, and possibly my ears from hearing.

In my periphery I was vaguely aware of a couple forking around me

'Hey, Lucy.' He greeted, enveloping me in a hug like it was the most natural thing in the world.

'Hi.' I managed. 'I didn't think you'd be here.'

'Why, didn't we say two?' he checked his watch. 'I know I'm a little early, but I caught up on a few emails. Do you want to head back to the room and drop anything off?'

I hesitated, not as tired as I was, but more sober than I'd been last night.

'I know a great pasty shop on the Barbican – have you eaten?' he asked.

I shook my head at the same time my tummy growled.

'Okay, then I thought we could do a boat trip – are you okay on boats?' I nodded again. No growling this time. 'Good, I know some people aren't great but it's a cruise on the River Tamar, so very gentle. What?'

My tiredness and nerves forgotten, I smiled. 'Your enthusiasm is infectious. I'm good to go now if you are?'

'Absolutely.' He stated, and I fell into step beside him.

We strolled along the path of the green, past spectacular topographical views of the rounded Art Deco lido swimming pool, down towards the familiar cobbled Elizabethan area of the Barbican. The view across the water was so blue and beautiful I kept stopping to absorb the spectrum of colour, dotted with silent, vivid white boats. I hadn't quite realised how grey London was, even though I'd lived there almost a third of my life.

'See that hill over there?' Cain pointed to the right side of the water. 'That's Cornwall, where I live. Well, that's south Cornwall, I live over on the north side, an hour or so away – much closer to the Atlantic, for the surf.'

'I love the patchwork green; great complimentary shades against the water.' I said, taking a few photos before we carried on down the winding path to the sea.

Seagulls swooped and skidded to a landing all around us, as people ferried between the shops and restaurants of the main street. We stopped outside a small bakery on the corner of a street.

'Here we go; best steak pasties in....are you vegetarian or anything?' Cain asked.

'No. Steak sounds good. As long as I don't have to cook I'm happy.'

'You don't like cooking?'

'There are other things I'd rather do.' I said.

'Like what?' he asked, as he opened the door for us to enter the small shop. The heat from the ovens and a baked deliciousness enveloped us.

'Like work. Umm, read. Watch a film. Travel.' I answered.

It was our turn in the queue, and Cain asked if I minded him ordering. I shook my head, moving closer to him as other customers entered the shop. The close heat made me dizzy, and I was grateful when I could pull away from him. I stepped outside, and he was right behind me, with two pasties wrapped in brown paper bags. We sat on a wooden bench outside the shop and he handed me the warm bag. I guided the top part of the pasty out and bit carefully into the pleated edge of the semicircular pastry, and was rewarded with a huge chunk of peppered steak and steam.

I finished the Devon delicacy just shortly after Cain, all the while people swarming along the streets as they made their way to or from the Barbican.

Cain disposed of the bags in a nearby bin, 'Good, right?'

'Absolutely,' I agreed, brushing golden flakes from my clothes, 'I have eaten a pasty before – there are quite a lot of foods available in the capital.'

'Yeah, but you haven't enjoyed a Devon pasty, and the Cornish ones are even better. But ask any Devonian and you'll hear a different story. Wait until the cream tea wars later. Ready to go?' I nodded and he continued, 'Let's head down to the wharf where the river cruise starts from. I have a couple of tickets that Jo had behind the bar last night. So, you like to travel?'

I nodded, amazed at his stream of chatter, how it was observational and inquisitive at almost the same time. There was a two-way chat going on, though, as I realised he was waiting for me to talk.

'Um, yeah, I've just returned from a research trip to Haworth in Yorkshire. And each summer I house sit for people in countries I want to visit. Last year I stayed in a lovely home in Martha's Vineyard.'

'And how does the British seaside compare to the American seaside?'

'Well, the food is great in both places – I love both fish and chips and lobster rolls. There are more flags in New England, in America, on every building, lawns... greens. There is a wealth of literature connections in both places, too - I got to visit Emily Dickinson's home in Amherst.'

'Who is she?'

'A nineteenth century poet. She's been on my to-visit list for a while. She lived a mostly solitary life, except for a few close relatives and friends. She was drawn to writing poems, although only around a dozen, heavily edited, poems were published in her lifetime, even though she wrote over 1500. She's my second favourite Emily in literature after Emily Bronte, who I'm presenting a paper on tomorrow morning.'

'Ah, so not just attending the conference, then?'

'No, there had to be another reason for me to trek all the way from London to the South West. The history is pretty spectacular in both locations, though, and I enjoyed a few days in Boston, covering the vast history and politics of the country.'

'Have you visited anywhere elsewhere in the States?'

'I went to California the year before, for a tour of Steinbeck's county. But I don't like driving on this side of the road, never mind the other, so I rely on lifts from the guest house owners, and local tours. I don't always have time for the big rail journeys it would take to explore the west. I'd love to see the Rockies one day.'

'Oh, they are everything you imagine and then some. I travel to Nashville every month or so, but I haven't travelled too far outside Tennessee – the country is vast compared to the UK, never mind little old North Cornwall.

'Nashville?'

'Yeah, I'm a songwriter. Musician.' This was the moment. The day could end right here.

'One of my favourite writers, Mark Twain, is from neighbouring Missouri. Over a hundred years after he's gone his works are so insightful.'

I released a breath with my shoulders. This was a good day. 'I hear New York is pretty walkable?'

'Yeah, it's a handy stopover – I was there last year for a night before taking the train to Boston. But I live in a large city, so I like the idea of a more relaxed summer. With a lot fewer people to navigate around.'

We'd reached the wharf, bustling with boats, people and gulls. The tang of the saltwater from the sea mixed with the scent from nearby fish and chip shops.

'There's a boat due to leave in a few minutes, come on.' We wound our way along the jetty just as the skipper was about to unhook the rope. Cain took my hand as we launched onto the deck. I didn't argue when he didn't let go as we walked through the boat to an empty bench beside the window. We sat and I pulled my hand away, enclosing my warm fist into my jacket pocket.

My eyes feasted on the surroundings, as the Captain talked us through the history of the River Tamar, and the local landmarks, including Smeaton's Tower, which was relocated to the Hoe and now a tourist attraction as opposed to a working lighthouse. Cain pointed out sea birds, and we kept a look out for seals – he said we'd have to visit Cornwall for a possible shark sighting, although the local Baskin sharks were vegetarians, apparently. I had no intention of going for anything other than a paddle in any water.

The cruise took just under an hour, and returned us to our departure point. We waited for everyone else to leave, the boat gently bobbing as people jumped to the jetty. When it was our turn to leave Cain held out his hand for me to cross onto land. This time he let go and dug his hands into his jean pockets.

'Thanks for a lovely afternoon-' I started.

'Do you want to go to a beach near-' Cain asked at the same time.

'There's a beach near here?' I asked, trying to remember the advice from the hotel staff.

He nodded and pointed across the jetty. 'The water taxi is just heading over to us now – takes about five minutes to cross.'

The sun was still warm and I had to admit to being excited at the prospect of walking on sand.

Why not make this a mini-break?

'Sure.'

He took my hand again, leading me through a queuing system with no organisation, and we arrived just as the yellow water taxi did. This time there were only a few passengers to embark so within a few minutes we'd set off.

4

Cain

I was a goner.

Equal parts energised and traumatised, I had had the best day in a long while, and even though it was nearing midnight I didn't want it to end.

I had talked for both of us as we walked all over Plymouth, but Lucy soon found her voice. What had originally begun as a lunch, and the opportunity to see if it was a post-show high that had me reacting the way I did last night, easily turned into an afternoon river cruise, a beach visit and afternoon tea, where I watched as she sank her teeth into the thick, clotted cream on top of strawberry jam and a fruit scone. She was a Cornish cream tea fan, and so was I now, having always preferred cream first. Then we'd stopped for drinks at a bar and taken on fish and chips on the Barbican.

We were on another slow walk back to her hotel.

And the night wasn't over yet.

I had to write with this woman.

I stopped at the hotel's doorway.

'I've heard the same riff playing in my head most of the afternoon, but the story isn't forthcoming. Do you think you could help me out, if I play it for you?'

I knew I was talking even quicker than I normally do. I sounded desperate. I was.

One simple, definite nod, and I pushed open the door for us, striding to the reception desk.

I quickly hired a meeting room and arranged coffee.

Lucy hadn't said a word after her brief nod. I had to retrieve my guitar case from my truck, and half-expected she'd have changed her mind.

She was pouring coffee into two mugs when I returned.

'Milk, no sugar, right?' She asked me.

'Good memory.' I smiled, unlocking my case, taking my notebook and pen out and placing them on the table. Lucy made herself comfortable in a chair as I tuned my guitar. She reached for my notebook with a raised eyebrow, and only opened the smooth, black leather pages when I nodded. Not even Jam had access to early drafts of my lyrics. When she'd read my half-arsed attempt at lyric writing, she placed the closed book on the table between us, her fingers smoothing down the covers.

My fingers brought the riff into the room and I closed my eyes, waiting for the story. I became aware of a pencil moving across paper.

Trepidation.

Atonement.

Fear.

Those were the only words I felt as the melody played.

The pen stopped. I heard Lucy move her chair I opened my eyes. On hotel paper she'd written: grey to blue, anguish, courage in renewal.

I nodded slowly and picked a faster rhythm. Lucy took the paper again while I played. We passed the branded sheet between us for who knew how long. At some point more coffee arrived and Lucy poured the welcome liquid into our mugs, opening small packets of hotel biscuits for us to share.

And then I felt it.

I knew the song.

Surrounded by water, two figures tell their fifty-year story.

It was the one I was ready to learn.

Lucy let out a massive yawn and I railed at time for continuing forward.

'Sorry,' she smiled. Her eyes sparkled anything but apology.

'No, no, I'm sorry I kept us up so late.' But still I didn't move. I couldn't.

'Is that how you write all your songs?'

'I've never written the start of something with anyone else.'

'Never?'

'You'll have full co-writing credit.'

I would never tire of her laugh.

'Can we play some of your songs tomorrow? I'm free around two again.'

'Oh, Luce, I'm Thomas-Rhett-happy right now.' I called out, placing my guitar back into its case.

'I have no idea who that is, Sunshine, but I'm happy for you.' She yawned again.

We tidied up and I walked her to the lift. She pressed the call button and I pulled her in to a goodbye hug. 'I'm so glad I met you.' I thought, as the lift pinged its arrival.

It was only as the doors closed on her *oh*, that I realised I'd said the words aloud.

Would I ever learn not to be so honest?

5

Lucy

All my senses were playing havoc with each other as the lift dawdled to my floor, and I walked to my room.

Today had been ... well. What had today been? I'd gone from not expecting to see Cain again to inviting myself to hear him play his songs in the space of ... what ... twelve hours? I didn't even care that my presentation was in a few more hours and I still had to sleep.

I paced the room, rehearsing an already perfected hook for my speech, then showered and dried my hair as I waited for my mind to slow down.

My body finally won and I passed out on the bed.

Even better, I'd had the foresight to set my alarm.

After breakfast and a brisk walk through empty streets, I arrived in my designated room at exactly the right time. There was barely any room for me and the three other speakers. I was on second, which gave me enough time to draw my head away from the beach and into the room.

My turn arrived. I walked to the table, inserted my memory stick into the PC and presented Emily Bronte's magnum opus, and her remarkably short life, at the same time as it felt I was looking down on myself and sensing subtle changes within. A slight seismic shift, barely visible on a Richter scale. The ripple from a pebble launched into the sea. The movement of a butterfly landing onto a petal.

My slides finished, I smiled at the audience, thanked them for listening and responded to, mercifully brief, questions. I removed my USB and returned to my seat. Considered movements, attempting to curtail my inward imbalance.

During the morning break I bumped into Debbie-Ann from the first night and she regaled me with tales of her Plymouth adventures, and how she and Gill were skipping out on sessions this afternoon so they could visit Bath. Did I want to tag along?

'Oh, I'm sorry, I have a pre-booked train. Have a wonderful time, though, Bath is a beautiful place. The Jane Austen Centre really explores her Regency heritage.'

'Museum? Naw, honey, we're going to the Thermae Spa – at night you can see the whole of Bath from their rooftop pool.'

Okay. 'I'm sure you'll have a marvellous time.' I refilled my travel mug and smiled as I wandered to my next session, grabbing a couple of packets of biscuits on my way.

I had very little idea what the mid-morning speakers were sharing. Either there were a lot of muddled thoughts, or yesterday's events were catching up with me. Although, I have survived on less sleep during my early years as an academic.

After my final session I caught a taxi back to the hotel, surreptitiously seeing if Cain was nearby. I paid the fare and stepped out of the taxi into the afternoon sun. He was probably still-

'Lucy.' My name cut off my thoughts, as I was once again enveloped by his warm arms. When he pulled away he asked, 'How did your presentation go? I felt so bad at keeping you awake so late.'

'It was absolutely fine, thanks for asking.' I smiled, my hands buried deep into my trouser pockets. 'Not too many complicated questions, either. How was your morning?'

'Really good. I recorded our song, which I can play for you in the car. Feels so good that the fragments now have a home. Have you checked out?' his mouth worked as quickly as my mind.

'I was just going to do that.'

'Good, what time's your train? Is there a later one? Would you like to go to the second best beach in Cornwall?'

Well, I did need to have my fix of shorelines before heading back to London.

He waited in the hotel lounge, near the table I'd written Elle's postcard from, while I retrieved my suitcase and checked out. I confirmed the trains to London with the hotel's receptionist - the last train was at half past eleven tonight. I would probably pass out from exhaustion long before then.

One day's sleep deprivation at a time.

Cain took my case as we left the hotel, his keys in hand. 'I'll drop you at the station later.' He offered.

Two days ago I wouldn't have expected I'd say yes to climbing into a car with a man I'd only known a few hours. But I did so, and readily.

'Newquay isn't far from here, just over an hour's drive. The views along the north Cornish coast are spectacular. Little Fistral is easily my second favourite beach, after the one I grew up at - Kynance Cove - down in West Cornwall. Jase and Cassie – my older brother and sister – and I were always in the water, winter or summer. The turquoise waters there will explode your mind,'

He stopped at a black Nissan truck and opened the passenger door for me. I rolled my eyes mock-dramatically at him, but was warmed by the gesture. Even if the attention sent tingles along my forearms.

He closed the door as I was seated, and put my case in the boot.

Inside, the truck was larger than I expected, and spotless. A media screen stared at me, and when he started the engine country music began to play.

'Oh, Johnny Cash!' I exclaimed, surprised at my own recognition of his voice.

Cain groaned and hit a few buttons on the steering wheel, increasing the volume. 'This is the Folsom Prison album, one of his finest. You have no idea what I'm talking about, do you?'

'Possibly not, but I can appreciate a good song.' I settled back into my seat, pulling my sunglasses down from my hair to place them over my eyes. As we left Plymouth behind, Cain told me about Cash's life, his family, his legacy, and I had to admit I wanted to hear other songs from him. Turns out that I quite like a three minute story. Some of these songs could even be used in lessons to teach imagery in creative writing. My students would probably appreciate a wander into the twentieth century every once in a while.

We drove through endless one lane roads, surrounded by overgrown hedges worn out from summer, like we were driving through some impossible maze.

And then, suddenly, two wide streaks of a vivid blue were in front of us.

'Is that ...?' I asked.

Cain nodded. 'Welcome to the Atlantic. We're not in Newquay yet, but this is Trevaunance Cove, one of my favourite surf spots'.

'We're not ...? I don't even ...'

He laughed as he parked the truck. 'Don't worry, we're not surfing today, but this is a great little beach for watching intense waves – great photograph opportunities, too.'

We stepped out of the truck, and the roar of the waves breaking over sand, the taste of salt in the air, was an instant relaxant.

How had I never visited coast like this in the UK? The scenery stole my soul, salt hitting my lips as the waves crashed around my ears. As soon as I returned home I would download an app to listen to the surf; it would definitely help after a late night marking session.

The depth of sky and sea and rock was bewildering. A few surfers enjoyed the swells, their bodies at times parallel to the water, before they crashed and began again.

There was no way you'd catch me on a surfboard, but even after a few days with Cain I could sense how his instincts would thrive on the open water; an eager Labrador chasing the natural rush of adrenaline and a higher order.

The energy needed to jump onto the board, fall off, and within a few minutes resume an almost identical position, sort of made me want to sit down and enjoy a latte. I was more of an observer, not a doer.

We stepped out onto the sand, our shoes in our hands, and walked towards the shore for a paddle in the ocean. The water was cool over my feet and I gasped, but after a few moments I relaxed as the magnetic push and pull of the tide washed over my toes in a familiar rhythm. I was glad I was wearing Capri trousers, and I rolled them up to my knees, wading out further, breathing in time to the waves. My hair was all over the place, at the complete mercy of the wind. I released the elastic band that normally kept the strands tidy and smiled as both wind and hair seemed to sigh their thanks.

I heard a click beside me, and realised Cain had taken my photo. I laughed and made a celebrity pose for the next click, my hands on my hips as I stared down the lens.

'I'll never tire of staring at a coastal line, it's my definite happy place. This is beautiful, Cain.'

'This is incredible, but I've seen other beauties. Come on, let's head to another beach, not far from here.'

I nodded and followed him back across the sand, glancing behind occasionally to watch the surfers and few brave people swimming.

Within a few more minutes, after a winding drive, following the deepest azure, we parked again. A wide, almost-white, sandy beach lay ahead, framed by two grassy headlands.

Cain was out of the truck and reaching for my hand before I could take a breath.

'Right?' He asked rhetorically, as we walked across the sand, and began to climb one of the headlands. My head reeled from the landscape below us; the Atlantic lay everywhere, two infinitely small beings watching a tide drawn to the rocks.

I took some photos of the ocean, and Cain photo-bombed a couple of the shots, but remained wildly active when I tried to train my lens on him, not the view.

Eventually we made our way back down to the sand as the sun began to lower behind us. Cain held out his hand for me as we navigated the grassy slope, occasionally rocky in places.

'Want to stop for afternoon tea?' He asked, as we walked beside the cafes. The thought of food made me hungrier than I realised I had been.

'Absolutely, Sunshine. And a massive pot of tea. I could already feel the taste of the clotted cream as I sank my teeth into its cool texture.

On the journey towards Newquay, Cain hit buttons on his media screen and turned to me.

'I'd like to introduce you to one of the greatest singer-songwriters from the seventies, Bob Seger. I'll start easy, with his Greatest Hits.'

I lay back and listened as a piano rhythm played, then suddenly a huge voice filled the truck, singing about a west-bound road and making a choice.

Apt, I thought.

But I liked what I heard.

I drifted off to the breeze from an open window, as the music lulled me to sleep.

When I woke up, the view before me was like something out of a National Gallery hanging.

The sun was nearing the ocean, a fiesta of orange and purple spread across the sky to welcome the night.

Friday night's sunset paled in my memory. How was that only forty-eight hours ago?

I opened my door to take a closer look, and Cain followed just behind. Silhouettes of rocks and rock pools added to the dramatic scene. I would love to teach a class here, on the impact of landscape in literature.

I inhaled deeply, staring around me to take in the stunning views.

Cain took my hand and led me to a natural seat on a rock formation. I hadn't realised he'd brought his guitar with him until he opened the case. After a quick tune up he began to play the song we'd worked on only last night.

Unable to draw my eyes from his fingers, watching their intricate waltz across the strings, I almost missed the sun as it hit the water, but the rays brightened momentarily, dragging my eyes away.

Cain continued to play, changing into a ballad that almost felt familiar. When he reached the chorus, my eyebrows raised. He nodded with me, as I searched my extremely short-term musical memory; his tempered voice belied the power I imagined him capable of, but it suited the contemplative moment.

'One of Bob's finest.' He sang and I finally nodded.

'Yes, from the car!'

'From everywhere.'

The sun sank below the horizon and I gave my full attention to Cain. He began packing up his guitar, and I shivered slightly. He pulled off his sweater and lowered it over my head.

'There you go, Luce.' He whispered, his fingers lightly brushing my cheeks. His words and his movement sent a surge of pink to their surface.

'Thank you', I whispered. 'And thank you for bringing me here; I've had a wonderful day.'

'It's my pleasure. This is my local beach, Little Fistral. The larger Fistral, where they hold the surf competitions is behind us, and where I'm normally found if I'm not touring or writing. They hold a music festival each August over on Watergate Bay a bit further along the coast.'

'This place must offer you so much.' I stated, burying myself into his sweater.

He nodded, pulling me towards him, rubbing my shoulders and upper arms to warm me, as we walked back to his truck.

I fit perfectly under his arm.

Once inside he put the heater on, and declared we would find more fish and chips before the almost-midnight train left Plymouth.

A tiny part of me wondered if it would be the worst thing if I didn't return home tonight.

We found a small cafe and I devoured another delicious fish supper and several pots of tea.

'Have you always lived here?' I asked.

He shook his head as he finished his water.

'No. I grew up in west Cornwall, near Lizard Point. My parents own a guest house. I started writing music in my last couple of years of school. Absolutely everything to do with trying to find a girlfriend, you understand?'

I nodded, not quite picturing how he would have struggled.

'Somewhere between endless practising and cursing I fell in love, and suddenly I was never home. Every chance to perform I did. This awkward kid, on a stool, with a guitar that seemed too big for him, at each school play, production, quiet five minutes. I was in love with melodies, and trying to create stories through my words.'

Falling in love with words was something I understood. The right ones resonated, and the rough ones could be rewritten.

'I played covers for tourists, and with new people arriving every week I definitely learned my craft, how to work an audience, how to keep the bar open a little later. And how to save for a flight to Nashville.'

'Has it always been country music for you?'

'I love any singer-songwriter who can capture an audience in a few seconds. But yeah, I struck gold when I happened upon a Waylon Jennings CD in my Mum's collection, and he opened my eyes to a life beyond Cornwall'.

Cain tried to pay for dinner, but I swatted him away, as he'd paid for everything throughout the day. We walked slowly back to the truck for the drive to Plymouth.

'I'd like to say I was an overnight success in Nashville, but all the city did was tempt me with what I could be. Unfortunately, everyone in Nashville has the same dream, and buckets of talent. So I was back home in three months. But I couldn't concentrate on anything other than writing. So I listened, and wrote and rewrote, and a year later returned to Nashville with a catalogue of songs I could at least play in bars. I threw them in on covers nights, and thankfully found an artist who wanted to record one of my songs. And I just kept going until I sold all the songs I had.' He shifted up a gear and turned the heater on.

'The next time I returned home it was with keys to my own place in Newquay. Took me about five years, but what a time. Now I have two families; Nashville is like a second home to me. It was only natural that that awkward kid found his way back to a stage. So, what's your story?'

'Me? I'm not that interesting. I love reading and writing, so I teach reading and writing. I couldn't imagine doing anything else.' And I wasn't spoiling the moment with tales of escape and anonymity.

'What music do you listen to?'

I bit my lip and paused.

'I don't really. I like the feel of a good book between my hands. When I listen to music it's on the radio. I have a few CDs from the musicals. I quite like a good soundtrack. Les Mis., Jersey Boys, Phantom.'

'Oh, I can get with that. My Mum is a theatre nut. When I hit my teenage years she was always dragging me to Plymouth to see a show – Jase and Cassie don't really understand music as much as Mum and I do; they're restless, like Dad. But driving over and walking all over Plymouth with Mum was where I picked up so much history of the place.'

'Ah, you are a great listener, then, even if you were a reluctant observer.'

'Well, I wouldn't say that. The first time I saw Evita I may have made sure Mum always knew when that was playing.'

'Oh, Evita, I love that show.'

He grinned, and turned the ignition, scrolling through the media screen until the opening bars of High Flying Adored came on. It was testament to how relaxed I was that I sang along with him, even though I know I don't sing. He was too busy laughing to show me up by actually singing.

Sadly, we were at the railway station all too soon.

He parked the truck and wheeled my case through to the deserted concourse, all the while holding my hand, even though there was no uneven surface beneath us. We read the digital information screen and he insisted on walking me directly to the platform.

I handed my ticket to the train guard.

'I'm okay to carry this on?' Cain asked, holding my case.

'Sure. We depart in ten minutes. You'll need to be off then, or pay for a ticket.'

I led Cain through to my room. I'd booked both beds in the two berth cabin, so I could have a full night's sleep without anyone else snoring, or interrupting me with conversation.

'Wow, this may be small, but it has everything.'

'Absolutely.' I flipped up the counter top to reveal a sink and smiled a ta-da smile. He stood in the doorway, his arms resting above his head on the frame.

'Hey, Luce.' He said, motioning for me to walk towards him. I walked halfway across the room to hear what he had to say. 'Closer.' He added.

I stepped forward, my concentration lost as I stared into his inky blue eyes, committing them to memory one last time.

He leaned forward, his hand reaching slowly around to the back of my neck as his lips found mine. I smiled, unable to move anywhere, even if the carriage had been on fire, instead of my skin.

I couldn't tell if the taste of salt was from the ocean or dinner, and in the time it took me to wonder, he'd brought our bodies closer together, deepening the kiss. It had been so long since I was so close to a man that I was grateful for instinct when my lips parted a little, and suddenly both his wrists rested on my shoulders, his thumbs caressing the delicate spot behind my ears.

I shuddered, pulled away first, badly needing to breathe.

His incredible smile would be etched onto my mind, too.

'I think I've needed to do that all day. Maybe since Friday.' He said, his hands lightly stroking the back of my neck.

My tongue darted out to moisten my lips and his lips followed its trail.

Just as my arms reached around his waist, the train guard walked past, announcing five minutes until departure. I broke away, nervously laughing. Cain returned my arms to his waist. His arms rested around me.

'I have had the best weekend, Luce.'

I nodded, rasping out a Swayze, 'Me too, me too.'

'I'd love to see you again. Can I have your number?'

I reached around to the back of his jeans and took out his phone. His smile lit up his face again, and I handed the gadget to him, reciting my number so he could key it in. He nodded and replaced his phone, bringing me close for another kiss before he had to leave. I would always remember the sea this way.

I pushed him away, although my hands lingered on his chest. His solid, surfer's chest.

I pulled my hands down, balling my fists, and stepped back into the carriage, just as the guard reappeared.

'Time to go, Sir. Or are you buying a ticket?'

'I have to get back, Luce.' I nodded and he reached for my hand. 'Walk with me to the door?' I followed him, and the guard disappeared to prepare the train for departure.

Cain stepped off the train, closing the door between us. He poked his head through the window and kissed me once more before stepping back behind the yellow line, laughing and waving at me, amid shouts from the guard.

I watched him on the platform, his hands burrowing into his jeans pockets, as the train left the station. When the cold night air kicked in I reluctantly returned to my bare carriage.

I was tired and wired, and downright exhausted.

Probably from all the sea air.

Probably.

I lay on the bed in my compartment and within minutes the gentle rocking of the train lulled me to sleep, where I dreamt of a hundred shades of blue.

6

Cain

I messaged Lucy as the last of her train pulled
away from the station, and at the instant ping
back with number unknown I was torn between
wanting to run after the train or drive to London
to meet it.

No, no, no, no, fucking NO!!!

She surely wouldn't have entered the wrong
number deliberately.

Would she?

No.

We had had the most surreal time this weekend,
but all of it had been that mix of comfortable and
charged. The beginning of something, not an end.

And the kiss?

Exactly.

No - I had no reasons to believe she'd
deliberately key in the wrong number. I must
have missed a digit in my haste to kiss her again.
If she hadn't wanted to hear from me, she would

have been honest about there being no reason to remain in contact.

I scrolled through my photos of her, her hair as wild as the surf spray, eyes half-closed, wearing a smile as wide as my heart.

What the hell was her bloody surname? Where the hell did she work? Some university in London; how many of them could there be?

Except tomorrow I was flying out from the UK for a two week stint in Nashville. Sarah would floor me if I missed that flight; my first meeting was with the label's new CEO.

I kicked a metal bin as I walked through the station, startling a pigeon.

Why couldn't I have done the missed call thing? Why couldn't I have given Lucy my number instead? Out of politeness, if nothing else, she'd have sent a thank you message, and I wouldn't be wishing I was Clark Kent outrunning the train through a Kansas wheat field.

I could drive to Exeter.

The train's last stop before the Paddington terminal - by both road and rail it was around a fifty five minute journey.

I was in my truck and heading down the Devon Expressway, as soon as I could.

I hit 80 miles an hour most of the journey, only briefly slowed by night time road works, with absolutely no one working.

A few 50 miles-an-hour zones also slowed me down, but the clock on the dash suggested I might still get to Exeter St David's station before her train pulled away.

No such luck; I heard the whistle from the station guard as I hit the handbrake.

The train had left on time.

I turned the car around and drove back to Plymouth. I couldn't stand to listen to any music on the drive down, trying to figure out how it had all gone so unutterably wrong.

I pulled up to the shared apartment I'd seen very little of this weekend and Jam and Seb opened up the back for their equipment and luggage.   We drove up to Birmingham for our flight in a silence I could stew in; they'd crashed out asleep in the back so I replayed memories of Lucy.

A few days later, after horrendous jet lag and back to back meetings, we were on a stage trying to do sound check for a gig that night.

'What do you mean we're out of time?' Jam asked me.

'It's all wrong. The beat doesn't match the lyrics.' I yelled.

'Fuck off.'

Seb said nothing, just watched the two of us, as he worked on his bass.

'Who the hell are you talking to?' I stomped over to Jam.

He came out from behind the drums, sticks in hand.

'An *arse*hole from where I'm stood.' He said.

His long limbs had always towered over me. I'd seen him haul people out of the surf, I'd witnessed him play drums for hours, his steady rhythm my supportive backdrop; he'd frequently pulled me out of trouble just before it found me. We'd been friends for so long. This was my own ridiculous temper I was furious at.

I held out my hand for him to shake.

'Sorry, man. You're right.'

He grinned and we gripped each other in easy forgiveness. Seb's responding riff indicated he was pleased with how our dispute had ended.

'You have been a prick ever since you returned from Devon.' Jam sat down on the stage. I joined him.

'I met a woman.'

He nodded.

'I lost her number.'

'Oh. She's a good woman then?'

'The one I'm going to marry.'

'Oh, fuck. I'd act like a prick, too.'

'Every time I close my eyes I see her.'

'So what are you going to do?'

'Play every university and college campus in London until I find her.'

'Cool. Need any help?'

I shook my head. 'Just tell me when I'm being an arsehole.'

'Will do, will do.'

We returned to sound check.

After the gig I couldn't sleep that night, as usual. But instead of amplifiers in my head, it was her distracting me. Again.

Her eyes, questioning me, wondering why I hadn't called. I could almost reach out for her, but she turned around, drifted away.

Was I already forgotten while she got on with her life?

7

Lucy

It had been over a month since I'd returned from the South West, without any messages or calls from Cain. I had at least stopped checking through websites every other hour, to see where he was performing, find possible answers as to why he might not have got in touch. He'd seemed so earnest. So honest.

I was walking across campus to my first year class when my phone rang.

I reached into my coat pocket and pressed the green circle.

'Everything all right, Sis?'

Elle screamed down the phone and I dropped my bag.

'What's happened? Are you okay?'

'I got in, Sis.'

I squealed as quietly as I could, retrieving my bag and its contents.

'Harvard?' I could almost hear her nod.

'Yup. I'm off to America next August. Just have to survive final year of A Levels.'

'And Mum and Dad.'

'I hardly see them, Sis. I'm either working or at school or at Bryan's.'

'Take care of yourself, Elle. Oh, I'm so happy for you. There are some great US writers from Massachusetts.'

'As long as they can teach me the business of getting rich, I don't care.' I laughed at her straight forwardness. She'd always been so confident. She had worked so hard for the chance to travel to the US. I couldn't wait to visit her, safely away from our parents. Watch her grow into the amazing woman I knew she was going to be.

We rang off and I headed to class.

I was so busy grinning to myself that I almost forgot to feel sad or annoyed. When would it become easier to feel my regular self again? I didn't want to take my bad mood out on other people anymore; I'd called out Moira the other day because she'd added new undergraduate meetings to my schedule. I knew I normally didn't turn down the chance to support students either, but I'd had a perfectly acceptable evening of wallowing-in-pity films planned.

Or revenge films. I hadn't quite made up my mind.

I looked around the lecture hall at the first year students.

The room was almost full, apart from the front row, which no one ever seemed to occupy.

By Christmas, the intake would reduce in size, once the work load came in.

Which I intended to increase today.

I switched on the PC monitor and an image of a graduate came up on the screen in front of the class.

'English is used everywhere. It's one of the world's strongest currencies.' I glanced around at the students, some even taking notes on their devices. 'This is not an easy class. Do not think it's an extension of A Level English, or that if you can speak it, then you can write it, and pass it.

'As a graduate the world will open up for you. As an English graduate you may feel that the doors occasionally close. Some of you may harbour dreams on writing your own books one day. Others among you will want to earn prizes for your investigative journalism. Some of you are here because your parents convinced you it was a good idea.' I paused to gauge the heads that popped up at this comment.

'There are two things you need to do well on this course to be successful. And you need to do them every single day: read and write. The more you read, the more you will question, and those questions are submitted as answers to me every fortnight.' The usual groans ran around the room.

'I trust you've all received the book list?' some nodded. Some nodded cautiously. 'How many of the books have you read?'

A hand rose up.

'Yes?'

'I thought those books had to be read all year?'

I shook my head.

Another hand rose up.

'I read most of the books, but couldn't find some of the smaller, obscure ones.'

'Good. Has anyone read all on the list?' A handful of people near the front raised their hands.

We were going to be in for a busy term.

'Hey.' Moira stood in my doorway, trademark coffee travel mug in her hand. I stopped writing and motioned for her to sit down. She shook her head; this was just a quick chat.

'How was the conference in Plymouth?'

'Oh, good. Good.'

'And?' She raised her eyebrows. Why on earth was she a details person?

I'd leave one key detail out.

'I met a few people from the mid-west. They run popular communications courses. Something we could look into here for an elective, perhaps draw in students from education who'd like to learn the performance aspect of their future career.'

Moira nodded. I'd passed the test, apparently, of having networked. Despite the fact I found out about the research Gill undertakes through an Internet search a couple of weeks ago.

'And how was Plymouth?'

Incredible. And so long ago.

'It's a lovely city. Great history.'

She nodded again. 'I didn't think it had gone as well. You've been remarkably quiet since your return. You should go to more conferences though. If you're after my job in the future.'

'Oh, you know how the students are, keeping me busy.'

'Yes, the students.'

She nodded once more and walked away down the corridor.

Of course, now all I could think about all afternoon would be Cain.

And why my phone hadn't rung.

And then berating myself for waiting for the phone to ring; as Jane would declare, I'm an independent woman with her own free will. I could go out tomorrow and meet someone else.

Should I so wish.

She didn't have a silent phone to deal with.

At least Wednesday was on the way to Friday, and distraction in the form of a Dinner Club Devito trilogy this weekend. On Friday Ash and Luke were showing Throw Momma from the Train, and I was just in the mood for Billy Crystal and Danny Devito banter. And if that didn't clear my grumps I'd watch DeVito, Douglas and Turner remind viewers why relationships were ridiculous things in War of the Roses on Saturday. On Sunday they were showing the so-bad-it's-brillinat Twins, which I always laughed at. No one did cinematic optimism quite like the eighties.

I packed away my work and locked up my office.

We were having a late summer rush of good weather. I still only wore a light raincoat to work, and even on the walk home it wasn't really needed. I pulled my sunglasses on, loving the sharpness of the red and gold leaf colours against the backdrop of an incredible blue sky.

Which didn't remind me of a Newquay beach, or long-lashed azure eyes.

At all.

I stopped at the convenience store on the corner, for a pizza and chocolate cake, and bought half-priced pastries for tomorrow's breakfast.

I let myself into my apartment building, securing and checking the lock. I scaled the stairs quickly and unlocked my front door. Even after all this time I still looked over my shoulder, even though there had never been any cause to. Manchester was a lifetime ago.

I double-locked the door behind me and kicked off my shoes, dumping the food onto the kitchen work top as I changed into comfy sweat pants and a long sleeve top. I was taking a night off work tonight, in favour of slapstick Pryor and Wilder; life was far too humiliating for it not to be laughed at regularly.

When I arrived at the Romantics seminar group the next morning there were only fifteen out of twenty students in front of me.

'Morning. Does anyone know where our friends are?' I asked the group.

Mindy, a second year Journalism student, filled me in on the absences, which may have been connected with a pre-sale for some US artist or something.

Just what I needed; they'd have extra reading next week.

'Okay, let's recap on the last session, shall we?'

Tallie raised her hand and was away with a neat summary of Victorian gothic horror. I'd heard good reports of her work with the drama students, too, so she was on track to her research trip to Yale.

Mindy interrupted her with questions, directed at me, although I encouraged all my students to learn from each other more often than they should ask of me. They had to start working out theories for themselves.   I wondered what kind of student Elle would be in class.

'Dr.?'

'Yes?'

'Do you think the Bronte Sister's should have assumed pseudonyms? Doesn't that reflect on the authenticity of their texts?'

'What do you think, Mindy?' I asked. 'What does anyone think?' I opened up the lesson, and some well thought out answers were forthcoming.

Tallie commented, 'rather than question the apparent authenticity of the text, we should question what would have happened to their books had they published initially under their own names. Would society have accepted the magnificent love stories, featuring madness and spirits and independent women, had they known from the start they were written by women?'

There was hope yet.

The new classes had started out as a welcome distraction, with new faces to learn, and characters and personalities to guide towards academic success.

But I was good at my job; we were only a few weeks into the new term and I had grouped my classes towards their specialist interests, set up mentoring opportunities for the likely graduate school candidates next year, and I had never had such a clean and tidy apartment.

I'd begun to stay at work later and later, before walking home and collapsing into bed. Usually Sundays were the worst. I was able to spend the day with The Dinner Club, watching whatever eighties film marathons that Luke and Ash had organised. But Kelly could sense something was off, and I was worried at one point she'd just pick a random stranger to sit next to me over our usual tapas and drinks. Male or female.

I woke up most mornings to the memory of Cain's eyes, his voice, his promise to call. Then I spent the day trying unsuccessfully not to think about him.

It was going to be difficult to seek more distractions.

Perhaps I'd take up the art class I'd always thought about. Or take up Kelly on her offer to watch back to back horror films.

After the Romantics seminar finished I'd taught my Semantics group and managed a quick dinner before spending the evening in a quiet study room in the library, marking some assessments, struggling to fight back a sudden cold. Maybe I wouldn't be watching all three Devito films this weekend.

I sneezed again, and again, and it took a few minutes to stop.

Closing my eyes, I awaited the inevitable coughing fit. New people and colder weather always meant an illness. I was ready for the end of semester. Or at least a break from talking. I reopened my eyes and tried to focus on the papers in front of me, but nothing made sense any more.

Time to call it a night and try again in the morning.

I unplugged my laptop, slowly packed away, and wrapped my thin jacket and scarf around me. It would be time for the winter coat this weekend. Quilted heaven. So long, autumn; hello winter.

As I opened the heavy doors, onto the crisp November air, my muffled ears picked up an all-too-familiar sound; a Cain Adams record.

I groaned and closed my eyes again.

Since I'd met that man he'd been everywhere on campus – student radio, essay topics, phone downloads, hurriedly hushed as I walked in. I hoped one day to catch a break, and not have to catch my breath when I heard first year undergrads exchanging his lyrics in poetry class.

Especially any song about a beach.

I buried my chin into my scarf and walked down the few concrete steps that led onto the college green. Only a few short minutes until home.

The sound became louder, and I suspected the shadowed group under the oak tree had turned up the volume on their i-gadget.

Except the music sounded different.

I paused at the side, noticing a guitar player.

The guitar player, with a baseball cap worn low over his eyes.

I glanced around at the group, who were appreciating the moment. No videos or mobile phones recorded him. It was a captivated audience.

Briefly he paused playing, and looked up, locking onto my eyes.

I hoped by remaining still he wouldn't see me, but I sensed his playing got a little faster, a little harder, to round off the track. I had about thirty seconds to walk away, but I simply had no energy.

No calls or messages, and here he was on campus; really, life - really?

The song ended and I opted for brazening out.

He was in front of me in moments.

'Luce'.

'No one calls me that.'

'Dr. Luce?'

In spite of my disappointment, my lapsed anger, my sheer exhaustion, a smile slipped out. Then I shivered.

He noticed the slight film of sweat on my nose and forehead, and immediately wrapped his leather jacket around my shoulders. It smelt of sweet sweat and the weight of it was like a warm hug I hadn't known that I needed.

Now that he had finished playing, a group of confident girls stepped in for a photo, despite the dark. Cain smiled and posed, signed autographs, all the while glancing over at me. I was leaning against a wall, not really sure what else to do, and with no energy to walk anyway. Suddenly my knees buckled and he was right there for me to fall into.

'Where am I taking you, Luce?'

I whispered the address and he carried me to his truck, immediately turning on the heat.

But I didn't feel a thing, except absolute exhaustion.

At home he unlocked the building's door, and guided me up the stairs to my front door.

'I might just lie down for a few minutes.' I clung onto my bedroom door handle to remain upright. 'Help yourself to coffee. I'll be out shortly.'

I kicked off my shoes, crawled under the covers and was asleep within minutes.

Thirst woke me up and light from another room illuminated a glass of water on my bedside table, which I downed. I fell back into unconsciousness, dreaming of Cain sat on a chair watching me, a copy of Wuthering Heights in his hands.

The next time I stirred, I could see daylight underneath my curtains.

My throat was no longer as dry, and my limbs felt like they were attached to me again. I turned over in the duvet, not quite ready to face the morning. A few more minutes in yesterday's clothes wouldn't hurt. Then I'd need coffee, a sure sign I'd escaped a serious cold; when I'm really ill I can only drink tea.

A few minutes later my growling stomach won and I slithered out of the duvet, stripping clothes as I stepped into my shower. The hot steam cleared what was left of my tiredness and I wrapped in my bathrobe, heading to the kitchen for coffee.

Cain lay sleeping on the sofa.

My worn copy of Wuthering Heights on the floor beside him.

A hundred questions rose in my mind, but before I could formulate a sentence his eyes flew open.

'Lucy. How are you feeling?' he sat up, trying to cover a yawn.

'You stayed.'

Why couldn't he have just stayed away?

'You passed out. I checked on you, and you were sleeping, not unconscious. But I didn't want you to wake up with me staring at you.'

'Like I just did to you.'

'I must have been more tired than I realised. What time is it?'

'Definitely time for coffee.'

He nodded, checked his phone.

'Oh, wow. Almost eleven.' He muttered.

'Then it's definitely brunch.' I amended.

He nodded, 'Mind if I use your shower?'

'Help yourself. The bathroom is ... well, you probably found it already.'

He nodded again.

I disappeared into my bedroom to dress, and try to engage with what was happening.

I met Cain in my living room again.

'There's a good cafe around the corner from here, if you're ready?'

'Lead the way.' He smiled, holding out his hand.

Stood at the front door, I realised I hadn't double-locked last night. For the first time in almost seven years. A wave of nausea collided with my hunger.

'Are you okay, Lucy?'

'I didn't double-lock my door. I always do. I need to.' My fingers rested on the mechanism that kept me safe.

I'd be extra careful not to let my guard down again. And Cain wouldn't rescue me a third time.

8

Cain

Twenty three campuses I'd played at, in between gigs, over twenty-one days. That's what it had taken for me to find Lucy again.

We walked to the cafe in an uncomfortable silence. I guess we had just spent an awkward night together.

No, Adams, not the time for misguided observations.

We sat in a booth, opposite each other. She was still as incredible as I remembered, though more hollow around her eyes.

Breakfast ordered, coffee on the way, I gently took the sugar packet out of her hand that she was mindlessly shifting up and down, like a tormenting hourglass. She twitched at my touch and I put my hands by my side.

'I'm so sorry I didn't call you.' I began. 'I didn't have all the digits of your number. I drove to Exeter to try to catch you, but missed the train by just a few minutes. Do you know how many campuses I've played at in the last three weeks?'

She studied me for a while. I wanted her gaze on me for very different reasons.

'It's okay, you don't need to make up a story – I grade them for a living. We had fun. That was that.'

I kept my hands still, careful not to make any sudden movements. She reminded me of a rabbit Cassie had looked after when we were growing up. Scared into a corner when Jase and I bounded up to her, only responding to Cassie's soft steps.

'You are so much more than whatever you think "that" is. What happened, Lucy, to make you doubt?'

'Don't think you're the first to make a promise they couldn't keep.'

'Tell me, Lucy. So that I understand.'

She wriggled in her seat, her discomfort saved by the arrival of our food.

'Maybe another time.' She said. I hadn't yet earned the rights to her stories, but there would be another time.

I nodded. 'I have about eighteen free hours. I'd like to spend them with you. Then I have a show to get to in LA.'

'I have classes this afternoon. Poetic Devices. You could come along. If you wanted.'

'I would love to see you in action.' I smiled.

That was the fastest two hours I'd ever spent in a classroom.

I sat at the back of the lecture theatre, marvelling at the literary *a cappella* performance I watched on the podium before me. Lucy was so knowledgeable, so engaging, when it came to sharing her love of poetry and the inner workings of elusive emotions.

This was why we had written together so well.

I couldn't believe I'd finally found her, U2. I would move mountains to earn her trust.

When the class finished, most of the students left but a few remained back talking to Lucy with questions that she was happy to discuss.

Lucy had every right to be pissed at me when I turned up out of nowhere, five and a half weeks after we'd last met, just singing on campus like that. But as quick as her guard had gone back up when she saw me - when I saw her teach, I saw the woman I was going to spend my life with.

I just had to figure out how.

A life on the road isn't any life at all.

Perhaps I could just record songs for others again - leave them to spend the time on the road.

I already knew that wouldn't be a possibility, not after having had a taste of performing. I've never felt that everything was so right, as I did when I stepped onto the stage for that first time, and every time.

Perhaps I could have a total career change and ask Jase to set me up with a job? Settle down like he did with Shelly; I might just make that phone call to hear his laugh.

Besides, could I settle down? Haven't I always been too much of a rambler?

I waited until the last person had left the room and strode up to see her.

'What did you think?' she asked, filing paperwork into her bag.

'We need a room, right now.' I demanded, almost losing it over her shocked expression. 'I have to write with you.' I added.

'I'm going to my office to prep for tomorrow's lesson – you're welcome to work in there, while I plan'.

I nodded and we walked the short journey to her office in silence.

Lucy poured coffee into mugs for us, added sugar to hers, and left the mugs on the side, switching on her PC.

For the next few hours I worked on a ballad I'd been playing around with, while she worked on her computer. A couple of times I caught her watching me, but she averted her eyes back to her screen.

Suddenly she stopped typing and looked up at me.

'Cain, you have all this ... this ... insight ... for your stories, so why are you writing in clichés? Don't you think you have something to say?'

'I have plenty to say, during every single sold out show.'

'Yes, but what songs are you writing about? A girl song. A drinking song. Another girl song. Another drinking song. You are capable of so much more.'

'And what do you know of my life?' I demanded.

'Absolutely nothing. I'm the perfect outsider, offering you an honest opinion.'

I paced the room, absently picking up and replacing books from a book shelf.

'No one has spoken to me like that before.'

'Yes, well.'

'It's been a long time since someone called me on my BS.'

'That's a front.'

'See what I mean?' I groaned, before sitting down again. 'A front for what?'

'We're all hiding from something. Afraid to go too far.'

'What are you hiding from?'

'The biggest cliché; the past. Aren't we all?' She held out her hand for the black leather notebook. I handed it over and played a ballad I'd been working with for a few years. I heard the slow, soft scratch of her pencil hitting the pages of my book as she began to write.

I knew that look - she was absolutely lost on choosing the right words. For my stories.

We worked and reworked the words until the imagery was just right.

I loved working with this woman.

At some point in the night we ordered in Chinese for dinner, and only stopped writing when Lucy let out a huge yawn. I checked my phone and realised it was somewhere after midnight.

'Bugger. I'm sorry - I get so caught up in writing with you.' I apologised.

'It's been a long semester,' she smiled, sleepily. Her hair fell over her eyes, and I resisted the temptation to tuck it behind her ear.

She followed me out to the truck and I drove us back to her apartment.

'It's late. There's a spare bed in my study – you're welcome to stay.' She said, before leaping out of the truck and opening her door.

I parked and followed her in. She showed me the room, and whispered good night.

Within minutes I was flat out asleep.

My phone alarm went off with an obnoxiously loud pop song and I quickly cut it off.

Bastard Jam messing around with my settings again.

I buried my face into the pillow, refusing for a few minutes to acknowledge that I had to leave her again.

I washed and freshened up in the bathroom, then padded towards her room and softly knocked on the door. When I didn't hear anything I opened it. There was no way I was leaving without saying goodbye.

'Lucy, wake up.' I urged gently. She fluttered her eyes open. 'I have to go.'

She sat up in bed, then. It was still dark outside. All I could hear was the thudding of my heart racing my willpower as I kept from kissing her like I wanted to.

'Six days and nights of interviews and shows, then I get a night and a day off – can I come and visit Friday, before I fly out to Atlanta?'

She nodded once.

'Good. Go back to sleep.'

Her eyes never left mine, and I found myself leaning down to press my lips lightly against her forehead. I tore away and she drifted back off to sleep.

9

Lucy

I had no idea what time Cain would visit, but I woke early the following Friday morning, and had bought a range of groceries for the weekend - and possibly a short siege - unable to decide on what we would eat. I've never been good at cooking; there's just no point going to all that effort for one. It's more efficient to eat out, so I can concentrate on reading research articles, or planning lectures.

Everything I'd experienced, everything I'd done to protect myself since starting over, evaporated when I was with Cain. His presence confounded me. What could explain the disappearance of the last five weeks? Or give meaning to the appearance of a woman who literally swooned in front of a man and had to be rescued, a second time, by him?

This time when I heard Cain's songs on the radio, I turned the volume up, needing to hear the lyrics, to hear what he was all about.

I'd just turned the corner to my street when I spotted a familiar truck parked up.

My body lurched to a stall.

He'd actually turned up.

Cain stepped out of the vehicle and walked over to me, a baseball cap pulled low over his eyes. He took the two bags of groceries from me, our fingers connecting briefly in greeting.

Sort yourself out, Rawcliffe, I thought. He's just a bloody man.

'Thank you.' I said. I walked with him to my front door, 'have you been waiting long?'

'An hour or so; I really should have taken your number again, so I could call ahead. I worked, though.'

'What do your days consist of? I wake up, teach, teach again, grade, eat, sleep.'

'I have my own routine, too, depending on where the shows are, or if we're writing. Now I'm readying for a run of shows in California this week. The new album will launch at the end of the month. When I'm not on the bus or a plane, I spend most of the mornings in meetings with either the label or press, which is my very least favourite part of a tour. I do all of this for that stage.

'Apparently Jam - my drummer - and Seb - my bassist - think I'm never satisfied. And they could be right. Sometimes. Where shall I put the groceries?'

I had forgotten his easy conversation.

'That's okay, I'll put them away – I wasn't sure what you'd like to eat, but I bought steaks and I'm very good with a baked potato.'

'Perfect. Let me just grab something from the truck and I'll come and help'.

Within minutes he was back, holding a CD out to me. 'It's the album's demo. I'd like you to have a copy before it's released.'

'Oh. Thank you.' I felt the heat rising in my cheeks and neck. 'Would it be weird if I played it now?'

'Not at all. Here, I'll hook it up. I'd like to see your reaction to the tracks.'

I was grateful of the distance between us. Suddenly, Cain's voice filled the room, and I stopped cooking. He was singing the lyrics we'd worked on in Plymouth. The song he'd played for me at the beach.

He caught my eye and, in spite of the last few weeks – and especially the last three days – I beamed.

'You are pretty good.'

His laugh jolted me, and he swept me up in a hug, 'Dear, dear, Lucy, you've made my week.'

I faltered, but smiled, and passed the cheese, 'you grate; I'll dance.'

Over dinner, the conversation turned to childhood.

Cain told me of growing up the youngest of three – so, pretty much getting away with everything, and blaming his older brother, Jason, for a lot. His Sister, Cassie, came next, and learned to survive growing up with two boisterous brothers. As did her boyfriends. Although, she learned to handle them herself.

Reluctant to steer the talk around to my adolescence, I asked him if he'd had any childhood sweethearts. He had the good grace not to rib me about my vocabulary choice.

He nodded, holding up his forefinger. 'Jamie and I met on our first day in high school. Hated each other at first – she was Cassie's friend and I thought she was a snitch, always telling Cassie what I was up to. But, y'know, then I changed my mind. She took care of herself a lot. Other boys started to notice, but I shoved them away – literally in the case of one poor guy. I tend to go after what I want.

'We were together through to our last year of school. Didn't think anything would break us apart. She went off to college, and I tried college, but I was always distracted by music. I guess we just grew apart. By our seventh year we were done. I'd moved to Nashville properly and was working all the time anyhow. I took on any and every gig, no matter if there was only five patrons in the bar, and all I got paid was beer. I was learning my craft.

'I heard from Jamie when my first song hit number one. That was about five years ago. She was with someone else, but prepared to give it all up for me.

'Except, I didn't have the same feelings for her. Couldn't trust if she missed me or liked the successful me. I'd heard a few things from Cassie. One night she came home in an absolute rage. I'd never seen my Sister that pissed, not since Jase and I had stopped tormenting her. Few years later Cassie told me she'd overheard Jamie describe her life as Mrs Adams. And it had little to do with any love for me.

'I didn't care that much. I was working, and er, socialising, when I needed to. There wasn't time for anyone to get close.

'What was your childhood like for you, Lucy?'

I shifted in my seat, swirling the base of my glass. My life was a world away from his, always had been. I took a drink and noticed how he sat patiently, seemingly interested in what I was going to say.   When I didn't say anything, he asked, 'Any broken hearts along the way?'

'Oh, I think we've heard enough memories for now – any room for apple pie? With ice-cream?' I headed for the freezer.

'I could get used to this, Lucy.' He followed me to the kitchen.

I faltered on his comment, wondering what he meant, then opted for the literal. 'These are the only two meals I can prepare – we're eating out next time.'

'Not a chance – I'm cooking tomorrow; you like pizza?'

'That's rhetorical.' I handed him a bowl and a spoon and took my own dessert to the lounge.

The thought of a tomorrow with him was equal parts tormenting and comforting.

In the lounge he headed straight to my floor-to-ceiling DVD tower.

'Woah, I haven't seen this many DVDs in one place in a long time. You must have, what a few hundred?'

'Umm, 341, give or take. I like films.'

'I stream everything.'

'Yes, well, you travel a lot – your equipment is probably more useful to you on stage than an eighties film obsession.'

'Oh, but you do have the best movies in here. Let's watch one.'

'Okay. I settled back into the chair – you choose.'

He browsed the titles, in category and then alphabetical order...reciting names as if he hadn't thought about them in years.

'Oh, wow, Tango and Cash. Cheesy classic. And Overboard.'

'Kurt Russell is very much underrated as an actor. The eyes, the hair, great comic timing.'

'Too true, too true.'

He skipped right past the Rocky, Indy and Die Hard films, heading straight for my John Hughes selection to read out the titles: The Breakfast Club, Ferris Bueller, Pretty in Pink, Weird Science. He paused at my John Cusack collection, and lingered on the Spielberg, at Back to the Future.

Then he held aloft the triumphant winner of Bill and Ted's Excellent Adventure, and air-guitared, before setting to work on the DVD player.

I curled up on the sofa; it was Friday night, and I was exhausted from a hectic week. I'd seen this classic film hundreds of times. And I was so cosy under my blanket.

10

Cain

Sitting with Lucy on her sofa was as good as I'd felt in a long time.

I loved the road, playing my songs to an eager crowd. But this was a different kind of energy. Like the opening bars to a Springsteen ballad. Raw. A slow burner. Something that nudges its way into your life until it feels like it was always there.

I'd never seen a woman blush quite so much, and it was adorable that I could bring out that reaction in her. I needed her sass, too, that she'd only tell me truths, no matter how painful. Who knew what would happen if I hung around?

I pulled the blanket slowly over her exposed toes and tried to concentrate on the comedy in front of me, and not the woman next to me.

I'd woken early this morning to catch a set of waves, and, after showering and throwing a few things in a bag for the week, I'd arrived in London just after eleven.

Then I realised I'd forgotten to take Lucy's number.

But I did at least know where she worked and lived.

There was at least twelve hours that I could have turned up in, and I didn't actually agree with Lucy on a time. She could have been working until five or six for all I knew. She certainly wasn't home when I arrived just mid-morning.

But I was getting better at waiting.

I'd parked up and paid the parking, and then I sat in the truck doing the social media thing that Sarah was always on at me for getting more involved with. Jam was the Twitter and Instagram fiend. I'd probably last used Facebook three years ago, before my first album flew, and there was a whole bunch of other stuff that I had no idea what it was all about. At least Twitter was easy to understand, if fast-moving. I could see how easy it was to become absorbed.

I'd been periodically looking up into my mirrors, to make sure I didn't miss Lucy, and suddenly she was right in front of me, laden with all sorts of canvas bags over her shoulders.

I threw my phone on the seat and headed over towards her, taking the bags.

And just like that I was at ease with her. She was still the same woman I'd met all those months ago, if perhaps a little guarded now; I know what

I'd be telling Cassie if a guy hadn't been in touch for weeks.

Bill and Ted played out their future hit song and I stretched out, letting out a yawn.

Lucy woke up, startled as if from a deep sleep. A worried sleep.

'I've made the guest bed up for you.' She stated. 'And the bathroom's next door, which is all yours. I have my own. For however long you stay.'

So, she'd planned that I'd possibly stay over?

I liked the thought of that.

'I don't want you to go to any trouble. I'm used to trying to sleep anywhere. Back of a truck, literally lying down on a jacket for a pillow, between amps and guitar cases.' I laughed at the memories of the early days. Before I had a team around me who booked hotels and provided meals and brought me back home to Nashville, which had always felt like home.

Until now.

Perhaps Music City had some competition.

'I'm free the whole weekend.' I'd said, following her out of the room.

11

Lucy

When I woke up I knew that something was different.

I stretched, blinking awake at the sunlight peeping in between the gap in the curtains.

Then the scent of bacon wafted into my room. And coffee.

Cain.

Cain was in my apartment and cooking.

He was in my apartment.

My clock read just after nine.   I quickly showered, threw on jeans and a long sleeved t-shirt, and swiped a toothbrush around my mouth. I pulled my hair back into a bun to tame the frizz and headed towards the kitchen.

I peered around the door of my open plan kitchen dining space, and witnessed Cain dancing along to the radio, frying pan in his left hand, spatula in his right, as he served up bacon onto thick, golden, fluffy pancakes. He smiled when he saw me and nodded towards the plates.

'Lifetime of growing up in a guest house – I cook a mean breakfast. Hope you didn't mind me making myself at home.'

'If it means pancakes and bacon, carry right on.' I settled myself into a chair and sipped from the mug of black coffee in front of me, adding more sugar, and stirring with the bottom of my fork.

He brought the plates to the table, and settled in next to me, automatically kissing my left cheek, which rebelled and inflamed at his touch.

'Morning.' He said, raising his coffee cup to mine.

'Morning.' I repeated, busying myself with forking bacon on to my pancake until the blush subsided.

'I was thinking, we could take on London as tourists today, if you don't have anything else planned?'

I hadn't really thought beyond, *will he turn up*?

The day was promising to be one of those late autumn surprises, the cloudless blue sky distracting me from a weekend of marking essays.

'No, I don't have anything I need to do. I could be a tourist for the day. Where do you want to go?'

'I want to know the hidden London. Where do you eat your favourite brunch? Where was your favourite place when you first came here?'

I thought for a minute, about my decade in London. I used to walk around the city a lot. I'd seen Buckingham Palace, the Houses of Parliament, Westminster, Big Ben, the London Eye....all of the postcard fundamentals. I'd shopped on Oxford Road, at both Selfridges and Primark. In the early days I'd wandered along the lights of Regent Street towards Piccadilly and the cinemas of Leicester Square. And the place I visited for calm, when my mind was a whirling mess.

'Actually, I really love the Portrait Gallery. It's just behind the National Gallery on Trafalgar Square, but except for a small side door, it's something you could miss. You'd love the collections.'

'Absolutely – it's a date.' He clinked our cups again as he continued to chew his breakfast.

A date.

Yeah, that wasn't going to make me feel awkward at all.

After breakfast was cleared we set off on foot towards central London.

I'd suggested we walk, instead of taking the tube, taking advantage of the sunshine. Cain renewed his parking, and we set off towards the city. He kept up a steady chat as we navigated the forty minutes around people and parks and southbound traffic.

He was so easy to listen to, so present, that it felt, I imagine, like walking with a good friend. There was no difficult conversation between us as we talked about films, about our shared appreciation of musicals, of the eighties as a genre. When he talked about film scores, particularly songs that played a pivotal moment in an artists' career, his face became even more animated.

When we neared the crush of Saturday shoppers on Tottenham Court Road, he took my hand in his, simply stating he didn't want to end up lost in London.

I didn't fall for his reasoning, but I didn't untangle our fingers. I should have sent him away but every sense I had overrode the logic I've always relied on. And I teach Romanticism.

I had to see this – whatever this was – to some sort of, hopefully mercifully short, conclusion.

We arrived onto Charing Cross road, lined with book stores and eateries to suit every taste and budget. After a brisk stroll through pedestrians and away from Underground expulsions of even more people, I pulled us towards the entrance to the National Portrait Gallery, at the back of Trafalgar Square.

The instant quiet had the same calming effect on me that I'd always felt soothed by. I let Cain's hand drop as we walked among the paintings.

For the next hour, we walked in companionable silence around the gallery, whispering about the paintings that made us stop and wonder at the painter's abilities, or the subject's pose. We spent longer staring at the musicians, and Cain inevitably had a story or two about the subjects.

When we'd reflected on every painting, the cacophony of urban noise as we emerged onto the London streets again was a little startling.

I tried taking surreptitious shallow breaths, focussing on the square of the pavement slabs beneath me. Cain took my hand and gently entwined our fingers, his rough thumbs stroking my palm. Breathing under control I glanced up at him, his smile reassuring. I couldn't have spoken had he asked me a direct question.

We paused to let a wave of students on a tour pass us, their backpacks and noise imitating a squall. Then we joined the rhythm of people as we turned onto the gathering place for millions of people each week: Trafalgar Square.

Cain bought coffee for us from a nearby cart, and we walked to a fountain, sitting on the wall. Everywhere around us families and students and tourists took selfies and group photos, capturing their opportunity to enjoy the iconic landmark.

The years of history this square has seen is phenomenal. Yet if I closed my eyes and listened to the water I could be at any beach. I really should make an effort to see more of London than the route between work and home.

A young man approached us with a sketch pad, offering to draw our pictures, to support his art studies, and my eyes blinked open.

'No, it's-' I started, at the same time that Cain voiced his agreement.

We looked at each other, and then the young artist, and I found myself acquiescing with a smiling nod.

The artist suggested Cain put his arm around my shoulders and motioned that we should sit closer together. Cain scootched closer to me, his arm draped around my right shoulder. The weight of his arm felt ... comforting. Steadying.

The man nodded, as his pencil flew across the page and Cain murmured lunch plans, remembering that Chinatown was only a few minutes' walk away.

The sun settled on the back of my neck, and I relaxed into the moment, caught between two men. I quelled the bubble of nervous laughter that threatened, just as the artist announced he was finished. He produced the picture for us to see and Cain roared with laughter, gripping the artist's hands in thanks.

I looked closer at the A4 paper and realised the caricature portraits had captured Cain's smile and my sideways glance at him pretty accurately. He'd over-enthused our body proportions, giving me a great hour glass figure, and Cain a pronounced jaw line. It was pretty impressive artwork.

Cain nodded and paid. I took the image for a closer look. The backdrop of the lion-guarded fountains was secondary to the clear relaxed pose he'd captured, as Cain and I sat amongst other tourists, on that beautiful sunny afternoon.

Cain looked at the art once more, imitating the pronounced jaw and hero-pose, and I folded the paper carefully and put it in my bag.

'Ready for lunch?' he asked, as I sipped the last of my coffee. He held out his hand to help me jump down, and we walked back up Charing Cross road. We turned left just after Leicester Square Underground station, and entered Chinatown.

After a satisfying lunch of more dumplings than I'd ever eaten, we waddled out into the streets.

'Where to?' Cain asked, his eyes skewering me with their presence in the late afternoon sun.

'Time for a drink. With history.'
This time I took his hand and directed us towards the embankment and the river, before veering left into Gordon's. We stood for a moment, letting

our eyes adjust to the wood panelled dark, before approaching the bar.

'Red or white?' I asked, handing him a wine list. 'The oldest wine bar in London.' I added.

'In that case, Merlot. For the chocolate vanilla. You?'

'Fat Bastard Chardonnay. Balanced acidity.' He roared his approval and I ordered.

As we waited for our drinks it was my turn to share my knowledge, of the seventeenth century diarist, Samuel Pepys and nineteenth century Rudyard Kipling connections.

'This bar feels like we're in the midst of Victorian London.' He said, looking around.

'Welcome to my world.' I nodded, raising my glass. He clinked his red wine against my white.

'To Lucy's world.'

Our relaxed conversation continued, and we ordered tapas to stave off dinner, and cocoon ourselves a little longer.

'Where would your next holiday be?' He asked, swirling the red liquid in his second glass. Or was it his third?

'I like to go somewhere close at Easter, perhaps Rome, or Prague or Paris, or Denmark, but one summer I'd love to travel across the States on the railway. Tucked up with a good book and a cabin, and dinner brought to me.'

'That sounds good. I'd probably swap the books for headphones or my guitar.'

'I have a feeling you'd be entertaining a small crowd in a corner somewhere, against the back drop of the Rockies.'

I could listen to his laugh all night.

'You're probably right.' We raised glasses again.

The wine had the expected powerful effect on my limbs, and I found myself leaning in to Cain a little more, the warmth from his body and the wine making me feel more relaxed than I had done in months. In six weeks.

'I couldn't believe it when you suddenly appeared outside the library.' I stated, glad of the confidence of wine.

'I visited seven colleges and universities each week, playing outside anywhere I thought you would be. I hoped at least someone would wander by your office talking about me. And then there you were. So still, stood in front of me.'

'If I'd have had the strength I'd have probably walked away.'

'I'd have followed you, to explain why I didn't stay in touch. Then, if you had wanted me to, I'd have walked away.'

'Cain.' What was happening? It felt like someone had removed all of the sound from the room, and all I could hear was the crimson blush starting at the base of my neck as it worked its way to the tips of my ears.

'Dr. Luce.' He replied, tilting his head in a light-hearted way. And the embarrassing moment passed. I smiled at his acknowledgement of how that night had gone and we raised glasses.

'Anyway. Where would you go on holiday?' I asked.

'Hawaii. Surf, surf, surf and a little climbing. And Mai Tais.'

'Sounds ...energetic?' I offered. 'I imagine the beaches are stunning.'

He nodded, enjoying the last of the wine in his glass.

Suddenly, I checked my watch and dragged him out of the bar, the blast of cold air very welcome.

'Come on.' I ushered us through the evening, heading towards my very favourite place in the whole of London – a little cinema down a back street.

'The Dinner Club?' Cain asked, looking up at the sign. 'I don't think I could eat anything else.'

'Don't worry, you'll love this place.'

I pulled him to the spacious Art Deco box office. Ash bounded over the counter and enveloped me in a massive hug – his typical greeting.

'Lucy, my lovely, I'm so pleased you could come...and you brought a friend, too...Kelly *will* be pleased!'

'Ash, this is Cain....Cain, Ash – co-owner of this amazing cinema.'

'Which only shows eighties films.....nice.' Cain added.

Ash hugged me again. 'Oh, you found a clever friend, too, who knows The Breakfast Club!' Ash declared, hugging Cain. Over Cain's shoulder he mouthed '*freaking hot, too*.' And I just shrugged, a little smile forming on my lips, before breaking their embrace so that Cain could breathe.

'What's on tonight?'

'Perfect date flick ... Scarface.'

There was that word again. Then, this was our second weekend together.

'Really? I haven't seen that film in years. Great performance from Pacino.' Cain announced, reaching into his wallet to buy the tickets.

'Put that away, hon. Lucy is a fully paid-up member of The Dinner Club, and that includes any friends of hers. Although, if you wanted to buy her ice-cream combo, that would probably pay this month's rent.'

'Ice-cream combo?' Cain asked, raising his eyebrows.

'Peanut butter, chocolate and vanilla ice cream, in a chocolate waffle cone, extra caramel sauce, chocolate drops, Flake; big spoon.' Ash and I chorused.

'We'll have two.'

'Didn't think you could eat anything else?' I asked.

'Well, dinner was half an hour ago now.'
Ash headed back around the counter and prepared our ice cream, then we headed to the screen room, which was full. I pulled Cain along to the first row of the upper tier, which was always reserved for the members of The Dinner Club. Ash and Luke were the owners of the cinema, Rich and Kelly were husband and wife, hooked on eighties horror films. Chris and her partner Sal worked for a film magazine, then housemates Ran, Carrie and Kelsey joined, who were in to vintage revivals. I became the tenth member a few years ago when I wandered in one afternoon and stayed for the three Christian Slater films they were showing: Heathers, Gleaming the Cube and Beyond the Stars. Complete escapism.

I popped into the foyer between showings for the ice-cream combo and got talking to Ash who whispered to me that Slater was his weakness; they were showing Pump up the Volume, Mobsters and Kuffs the following Sunday, if I was interested. I was and I did.

I was grateful Kelly was on the other side of Rich as we nodded hellos, and that the film was about to start. No one talks through a showing, unless the film is Top Gun or Dirty Dancing, which are both fair game for heckles.

I thought briefly about leaving with Cain before the end of the film, but I could almost feel Kel's eyes warn me to stay put. After years of her trying to set me up with various friends – and sometimes customers of hers – I'd actually turned up with someone, and she definitely wanted to say hello. If I could head off her twenty questions then we'd all feel great. One quick hello and we'd be out.

As the closing credits played, she almost floored Rich to ensure her hand touched my arm. She gave me her warmest detective expression, the one that meant no harm, but was going to be absolutely intrusive if she could get away with it. Rich shrugged his shoulders, a good-natured smile on his face. I pulled Cain's ear towards me and whispered a brief sorry, as we left the room.

'Lucy, so good to see you. And who's this?'

'Cain.' He reached out his right hand to shake hers, and effortlessly draped his left arm around my shoulders. Scarface cool. Psycho-killer aside.

'It is so good to meet you. I'm Kelly, this is my husband Rich.' Cain shook Rich's hand, too. 'We did not know that Lucy was bringing a friend tonight?' She raised her intonation at the end, daring me to correct her.

'Oh, this was an unexpected surprise for me, too.' Cain said. 'We've had a great day, and I thought we were heading home, after the best afternoon in forever, before she dragged me into this amazing place.'

'Home?'

'Yeah. I'm staying at Lucy's for the weekend.' Kelly's eyes could have been straight out of a surprised teen's face in the eighties horrors that she adores so much.

'So, we'll give tapas and drinks a miss if that's okay?' I said, moving towards the door.

'No worries at all, Lucy, we'll catch up next time.' Rich said, as the four of us said good bye to Ash, and headed our separate ways from the cinema.

'I'm sorry, I couldn't resist over-sharing. I suspect you're going to be interrogated next time you see Kelly.' Cain said, as we walked north to the tube station.

'Oh, that's okay. They're all really lovely. But incredibly inquisitive.'

He stopped walking and turned to me, reaching for my hands. 'I meant what I said, though, I have had the best day'.

I could only nod.

As he stepped closer.

As he dipped his head lower.

As his lips brushed mine.

As his fingers caressed the back of my neck.

As London stopped moving.

When he pulled away I tilted my head, punctuating the day with a more-confident-than-I've-felt-in-a-while 'Cain' and linked my arms through his as we continued to the Tube.

'I love the idea of an eighties-film film club. Your DVD collection makes more sense now'.

I was glad something made sense in this Lear poem of my life.

12

Cain

I woke to my nose twitching, as Lucy's hair tickled my nostrils. I could smell the freshly washed coconut scent from her late night shower, after we'd spent the day devouring London.

I had vague images of us sinking into her sofa to watch The Breakfast Club, and it had been well after midnight then. She knew as much about cinema in the eighties as I did about music from the era. We'd reminisced through the films of Judd Nelson, Ally Sheedy, Emilio Estevez, Molly Ringwald and Anthony Michael Hall without any support from *imdb.com,* except when I thought she was wrong; I'd checked the website and found I was the year out. Jam and Seb were going to love her.

I was going to miss this woman more than I should.

I had an album to promote, a tour, rehearsals, US meetings. I did not have the time to zone out watching movies.

But it had been so long since I'd had down time that I couldn't help myself.

I opened my eyes, not wanting to wake her from her position across my chest.

I watched the hands on the wall clock slowly move towards eight and then closed my eyes again, ignoring the dull ache along my right thigh, where her body rested.

She was absolutely flat out. I was used to sleeping anywhere I could catch five minutes between gigs or meetings, or on the road, or in the air. Most women I'd met along the way wouldn't have been caught dead snoring, albeit lightly.

She stirred slowly, raising her head up to meet me, the most startled expression across her face that I had to laugh. She laid her head back down and groaned, the vibrations tickling my chest through my t-shirt.

'Morning, Luce.' I said. She looked up at me then, a soft smile on her lips.

'Morning, you.' I settled my arms lightly around her waist, and was selfishly glad she didn't wriggle away.

I stretched out on the sofa, waking from the contentedness of a perfect forty-eight hours.

She pushed her glasses on top of her head and rubbed her nose. I wanted to hold on to her and never let her go. I wanted nothing and everything from this woman.

'Weekend over?' She asked, sitting up.

I nodded. 'I do have to fly to Atlanta later. I'll be away for a few weeks. Could I see you when I'm back?'

'Don't you have other places you need to be?'

'Luce, there is no one else I want to spend my time with.'

I sat up on the sofa, resting my arms on my knees, and reached out my hand for hers. She placed her fingers on top of mine. I flipped my hand palm up, and wrapped our fingers together. I could feel her heart pounding from here. All I had to do was lean forward and our lips would touch.

It could be the end of something beautiful.

But I didn't think it would be, so I did.

She met me half way.

13

Lucy

My heart pounded so hard I thought it was going to burst out of my body.

I was lying down and I couldn't move. I couldn't open my eyes. I could only hear the rush of the wind and whispered voices that I couldn't understand. My limbs ached, my stomach didn't know which way was up. A flurry of sounds left my mouth, the words just out of reach. Why was my mouth sore? Was I gagged? Where was I?

Then a rush of anger.

Not in me, towards me.

Tim. In my arms. Blood draining from his body.

Danny.

I sat up and screamed.

When I opened my eyes I was in my bed, curled fingers on my left hand stroking the small white scar on my palm.

My screams stopped.

Air whistled through my nose, as my chest raced for breaths.

Desert-dry mouth.

Immovable tongue.

Through the dark, a shimmer.
Azure sea.
Cloudless blue sky.
Thin navy line.
Blue horizon safe space.
In, one two three.
Out, one two three.
In. Out. In. Out.
In.
Out.
Thank you, blue.
My hands felt damp.

I didn't need to look down to know I'd wet my bed again.

I peeled my eyes open in the dark morning. The green digits on my clock radio illuminated 04:02, but the chance of sleep had gone.

Maybe it would have been better if Cain had never returned, had just remained a memory of a weekend away, when my defences had clearly not been working.

With more time, perhaps his memory would have faded, but my body had decided to act out its own retaliation.

I showered, threw the laundry into the washing machine and changed my bed.

Then I made tea and toast, returning to the lounge to watch the sun come up over another autumn day in London. There was something uplifting about November days, when it had started to chill at the beginning of the day, but the blue sky and lunch time warmth made you feel as if summer wasn't so long ago.

I wondered what Cain might be doing right now. It was the end of the night in Atlanta. His gig would have ended a while ago. Would he be with friends? Would he be fast asleep? Would he be in his own bed?

He'd said he was back in the UK in a couple of weeks, and had asked me if he could visit again.

What would he want with a grown woman who still wet her bed?

I returned my cup and plate to the kitchen and got ready for work.

As the days progressed, I struggled with classes. Flu season had reduced the numbers of students, but also the enthusiasm of those who remained. Everyone wanted to sleep, stop thinking, plan for Christmas.

I hadn't slept more than a few hours at a time, terrified of what I'd wake up to. By the third Sunday afternoon there wasn't enough coffee in Costa Rica to settle my mind and body.

I ran a hot bath and submerged into lavender oils. Through half-lidded eyes, I kept the hot water topped up until I could feel my eyes drift closed. I climbed out of the tub and wrapped my exhaustion up in an oversized white towel. I curled up on my bed, for just a few moments.

I woke with a jolt disturbed by daylight.

The dark hair and easy smile of Tim lingered on my mind.

I lay absolutely still, in case I could go back to unconsciousness, or was wet. But I was dry, and actually felt okay. I checked the clock and shivered from the time and the damp towel. Twelve hours sleep had different side effects; now it was time for air and breakfast.

Once outside, wrapped in my favourite layered knits and quilted jacket, I took the long road towards a Starbucks, away from campus, away from home. I found a quiet table in the corner where I could eat my blueberry muffin and drink my peppermint mocha calmly, and listened to the rest of a travel podcast I'd started a few weeks ago. Maybe a little trip planning would realign my mind. I could do with a few days away at Easter. Maybe see if Elle wanted to join me. Rome was supposed to be lovely in the spring, and I hadn't been for a few years.

A message interrupted my wanderings and I opened it before I realised it was from Cain.

Arrived back in the UK, missed you. See you later for fish and chips? Been craving so bad. I can bring them on my way. Be with you about six.

Maybe I could go to Rome this afternoon, then I wouldn't have to see him again?

Maybe I'd go to the Moon first.

Could I stave off a panic attack in the next four hours?

A class on madness in the nineteenth century should be suitably distracting.

14

Cain

When Lucy opened the door to me she looked absolutely shattered.

Her eyes were dull, not like she was ill, but like there was something she was holding onto.

Or holding back from.

Worry replaced my smile as I stepped inside the hallway and followed her up the stairs, closing the door behind me. In her kitchen she had plates and drinks out and she asked me how my journey was across London. But her smile was one of politeness, not reaching her eyes the same as it had in Trevaunance as the wind whipped her hair, or the weekend we explored London, ending with her body relaxed on mine.

We plated up the fish and chips and I told her stories of Jam's exploits on tour. He was the prankster on the bus, but was more of an annoying little brother than someone out to cause serious mischief.

Lucy seemed to soften as I shared tour stories, but I sensed that if I asked her directly to talk to me that she'd simply answer she was fine. Or perhaps shut down. I had to fight every instinct not to pull her close to me until she trusted me enough to let me in. That never worked for Jase when Shelly had something on her mind.

'Mind if we watch a DVD?' I asked. 'I'm afraid, I'm desperate to cut Footloose. Seb was playing Kenny Loggins tracks on tour, which Jam was convinced he could dance to, but his rhythm is not in his feet.'

I loved hearing her laugh, even if the sound was brief. She nodded and I said I'd clear up while she went through to the lounge.

When I came through with coffee, I handed her a CD.

'I put together a few country stories from the seventies for you, some number ones, and outlaw music, songs that were bigger in the US. I think they're stories you'll enjoy hearing, even if they're from the twentieth century.'

'Cain.' She started, and then seemed to lose her trail of thought. She moved towards me, wrapped her arms around me, and held on. I didn't say a thing. I couldn't.

I just held her until she broke away.

I sat down first, at one end of the sofa, and she sat at the other. We outstretched our legs until they were touching.

I tried to concentrate on Kevin Bacon trying to understand that a whole town isn't permitted to dance, and enjoy one of the best soundtracks to a film. But all I could do was steal glances at Lucy. One say so from her and I'd...well, I had no idea. But I had strong instincts.

When the film ended she didn't move, and I wondered if she'd fallen asleep. I gently moved my leg and she immediately looked at me.

'Sweetheart, why don't you head up to bed? I'll tidy up down here and then call a cab.'

One raise of her eyebrows conveyed more than all the talking that I could do. I knew what self-doubt looked like.

I yawned dramatically and stretched my arms over my head. 'Although, I am travel-shattered. Would it be okay if I stayed in your guest room tonight?'

One tiny nod, a smile that almost made it to her eyes.

'Thank you. Okay, you go on up.' I patted her legs and immediately moved my hands as I caught the merest of flinches. She sat forward, swinging her legs off the sofa and rubbed her eyes.

'Help yourself to anything you need, Cain. I haven't slept much this week, so maybe I'll feel better in the morning.

I nodded and said goodnight, then cleared away the cups and headed upstairs for a restless sleep.

I found it difficult to relax in long bouts during tours, but I managed six hours before I stirred.

I listened for sounds of Lucy moving around but didn't hear anything. I stepped into the bathroom across from the guest room and made myself more human. Coffee would also help, and I had a hankering for a bacon bap.

I moved quietly to the kitchen, and Lucy was already up. Dressed in jeans and a bright pink top that lingered just at the right place on her backside, I allowed myself a moment to drink her all in.

She was putting her hair in a top knot on her head, and I was so fascinated I forgot to alert her to my presence.

'Oh.' She murmured, her hair falling out of her grip, when she turned around and saw me leaning against the doorway.

'Sorry, I didn't mean to startle you. Good morning.' I smiled. 'I thought you were still asleep.'

'I think I passed out and didn't move all night. I feel much better this morning.' She pinned her hair up and poured coffee for us. She certainly looked good. Compared to last night. 'Bacon butties okay for breakfast?'

'Absolutely. Want me to make them?'

'It's okay, the bacon's almost ready. You could put the country CD on, though. I'd like to hear the stories.'

I nodded and set up the music to play out of her digital radio. In a moment a teenaged Tanya Tucker's vocals took over the room with Delta Dawn, the story of lost love and lost youth that is still played four decades on.

Over a long breakfast, and more coffee, we chatted about the other artists I'd chosen for the CD Kenny Rogers, Glen Campbell, Waylon Jennings, Willie Nelson, Billie Jo Spears, Bobbie Gentry, were the Nashville legends from the seventies.

'I'll gather some eighties tracks for you, if you'd like, before we introduce you to the nineties country revival?'

'I would like that, thank you. If you'd like I can find some short stories for you. Might pass the time on tour?'

'Yes! Anything to distract me from Jam's terrible jokes!'

However you want to let me in, Luce. However long it takes for you to trust me.

'Actually, Tuesday is my reading day. There is some work I need to do, from home, I don't need to go to the office. Some articles have been published on a Du Maurier novel I need to annotate.'

'No problem, I can head out and do a few things.'

'You're welcome to stay. Or go. It's up to you.'

'There's something I need to do in town, but I'll be back shortly. With pastries?'

I didn't often go to gigs for fun because my mind was continually working, analysing production, the set list, crowd response. But I'd managed to get us tickets for the music-making legends that are Brothers Osborne for tonight. The venue was small and standing mostly, but not far from where Lucy lived.

'You want me to see a band with you?' Lucy asked. I rolled my eyes and brought her hands to me.'

'You catch on quick, Sunshine.' I borrowed the endearment she had called me in Cornwall. 'Not just a band. Legends. Southern-rock-fusion brilliance.'

'I don't like live music.'

'You just haven't heard the right stuff.'

I could see she was thinking about the idea.

'I suppose you probably know what you're talking about when you say the band is good.'

I nodded, as sagely as I could. 'I'd trust your film recommendations.'

She snorted. 'Below the belt...Sunshine. Okay, okay, what does one wear for a concert?'

'A gig.' I corrected, glancing down at her jeans and sweatshirt. 'You may want a cooler top.'

'It's November!'

'Wear it underneath your sweater. And if you need me to keep you warm, I absolutely will.'

'I could always wear a coat.' She yelled, climbing the stairs to change.

I sank onto her sofa, reaching for a book that lay pages down, like she was halfway through reading it. A poetry book. I almost put it back down, but I realised it was comic poems. And they were short. I chuckled at the imagery some of them created, surprising myself by remembering some from my school days.

A few minutes later Lucy stood by the sofa. She was wearing a lightweight jacket over her sweater and jeans.

'Ok, let's go.' She threw a cross body strap over her, the small leather bag landing with a soft thud at her thighs.

I nodded and led us out of the room, welcoming the cool evening air.

'So, will these Brothers have recorded anything I know?' Lucy asked, easily falling into step beside me, as she put her keys in her bag.

'Nothing in the UK...in the US they have had a few hits that made it to radio...It Ain't My Fault, Stay a Little Longer....which has an incredible three minute guitar solo. And they won two CMA awards last week.'

I groaned at how blissfully unaware she was of music. 'Maybe I should have played you a few tracks before we left.'

'I'd rather just hear them live – if they're as good as you say they are, it'll feel more of an experience then, won't it?'

We arrived at the club just after eight, and headed straight for the security team. I showed our tickets and we headed in, before anyone in the queue could recognise me. Inside I removed my cap and went straight through towards the dressing room, again showing our tickets.

'Who are you, Bond?'

'That's Mr Bond to you.' I squeezed Lucy's hand and I heard John tuning up before I saw the presence of six foot four vocalist TJ – I couldn't wait to watch Lucy's reaction when his bass vocals rang out around the room.

We had a quick catch up in the cramped room, as crew worked around us, and the Brothers invited us to watch from the side, but I wanted Lucy to feel what it was like to be part of a crowd.

I pulled Lucy with me towards the bar, ordered drinks and looked for a spot in the crowd to hear the best sound. The lights dimmed as John and TJ walked out on set, and the room went wild. I wrapped my arm around Lucy's shoulder and pulled her close to me.

TJ's vocals boomed through the room and for the first few songs I couldn't gauge Lucy's reaction. I should have realised the nineteenth century specialist would probably be a bit disengaged listening to drinking songs. I downed the rest of my cider and whispered in ear that we could leave anytime we want to.

'Why?' she mouthed back.

'It's okay if you're not enjoying it.'

'But I am.'

She looked genuinely confused, then shook her head and turned her attention back to the stage. I studied her again, viewing her differently. Her eyes never left the stage. She was taking everything in, alternating between watching the brothers and the band.

She wasn't reacting in the same way as a crowd does, because she didn't know how to.

We needed to dance.

I reached for her fingers in mine, and tapped them in time to the music I knew so well.

The brothers had only been around a few years, but their talent was recognised on both sides of the Atlantic, across musical genres, both critically and professionally.

They slowed their performance and TJ's raw vocals, and the blues guitar sound, wrapped the room up in his unfolding of a love connection. Lucy briefly closed her eyes, losing herself in the music. I wanted so badly to know what she was thinking.

The song ended and an audience participation song came on, sending the room into an enthusiastic frenzy.

I wasn't sure if my protective instincts brought Lucy to me, or she nestled into arms, but I knew I wouldn't let her lose me in the surge towards the stage.

15

Lucy

When my alarm went off the next morning, I surprised myself with how rested I felt, despite not returning home until after midnight.

The show had been something else. The music seemed to reach in and show me what to think, of how stories can become three or four dimensional. The set had been charged. I was recharged.

I walked quietly through to the kitchen, pouring coffee into my travel mug. I left a note for Cain by the coffee machine, with my spare keys: Make yourself at home (anytime); I'll be back later.

Then I grabbed a banana and left for work.

When I returned home, under a downpour, the late night was catching up with me and I yawned as I fumbled with my key.

I unravelled my scarf as I climbed the stairs, removing my hat and woollen winter necessities in my bag.

I could hear Cain playing his guitar as I opened my front door, and I quietly listened to the melody as I spread out my soggy knitwear. After last night I was starting to appreciate the skill that came from creating on a beautiful piece of steel and wood. He paused strumming, then launched into an upbeat song I recognised from last night.

I grinned and found him in the lounge, laid back on the sofa with his guitar across his lap. He continued playing but smiled as I walked in, raising his cheek towards me. As I crossed the room I was rewarded by the depth of blue concentrated in his eyes. They pulled me towards him as I rested my lips on his cheek, at the last minute redirecting my attention to his lips. He continued playing, taking us into the familiar notes of the beach song. Staccato rain drummed on the window and I closed my eyes.

Feeling.

Feeling like I was in the middle of something.

As his lips welcomed mine.

Feeling happier than I'd ever been.

As Cain lay underneath me.

Feeling unsure of what was happening, and content that it was happening.

My stomach suddenly growled, breaking us apart into laughter.

'Time for pizza, Luce?'

'I'll call for delivery.' I took my phone out of my pocket, but he placed his hand over mine.

'Wait, wait, wait.' He placed his guitar on a stand and I followed him through to my kitchen. 'Let's see what we have in here.'

He started on the fridge freezer and worked through the cupboards, pulling out ingredients. I stood back, fascinated as he moved around the small space, quite glad I hadn't stocked up on emergency pizzas; I saved that shopping trip for the darkest winter term.

He placed flour and herbs and the barbecue sauce on the counter, then cheese and bacon and some frozen vegetables I'd had in probably since the summer, when I tried to be healthier.

In a few minutes he was walloping dough around my table, actual from-scratch things created in my kitchen. The flat bread was lightly fried awake while he continued to look through my cupboards. He turned up a tin of hot dog sausages – for sick days, usually – and started chopping them up, adding dried herbs and cheese and frying up the bacon.

I never knew my kitchen could produce such enticing smells. He brought out the bread and added the barbecue sauce, sausages, cheese and defrosted broccoli, more cheese and herbs, the bacon and some peppercorn he'd unearthed. Then popped the whole lot onto a baking sheet and in to the oven.

I turned my attention away to drinks and found a bottle of red. To be fair that was even easier than you can imagine; my wine is always well-stocked for impromptu Dinner Club dalliances. I also found a peanut cheesecake in the freezer, which I plated up so it would be ready later.

'Sofa or table?' He asked, holding the two plates of pizza-calzone in his hands.

'Absolutely sofa. Lethal Weapon or Beverly Hills Cop?' I carried the wine and two glasses through to the lounge, right behind him.

'Oh, tough. Eddie Murphy banter. Do you have Trading Places?'

'Do I? Can you make delicious food from my kitchen?' I called out.

We managed to watch 48 Hours, too, but didn't have the energy for Another 48 Hours.

'Lucy, Lucy, Lucy.' He called out, stretching along my sofa.

I knew what he meant. It shouldn't feel this comfortable to share my space with someone else.

Especially someone I'd only known for four weeks.

Someone who wasn't Tim. Or Danny.

By the time we'd finished the pizza I was yawning again; how can a day of doing nothing be so exhausting?

'Time to head on up to bed?' Cain asked. My phone told me it was nearing eleven, and although I didn't want to admit it, the day was over. I was terrified by what the night would bring.

I nodded and we headed to the hall. He reached the guest room first, and turned to wish me good night, his hand on the handle.

I was stood outside my door, but I couldn't go forward. The air felt like it had been sucked out of the room. My mouth felt dry and awkward.

He walked over to me, reached his arms out to embrace me in a hug.

'Stay with me tonight?' I whispered. For the first time, I couldn't be alone. I couldn't be without Cain. And I couldn't think it through.

'Luce?' he pulled away, his arms still around my waist.

'I mean, if you don't mind? Could I just lay on you?' Keep the dreams at bay.

He nodded opening my door for us to step into the room. He lay down on my bed, stretched his legs out, and held out his arm for me.

I curled up to his warmth and he pulled my blanket over us.

'Thank you, Cain.' I whispered, wrapping my arms around his waist, sighing as I closed my eyes.

He stroked my hair until I fell asleep.

I jolted awake, as if from a shock. My hands flung to my sides. Dry. I sighed quietly.

When my heart beat returned to steady, I noticed Cain was awake.

He lowered his head to mine, his kiss soft on my lips.

'Morning, Luce.'

'What time is it?' I asked, stretching awake.

'Almost seven. I'm afraid I have to go soon.' He said.

I sat up, then.

'Come here.' He waited for me to curl up again into his waiting arms, and kissed me properly awake.

'I have had a perfect non-weekend weekend, Lucy. Thank you.'

'You're welcome. It has been good, hasn't it?'

He nodded, brushed the hair from my eyes. 'Can I come back a week on Saturday?'

I nodded. 'That would be good.'

'But I'll have to leave for rehearsal on Sunday.'

'That's okay.' Even twenty minutes with him would make my weekend. But maybe an hour or so would be better.

'I'm going to get ready – you go back to sleep. I'll say goodbye before I leave.'

I nodded, and snuggled back under the blanket, enjoying the new smells on my bed.

He was back, freshly showered, fifteen minutes later, bearing coffee.

'Oh, my God, yes.' I dived towards the cup, my fingers brushing his.

Cain stilled the cup and leaned in for a kiss. It had been a long time since I'd had a start to a work day this good.

16

Cain

I parked my truck on Lucy's drive, and stared at the clock revealing an unearthly hour of six am, wondering if I should wake her. I'd glanced up at her apartment. I could see a faint light, perhaps from a floor lamp. She had told me I was welcome any time, that's why she'd given me the keys. But what kind of man turned up on a woman's doorstep at this hour, especially on a Saturday? I should go for breakfast and call her later.

The journalists hadn't wanted to leave, then we had the meet and greets, and the show started later than planned. And it was an amazing show; the crowd knew all the lyrics, even to songs we'd only just put out there. We played for almost two hours, throwing in a few Cash covers, which they went wild for, and came back for an extended encore.

I even forgot about Lucy for a while.

But after the gig I didn't even change my shirt, just headed out back to where a few fans had gathered. Then a few more, and a couple more. Jam and Seb even got in on a few photos. They're always amazed at how they're recognised over here, and the fans want all of us in the shot. I signed, and as the last fan left I saw the crew load up the last of the equipment in the bus.

Jam headed out to Manchester's bars and clubs; he's in the independent Northern Quarter every time we play in the city, finding drums and a welcome audience whichever cafe or bar he turns up in. I have to admit I may have joined him – Manchester has a great vibe, and you never know what's going to happen on a night out – but I was headed straight for my truck. Straight to Lucy.

I played Bob Seger tracks to keep me awake – loud rock stories, spanning decades. When   Turn the Page came on, about life on the road, I pressed the repeat button.

Bob knows; this life on the road can be tough on a body.

I was just outside London when I needed a quick stop to remain awake.

There is nothing lonelier than a Motorway service station at four am. Red-eyed people searching for a release from whatever road hell they've found themselves in. The stores are closed, the car park eerie.

I'd climbed back into the truck and thought about Lucy. She'd be fast asleep now, flat out on her bed, probably a novel nearby. I should read more. If I was going to spend more time driving across the UK, then a few audio books might be good company.

I could ask Lucy for more recommendations; she could read to me.

I shook my head, unable to linger too long on an image of me and Lucy curled up on the sofa as she brought her stories alive for me. I wanted the real person so much.

I turned my thoughts to how she'd grown up.

My life had been so noisy, full of family and friends, and neighbours, and holiday makers to show off in front of. So quiet in comparison. And when I was young I never got away with anything. Until I learned how to hide a little better.

143

How would Lucy and I have grown up together? Would she have tamed Cassie's wild streak, where Jamie encouraged my Sister to commit to dares? Would I have found myself drawn to Lucy's bookish nature, when all I needed was an audience? Would I have fought Jason for Lucy's admirations?

Absolutely.

I wound my way through the arteries of north London, towards Bloomsbury, towards Lucy. The city was waking up, as workers cleaned the streets from evidence of the night before, and prepared the pavements for a new day. Lights in tower blocks flickered on as I drove past, a million computer screens awaiting instructions, a Saturday just like a Monday. As I drove nearer, the buildings dwarfed me, their presence reminding me that I was just one of an infinite number of dreams. It was a different sensation, being on the water, or on the moors. If I wasn't driving towards Lucy, I'd have woken early to hike, surrounded by ancient gorse and the wind, reminding myself that I was only one person in the bigger picture of nature.

I rubbed my face, faltered for the first time over my direction. Head or gut, which was going to win?

But I needed to see her. And after the week I'd had, I just wanted to feel her smile.

I climbed out of the truck and quietly let myself in, remembering to double-lock the door, and climbed the stairs to her door, unlocking and locking slowly. I turned the corner to the living room, following the lamp light. Lucy lay curled up on the chair, asleep, a book opened on her lap.

I hardly dared to move.

Wherever Lucy a feeling of instant calm washed over me that I'd only ever felt one place before. Home.

She stirred, and I walked over to her, gently stroking her shoulder.

She was instantly awake. Initially startled, until she recognised me.

'Hey, you didn't have to stay up.' I whispered.

'I was reading.' She lifted the book from her lap, her gaze never leaving mine.

'Our interviews went on too long.'

'Hmmm, interviews.' Her sleepy voice drew me in and I understood her needs. They were my needs, too.

Smiling, I leant down to drop a kiss on her sweet lips. She sank back into the chair, her arms seeking out my neck to draw me closer.

I lifted her off her feet and twirled us around the room.

'It's so good to have you back in my arms, Luce.'

'Welcome back.'

The moment stilled around us. I wished I knew how to respond to her thundering heart without it breaking.

'You have anything to eat in that kitchen of yours?' I asked, carrying her through the doorways.

'I bought a peach pie earlier.'
My stomach growled and I set Lucy down and opened the fridge.

'So, how was your week, Luce?'

'Exams are on their way, so lots of worried students, hoping they'll get through to the second semester.'

'Man, I may be tired, but I'm so glad I don't have to take exams again. Kids still stay up all night studying?'

'Some do; most play computer games.'

'Yep, that'd have been me.'
I delved into the pie, and caught Lucy smiling at the speed it disappeared. I nodded my appreciation, and then let out a huge yawn.

'The room is already made up for you. Or.' She faltered.

I wrapped my arms around her, 'I'd sleep better with you on my chest'.

She nodded and was about to say something but I just smiled and dropped a peach flavoured kiss on her lips. 'I know.' I whispered, holding on tighter to her. She'd built a wall around her heart, and I would wait as long she needed until the bricks crumbled to the ground.

'Night, Luce.' I whispered, flopping down onto the bed fully clothed while she settled herself across me.

I woke to the smell of something cooking, and stirred under the duvet I don't remember climbing under. My boots had gone, too, and there was a glass of water on the side.

I followed the smell to the kitchen and found Lucy dancing around, to one of my earlier songs, in the sexiest unsexiest flannel pyjamas I'd never forget.

I leant against the doorjamb, the bacon and eggs temporarily forgotten, as I watched her sway and pop her hips in time to Jam's beat.

She popped a piece of a pastry into her mouth, and nearly choked when she caught me grinning at her.

'Mornin', Darlin'' I drawled, going to pat her back, even though the cough was under control.

'Cain!'

'Seeing you dancing around to my song, in the cutest outfit, smelling of coffee? What a start to the weekend.'

I leaned over her, my lips brushing hers as I inhaled her scent.

'I'm sorry I woke you so early.'

She smiled, and turned to the brunch, but I'd already seen the deep pink in her cheeks.
I took the plates from her and carried them to the table and enjoyed the best meal of my life, with the woman I was completely in love with.

That afternoon, rain stopped any thoughts of going out.

We sat in her living room quietly working side by side, in the few hours we had left together, before I had to leave for interviews and a gig in Glasgow tomorrow night.

'I could stay here all day like this.' I said. 'Your home is such a comforting place for me. Thanks for letting me stay, Luce.'

'I'm glad you feel welcome here – you really are. Despite our differences.'

'Our differences?'

'Don't make me say it.'

'I'm confused.'

'I must be the only girl who has no idea what to do with a man around the house.'

'Ah, you feed him, let him sleep, feed him some more. Pretty simple, really.'

'I think you know what I mean.'
I took her hands in mine. 'I have no idea what's happening between us, but you are all I think about seeing when I've finished work. When I'm driving across the country to visit you, Luce. I feel

so good around you. We have plenty of time together, I hope, to get to know each other.'

   She nodded and smiled. 'I look forward so much to seeing you at the weekends, Cain.'

  'Good – want to go to a party?'

17

Lucy

A party? Oh, I didn't think so. I gulped, licked my dry lips.

'It'll be fun. You and me, a few margaritas.' Cain laughed, salsa-ing around me.

It would be different, wouldn't it?

I felt like Andi in Pretty in Pink when Andrew McCarthy's character suggested they go to a house party.

Too many people I didn't know. Rooms with hidden purposes.

I was all ready for a night of films and talking with Cain, not to be abandoned to who knows what, as he caught up with people he knew.

I tried to convince him to go alone but he wasn't having any of that.

I'm a big girl. This wouldn't be like the Manchester parties. And I could always call a cab, or arrange an Uber from my smart phone, possibly, and head home by myself.

'Let's go out, Lucy.' Cain paced the lounge floor, restless energy from the run of shows and drive over burning him up.

I looked down at my favourite sweat pants and t-shirt, not really feeling the going-out tendency. For one thing I didn't want to be seen with Cain by my students.

'You, me, a few margaritas, a few friends.'

Being with strangers was only marginally better than being with students. I'd have no one to talk to when he was catching up. People tended to wander away when I started talking literature.

'Why don't you go out? I have plenty of work to do.'

'Nuh-huh. It's a Saturday. It's a dancing day, not a work day. And it's a you-and-me day.'

He held onto my hands, swayed his hips just long enough for me to take a deep breath and nod.

Reluctantly, I headed to my room. And then I remembered my wardrobe was work suits and workout clothes. Faltering, I glanced back and Cain was holding his cell phone, the party clearly already underway.

This wouldn't be like other parties; first sign of cocaine and I was out of there.

It always affected Danny badly.

I shook my head at how fast seven years could come rushing back and searched in my wardrobe for an outfit. I knew I wouldn't be wearing a dress.

And I was going to the party with Cain, not Danny.

Eventually I returned, wearing navy jeans and a red blouse, both items I could move freely in.

Cain met me in the doorway, his stunned silence a positive welcome. He held out a hand for me and pulled me into his arms, twirling me in time to a hummed melody.

'Beautiful.' He stated, and as I looked into the tenderness in eyes, I was beginning to feel it.

'Shall we go?' I asked, slipping into my coat. He simply nodded.

We walked across town to an address just outside Islington. Cain talked about his week, and asked about mine, but I was just trying to settle my nerves. If things looked bad I'd just explain a headache, which wouldn't be far from the truth, and call a taxi home.

I heard the music as we rounded the street corner. Ahead I could see pastel fairy lights strung across a garden. As we walked closer I could make out laughter and guitars being played. Cain's grip tightened on me as we surged into the crowd of drinkers and talkers. We walked through to open patio doors – the bi-fold type - into the kitchen.

'Dude!' A tall man worked his way over to us, enveloping Cain and handing him a beer. Then he turned to me, and after a brief hesitation scooped me into a hug, too. He smelt of clean laundry. When I pulled back, Cain took my hand in his again.

'Lucy, meet Jam. The man who has been at my back for the last five, six hundred years. He's the drummer.'

'Lucy, it is the very absolute pleasure to finally meet you.' Jam mock-curtseyed, his twinkling eyes suggesting fun was a priority. 'What will you have to drink?'

'An orange juice?'

'With...?'

'With a glass...?'

'Coming right up.' He spun around and headed towards drinks. At least he'd been kind enough not to mention my lack of drinking. I couldn't relax until I felt safe. I mean, safer than being so close to Cain. He pulled me into him as I took in the party-goers. More fairy lights decorated the open plan space. Groups of three and four people were dotted around, talking animatedly, but good-naturedly. Several large sofas took up one side of the room, where a group of people watched a trio of guitarists.

People milled past us, acknowledging Cain and moving on.

Jam returned with a sealed orange juice carton and a tall glass.

'M'lady.' He bowed out, dancing to the tempo of the music.

Cain took the carton from me to open it and poured out the juice into my glass.

'Say when.'

I nodded as the juice neared the top and he stood the carton on the side, picking up his beer.

'Cain.' A woman came jangling along, her arms full of metal bangles, wearing several rings on her fingers.

'Sarah! I've finished the vocals, you'll--'

'Relax, Cain, this is a party.' She cut off, clinking his bottle with her short glass.

'Sarah, this is Lucy.'

'The Lucy?' She asked. He nodded and she wrapped me up in a hug.

'So lovely to meet you.' She said, then deciding, 'you both should dance' taking my glass and placing it down, away from me. Cain picked it up, downed his beer and followed us to the centre of the floor.

The guitarists picked up the pace, and Jam pulled out drum sticks from his back pocket and added a beat on a nearby bookshelf and coffee table.

I followed Cain's lead as we danced to the energy in the room, downing my drink and leaving the empty glass on a table.

One of the guitarists was swapped out, and he headed over to us.

'Cain.'

'Man, good to see you. Lucy, this is Seb. Best Bassist in Islington right now. Possibly in London.'

'Such an accolade. Lucy, welcome to one of Sarah's legendary parties. Where no one's going home until the sun comes up. Or the music stops. I figured I'd keep an eye on Jam, you know how into things he gets?'

I liked this man. It felt like I could almost trust him in a catastrophe, absolute stranger aside.

'Lucy, can I get you another drink?' He asked.

'Hmm. Maybe a little something with orange juice?'

'Coming right up.'

'You just have those two around to fetch you drinks, right?' I asked Cain.

Oh, hell, that smile of his. So infectious.

I needn't have worried that I'd have no one to talk to – Cain never left my side, and when he talked to people, my hand in his, he included me in conversation. He really was a ball of energy that just had to dance, and drink, and give himself up to the music.

And I had to admit the margaritas were relaxing my dance misgivings.

'Cain, I need a little air.' I whispered, and we headed up to the roof garden, the December chill welcome on my face.

'You okay?'

I nodded, and he pulled a bottle of water from a barrel, opening it for me.

'I never liked parties at uni.'

'I never liked university.' He grinned, tipping his beer back, before wrapping his arms around me. I settled in to their welcome heat.

'So you never got to experience the after-party?' He asked.

The heat rising from his hold shot straight to my face and I shook my head, embarrassed by my blushes.

Suddenly, his lips were on my cheek, his mouth trailing down to nuzzle my neck.

'A guy and his girl sneaking away from the crowd', he whispered, 'to slow dance in a corner.' His leg widened my thighs, ever. so. slightly.

He threw my arms around my shoulders, and caught me up in a Latin move I'd only ever seen in the movies.

'I got you, Luce.' He continued, as I mirrored his movements, feeling myself fall into his gentle touch.

Sexy.

I suddenly realised what I was feeling and I kissed him quickly, emboldened when he let out a little groan.

'I guess there was a little making out?' I whispered, and he slowly pulled my head towards his, nodding, his mouth seeking mine.

'Maybe a little of this?' I asked, my finger tips finding his belt loops, pulling him towards me. He nodded a little more; I felt his smile on my lips and pressed him lightly against my chest, wondering whose heart was thundering the loudest.

One hand wandered down to my lower back, stroking the apex of my backside.

I hesitated and he raised his hand back up, stroking my spine, pulling away from my lips to whisper. 'We can stop anytime, Luce.' He stroked my face and I leant into him, wishing I'd had more good sexual experiences, to respond as confidently as I wanted to.

'Now it's my turn for too much energy', I sighed. He pulled me into him, his tongue slowly stroking, tasting my lower lip.

'I deal in energy, Luce', he ground out.

'Let's go home, Cain.'

We somehow made it out of the party and into a cab.

Once inside, he stopped at the bottom of the stairs and wrapped his arms around my waist, planting soft kisses on my lips.

'Lucy. Just tell me and I'll stop. Anytime. Okay?'

I nodded, and followed him to my bedroom.

He sat on the edge of the bed, and pulled me towards him so that I straddled his thigh. His surfer's thigh.

He rained light kisses along my jaw line, my neck, at the base of my throat, his hands gently releasing a blouse button at a time, his lips never leaving my skin.

'Stop.' I managed, struggling to breathe, disoriented.

He pushed me back, gently, his midnight eyes seeking approval to go further, and the gap between us sobered me. I nodded. The last of the buttons opened and I gasped at the slight chill on my exposed flesh. I looked down at my lace bra, and stilled.

He tilted his head to one side, waiting for me to breathe again, waiting for my nod, waiting for me.

His thumbs stroked my back, like we had all the time. I nodded again, and he pulled me to him, claiming my mouth with his, as he undid the clasp on my bra.

'Luce, tonight, it's all about you'.

His voice reverberated through me. I felt like I could spin out of control, but his eyes, those perfect Atlantic Ocean eyes would anchor me to him.

'At any time I will stop. I promise you.'

And I believed him.

That was all it took.

His tongue drew out every one of my senses, until I understood the meaning of the word senseless. I felt myself tighten.

'Cain.' He whispered, his voice calling me back.

'Cain, Cain, Cain.' I ground out, as he lay me down on the bed, his fingers easing down my jeans, my knickers, until I lay there naked.

I started to squirm under his intense gaze, and he lay down on his side next to me, kissing me, until I relaxed again. His fingers lazily stroked me everywhere.

'Cain.' He repeated. 'I want to hear you call my name.'

'Cain.' I obliged.

His fingers lightly traced the curve of my body, to my hips, dipping lower, lower. I struggled to breathe again, but when his fingers stopped moving, I cried out, biting my lip to stop the sound.

He threw one of my legs over his and leant up on one arm, his fingers finding me, stroking me, as he kissed me. The kisses came faster, his fingers dipping in and out of me until I arched my back.

'Open your eyes, Lucy.'

My eyelids fluttered open until I found his eyes.

'Cain.' I cried out, unable to think as I let my body control my mind for the first time.

'Cain.' I whispered, again, shattered and rebuilt.

He pulled the duvet over us and I drifted to sleep, the last thought on my mind was how someone could willingly offer up so much pleasure to another; what would he want in return?

A little while later I stirred, and looked down at a sleeping Cain.

I nestled into him, and he reached out an arm to cover me. He was beautiful.

When I opened my eyes fully, he was looking at me.

I just dreamt that, didn't I?

But I was naked, he wasn't, and I had a lovely ache where I'd never had one before.

'Morning, Gorgeous.' He drawled, reaching over to kiss me.

'Hi', I whispered, completely mystified as to what we were or what we were doing.

'Sleep well?' He asked.

I nodded, blushing.

His thumb stroked my cheek.

I smiled, unable to speak. I'd never been so lost, and safe.

'Fancy doing that again sometime?' He asked. I possibly blushed even more. 'I wish we had more time together.' He leant his forehead against mine. 'I just have time to make breakfast now, before I need to head off.'

I nodded again, a slight chill in the room making me shiver.

Cain wrapped me in the duvet, his lips landing softly on mine, before slowly pulling away.

'I'm on tour now. I'm not sure when I'll be back before Christmas. Come and see me though, please?'

'I'll be at the Manchester show.'

'Good. I'll leave passes at the front desk. Come say hello before.'

I smiled, knowing I'd already bought tickets for me and Elle.

His alarm rang and reluctantly he released me.

'Sleep a while; I'll shower then make breakfast.' He leant in to kiss me. 'We have a wet room at the show; I'd love to hear you moan my name again. And again. Under water. Again. And again. And again.'

I threw the duvet over my head and heard him laughing as he left the room.

18

Cain

As I soaped my body under the running water, I was amazed at my own strength of the night before. I'd never had such a one-sided night. I'd been completely intent on pleasing Lucy, gaining her trust, needing to ease some of her hurt.

For the first time I cursed the album launch, where long distance shows collided with my personal life. She couldn't just follow me on the road. I didn't want that lifestyle for her - too much chaos, too many people, too much travelling.

I rinsed and wrapped myself in a towel, padding into the study to dress.

By the time I'd plated breakfast, Lucy was dressed in her favourite sweat pants and a t-shirt. It took me a moment to realise it was one of my recent tour shirts.

I groaned and she let out a throaty chuckle. 'Thought you'd appreciate the sentiment.'

'I could have picked you one up.'

'Never let it be said I don't support music that I like.'

'Or co-write.'

'That, too.' She smiled, as I wrapped our bodies together, inhaling her paradise-scented shampoo.

'Thank you for last night.' She said

'Hey, no need to thank me. And this isn't a goodbye – I'll see you in Manchester?'

She nodded, nuzzling my chest, her body starting to respond naturally towards mine.

Suddenly she pulled away and sat down, the past written all over her beautiful face.

'Tell me about him, Luce. The guy who stopped you believing.'

And this time she did, as we held hands across her kitchen table.

'I fell headlong into the arms of Danny during Fresher's week. For four years I was never good enough, for him – I was always too ambitious, too shy. Too uptight. I wasn't allowed to have any friends; the same crap from a different source; my Father loved him.

'I'd never made those social connections in school that would have taught me to run as soon as he landed the first punch to my ribs.'

My own fists clenched in response. My Luce. She placed her hand over mine, breaking my fury. I opened my hand, to hold hers, while she continued.

'Thankfully, I was offered a place in London to study my graduate degree. I got in that car in

Salford, and I didn't stop until I ran out of petrol. Then I repeated the journey until I arrived here.'

'What happened to him?'

'The last I heard he was in prison. For something else. The thought of a party terrified me. He held very different gatherings.'

'I would never have pushed you into going.'

'It's okay. Turned out to be the best party I've ever been to.' She kissed me softly, her hands either side of my cheeks.

'You haven't let anyone get close ever since.' I stated.

'Well, there was this guy in Plymouth,' she took a deep breath. 'I want to believe he'd never hurt me, but I don't know how.'

I pulled her close to me, resting her head on my chest.

Why did I have to go so soon?

After breakfast, my bag in my hand, I opened the door to leave and a flash popped in front of my eyes.

'Mr Adams, is it true that you haven't written any songs on the album, but in fact they're all written by Dr. Rawcliffe, who you paid to keep quiet?'

I glared at the crowd on the street and immediately slammed the door.

'Luce!' I called, filling her on the situation.

I checked my phone and saw links from Jam and Sarah – a story had broken about my *affair* with a university lecturer, who was responsible for writing half of this album and my number one hits for everyone else.

'Don't worry, sweetheart, my team will be all over this and it'll be squashed before the afternoon.   I'll find out what happened and heaven help the bastards. I'll stay here until it's sorted.'

'You'll do no such thing – you have a full schedule coming up. I can handle a few writers.'

'Some journalists really are animals. You don't know what they're capable of.'

'Yes, yes, I do, I've trained quite a few. If your team will sort this in a couple of hours, I'll stay inside until they're gone. There's no point you missing interviews and rehearsals, or stepping into bother.'

'I'm so sorry, Luce.'

'Don't be – it's not your fault.'

'Shitty stories are the part of the job I hate.'

We hugged goodbye and I pulled on my sunglasses and surged through the crowd to my truck.

Of all the mornings to have to skip out on Lucy, this morning, this day was a shit one.

How can the best 24 hours turn into the worst?

I genuinely would have stayed with her – like I needed an excuse – so that she wouldn't have had to face writers at their worst. But she pushed me out of the door. I hope it was only because she knew I had rehearsals to get to, and not because she needed to think about last night.

The only thing to think about was when I could see her again.

When I played the Academy, that's when.

When I could get her all alone in that changing room.

I arrived at the airport with a little time before my flight. I took out my phone and called my parents.

After the family catch-up, I asked Mum about Nan's ring. The one Granddad had given her on the night he proposed.

The one that saw them through sixty years.

'What do you want that for, Son?'

She knew.

'I've met the woman I'm going to marry, Mum.'

'Well, that's wonderful, when are you going to propose?'

'I don't know.' I told her truthfully.

'Well, do we get to meet her first?' I thought of Lucy in amongst my family and neighbours and crowds and chaos; at least the main tourist season was over so there would be fewer strangers.

'Soon, Mum. Listen, I need to head off. Can you send it to the hotel I'm staying at in Nashville? I'd like to keep it with me.'

She agreed, and I boarded my flight, but not before I rang Lucy.

'Hey, Luce.' I said. I just wanted to be wrapped in her arms, to make sure she was alright after today's chaos.   'You okay?'

19

Lucy

I closed the door on the last reporter and sank against the wall.

No comments had taken all day, until finally another news story had broken, and they'd driven off, almost as quickly as they'd arrived.

My stomach rumbled and I eased myself from the wall, padding barefoot into the kitchen.

I retrieved a microwave lasagne from an almost-bare fridge.

As it heated, I poured a glass of chilled Pinot.

The apartment was deafening without Cain.

I knew he had a run of shows and work commitments, which meant I wouldn't see him until Manchester, in just under a month's time.

How quickly this small apartment had accommodated another person. His large frame had curled around his guitar easily in my study, as he scribbled notes and I prepared assignments for class.

When the microwave dinged, I plated up dinner, and went through to the lounge. I was unable to work tonight; I just wanted to unwind with a film or two.

Definitely not a romantic comedy.

I was halfway through the third Back to the Future when my phone lit up. Cain's number flashed on the screen and I took a sip of wine before answering.

'Hey, you.' I whispered.

'Hey, Luce. You okay? I didn't wake you, did I?'

I settled into the sofa. 'No, I was time travelling with Marty McFly'.

'Which one are you watching?'

'I'm on the third now. Didn't have the energy to work tonight.'

'I'm sorry you had to deal with the press. They can be ruthless.'

'They had a worse day – all they got from me was No Comment. Finally closed the door for the last time around seven o'clock.'

'Shit. They were with you all day?'

'That's okay. We shared pizza; they just have a job to do.'

'You are something else, Luce.' He chuckled, and the warmth of his voice spread through to my toes.

'How was your meeting?'

'Good, good. The new songs are going down well. Can I play one for you?'

'I'd love that.' I snuggled further into the sofa, covering myself with a blanket while Cain tuned up his guitar.

'Okay, here goes.' He began to play, whispering out the lyrics to a drinking song, a summer night, a long-haired girl. His voice added extra depth to the sexiness of the song, and I closed my eyes.

Comedies hadn't distracted me from his absence at all.

I needed to be wrapped up in his arms, finishing what we'd only just begun. A terrifying thought.

'Well, what do you think?'

'You don't need me to tell you how good you sound.'

'True, but I'd like to hear your thoughts.'

'It's good.'

'Luce.'

'It has definite potential.'

He let out a deep chuckle, 'It's the last verse, right?'

'Hmmm. Play it again.'

He obliged, and I heard him hesitate over the phrasing, humming instead, to keep the melody going.

'I like the lilt at the end. Like the night doesn't actually have to end.'

'Hmm-hmm.' His voice quietened and I could hear him scribble.

'What if the girl was a memory? One that he couldn't let go?'

Cain played the song again, adapting the words, playing it through to the end.

'Much better.' I smiled sleepily. 'Go to bed, Cain, I expect you'll have Sarah waking you up in a few hours.'

'Worth every minute. Sleep well, Luce.'

I woke to the sound of my phone going off again, and found it under my cushion.

A link to a video had been emailed to me. I checked the time and groaned when I saw it was only just after six.

I turned over on the sofa, and pressed play. Cain, Jam and Seb appeared on the screen, playing the tune from the night before. Seb's bass added melancholy to the sound, as did Jam's percussion.

The song sounded much better with the three instruments layering the emotion of an everlasting torn memory.

When the video ended I tapped in a smiley face and found my way into the kitchen for coffee.

I readied myself for afternoon classes and wandered across the manicured lawns of the school green just after lunch.

'Dr. Rawcliffe, can I have a word?' Mindy, one of my second year undergrad students caught up with me.

'Sure. Walk with me to class.'

The rest of the week passed much as it always did.

I fended off students' concerns about work, reassuring them that if they followed the information in class, put in the homework, and read around the subject, they would do well. Some tried to negotiate with me about grades. It never worked, but I liked their imaginations.

By Saturday afternoon I'd had enough of books and films and had gone to a Starbucks for a seasonal latte, temporarily relieved by the distraction of shoppers and their families.

I sent Cain a photo of my creamy drink, the emergence of a comedy moustache just visible above the mug.

Seconds later my phone rang and I quickly wiped my mouth.

'Hey, you. Thought you'd be at rehearsals?'

'Just stepped out for a minute to catch up with you.'

'Where are you tonight?'

'Belfast.'

'Awww. I couldn't see you anyway.' I declared, 'I have a date later.'

He was literally stumped for words. Maybe I'd enjoy flirting with him on screen; it was much easier when he wasn't so distractingly close.

'With Wolfgang Amadeus Mozart.' I chuckled, knowing in a heartbeat the film would be abandoned for an hour in Cain's arms.

He swapped the call to video and pointed at a Starbucks sign above his head. 'What are you drinkin' Luce?'

'A Mocha Valencia with cream.'

He ordered the same from a barista, who wished him a good show for tonight. Then he took the order to go.

'I'm not sure whether I should eat or drink this. What's your solution, Dr.?'

'You need a spoon, to enjoy the whipped cream.' He groaned, and I sipped my drink.

'Luce, I can't wait to see you in Manchester. Only fourteen more days. Then we can continue where we left off. Ahh, your blushes are killing me, Luce.'

'My sister, Elle, will be with me. I bought the tickets for an early Christmas present. She's very excited at hearing you play for the first time. She can't believe I've even heard of you, because you don't play nineteenth century sonnets.'

'You should both stop by the dressing room and I'll sign a bunch of stuff. Be good to see you.'

I struggled with that idea. I wanted to see him again, but he was just being polite. There'd be lots of people around, and I'd have nothing to say.

'I gotta run, Luce. Thanks for the coffee. Look after yourself.'

I nodded, waving at the screen until it went black.

20

Cain

Sarah had thought I was crazy when I asked her to book a flight to London. I knew I only had a day between shows, and I shouldn't be spending half of those in the air, but I had to see Lucy.

The last time I'd seen her, well, we'd been rudely interrupted by the press. Her handling of the situation had been amazing. And talking on the phone was one thing, but my arms were aching for her again. I'd never understood Otis Redding so much since I'd met Lucy.

I'd messaged her to say we were between gigs, asked what she was up to. As expected she was still teaching. I hadn't told her that I was back in the UK.

I could see a light on in her flat, and pressed the intercom. I announced pizza, balancing the box with my bag, then turned my back.

'Hello?' She asked, cautiously pulling the door back. Then, 'Cain?'
I turned around, and the smile on her face was worth the jet lag.

'Are you pleased to see me or the pizza?'

'It's a close call.' She grinned, taking the box from me and pulling me in for a long hug.

We stepped inside the warmth of her building and climbed the stairs to her flat, stepping into the kitchen.

I pulled her towards me and kissed her like I'd been dreaming about all day. Possibly night. I had no idea what time it was. She wrapped her arms around my lower back, holding on to me, her head resting on my chest, while the pizza cooled.

I'd made the right choice flying over. Feeling her lean into me was better than any whiskey-induced coma.

I reached down to kiss her again, and she held on tighter. When we broke apart she had a slightly dazed look in her eyes, which I suspected mirrored my own. There wasn't enough time to rush our time together.

She blushed and stepped back, opening the box.

'Yes, your side has pineapple'. She grabbed a slice, downing it quickly, and I joined in. She poured wine for us and gabbled away about how she thought I was crazy to just fly in for a night.

'I had 24 hours between gigs and there was only one place I wanted to be.'

'Cain.' she whispered.

'Luce.' I smiled, continuing to eat.

'What time is your flight?'

I groaned. I did not want to think about leaving. 'Five. AM.'

Her eyes widened and she checked her watch.

'We have five hours together?' I nodded. 'Expect you'll need a lie down then?'

'Oh, definitely. I pulled her towards me and somehow we made it up to her room. I remembered being here last time only too well. Before the press carnage.

As much as I needed her, I didn't want her to feel rushed into anything before she was ready.

I lay on her bed fully clothed, and patted the space next to me. After only a brief hesitation she curled up next to me. We kissed and I stroked her until her limbs stretched out, and she put her leg over mine. Relaxed was my second favourite state I could draw Lucy into. Being around someone you need should be as natural as breathing.

'I'm glad you're here, Cain.'

'Me, too.' I couldn't hide my drowsiness. She pulled the blanket up over us, and lay on my chest. I went to sleep the most shattered I had been in a while.

And I'd have done it all again for these few hours in her arms.

My alarm went off at ridiculous o'clock, stirring us both.

'Any chance you fancy coming to Chicago with me?' I asked.

She chuckled. 'Only a crazy person would fly to another country for a night.'

'Crazy about you.' I kissed her softly. 'Go back to sleep, sweetheart.'

She shook her head, and climbed out of bed.

'I may as well work. Plus, I get an extra five minutes with you before you have to leave. It's the least I can do.'

I wrapped us both up in a hug.

'What are you doing for the holidays, Luce? Which roughly translates to when can I see you again? Stay in Manchester with me, meet my family?'

I felt her stiffen in my arms and she pulled away.

'I would. But it's probably time I went home. It's been ten years. It will probably be Elle's last Christmas at home, too.'

I couldn't say I wasn't disappointed but I understood that my family was larger and louder than Lucy's family. I also knew that Lucy's family wasn't the most welcoming, and if she hadn't been home in ten years, their response might be difficult. 'You want me to come with you?'

'Thank you. But I guess I'm a big girl, with independent means. I'll say hello, and if conversation is absolutely horrendous, will escape to my room for a Christian Slater binge.' Although I wasn't overly festive, nothing should be labelled as potentially horrendous over the season. I brushed her hair back from her face.

'I'm flying out to the States on Boxing Day, until New Year, for some shows and meetings. Can I come see you when I land? I promise it'll be longer than five hours.'

'Of course. It will be lovely to see you, for however long.'

My phone rang and I knew that was Sarah making sure I was on my way. It'd go to voicemail, but I'd bring her Cadbury's back from Heathrow for the inevitable tizzy she was working herself up to.

'Merry Christmas, Luce. I'll see you in Manchester on the 24th?' she nodded and we kissed goodbye.

21

Lucy

The train slowed as it wound its way through the Victorian red brick and modern glass-fronted city to arrive at Manchester's Piccadilly Station. I hadn't been back here since I moved to London. Seven years had passed since I stepped foot in a city once so familiar to me. The last time I'd seen Danny. The last time I'd seen Tim.

Lights twinkled from shops, hotels, the streets, all celebrating Christmas Eve. I was due to catch another train for the short ten minute journey to Salford Crescent, where Elle would meet me. My head was pounding, but it was too dark for me to wear my sunglasses, and I'd packed my headphones in my case, ready for my film-binge later.

There was too much noise and activity.

I knew what was about to happen.

I slouched against a wall, sliding down, as I fumbled in my coat pocket for my phone. I needed the blue.

Trembling fingers battled with too many apps as I located my images.

In in in.

Out out out.

In in in.

Out out –

'Are you okay, Miss?' A passing man asks.

I nod.

Stare at the collage of photos on my screen.

See his feet walk away.

Scroll through the sea shots, not really seeing them.

I need to calm my breathing first.

I close my eyes, cling on to my phone, feel its four-sided shape with my thumb, over and over and over, clockwise.

In, in, in.

Out, out, out.

In. in.

Out. Out.

My heart rate slows.

I peek at my phone, seeing the horizon on the Andaman sea, from my trip to Thailand four years ago.

In.

Out.

Caribbean blue. Long navy line.

In.

Out.

My fingers stop trembling.

In.

Out.

Cornish blue. The north Atlantic coast.

I can hear again, though it will be a few minutes before I can stand.

I'm okay.

I sit, slowly tuning back in to the rhythm of students and oversized suitcases, commuters and their endless gray, interspersed with the high tinkle of party-goers using alcohol, instead of outer clothing, for warmth.

Okay, I can do this.

I text Elle to say I've arrived, and I'm just buying us donuts. Will meet her in an hour or so, once the tiredness has lifted.

I find the platform for the northern bound train which will take me back to the house I grew up in.

There isn't enough sugar in the world to prepare me for this.

Should I have gone with Cain to spend Christmas with his family? With a bunch of people I'd never met? Time would tell.

As with the rest of the UK, most of Manchester's buildings were either under construction or empty from over-priced rents. I'd travelled across the world, but one of my favourite train journeys was the scenic winding through Manchester on the way to Salford. Victorian architecture, steel and glass skyscrapers and life of all ages sit alongside the River Irwell.

I used to love doing this journey as the sun was setting. Tonight the city was lit up with Christmas lights and the markets by the town hall.

I'd needed to stay in London as long as I could before coming back.

I had wondered if I'd see Danny again. But Elle had told me he was still in prison.

If I had seen him again would it have mattered? He wouldn't recognise me from the bruised girl who fled to London on the night Tim died.

I heard my sister squeal before I saw her. A few other passengers turned around, as the tall pink-haired woman came barrelling towards me.

'Oh, it's been too long, Elle. Let me look at you.'

We drew back, connected only by our arms. 'Are you sleeping and eating well?'
Elle rolled her eyes and nodded. 'I have finals this year. Nothing is stopping me getting out of Salford and all the way to the USA!'

'Let me know if there's any work you want to go over while we're together.'

'Nu-huh. Tonight I need to party. After we've dropped your suitcase in your room. Mum and Dad are round their neighbours tonight, so you won't see them. And YOU need to tell me all about how you know Cain Adams!'

'What do you mean? I asked. There'd been no further stories in the paper.

'I couldn't believe it when you told me you had tickets – how does a rock singer catch the attention of a woman firmly stuck in the nineteenth century?'

 My mind stalled as we walked the short journey to the house I grew up in. I had no idea what was happening between us, so I had no idea what to share with Elle. The last few weeks, as Cain had been on tour, had been like before I'd known Cain, but emptier, because I had known him.

'I mean, did they even have radio in those novels you're always reading? Bet your students play him a lot on campus, though, that's how you heard of him, right.'

We reached the red brick end-terraced house of my youth and even though our parents weren't in, Elle sensed I couldn't quite step over the threshold just yet. She took my case, unlocked the door and headed straight up to my room. I had no idea what I was going to face, but I wasn't ready yet. She was back in minutes, door locked, and we were on our way back to Manchester for the show. And alcohol.

I chewed my lip, thankful we were walking side by side through the station, and that my effervescent Sister was talking too much to pay attention to a possibly awkward silence.

'So, what time is the show? Can we get there early to buy a t-shirt? But I need dinner first, I'm starving.'

When we arrived at the Academy there was a queue most of the way around the building.

Mostly gorgeous women, in various teeny shorts and Cain Adams shirts. They were dressed much the same as Elle, but so many more of them. My confidence in my own jeans and sweater combo faltered. There was no way I could endure the comments as I walked past these women to the box office to ask for the passes. What if I got the wrong place, and there was nothing available for me? I'd be mortified, as would Elle. No, the queue was beginning to move, and Elle was chatting with the girls behind us, enthusing about which tracks she wanted to hear.

Sucking in the disappointment at not seeing Cain personally tonight, I followed the women into the building. The merchandise stalls were crammed, but Elle easily got served, and picked up a few signed CDs to give out to her friends at school after the holidays.

We ordered drinks and found a place to stand near the bar. Elle didn't seem to mind that we were quite far back, to the left of the stage. She took selfies on her phone, tagging us in on social media, and danced along to the backing music.

Suddenly the lights dimmed and the roar of a thousand people bounded around the walls, as Jam and Seb took to their instruments. Half a minute later Cain strode to the stage, and they broke into the first song, about a beach. Elle danced and sang every word, while I tried not to tremble like a hormonal teenager, my eyes fixated on Cain. The man who had been sprawled on my sofa most of the autumn, now thriving on the progesterone in the room.

As the song faded they crashed into another song, and he was prowling the stage, playing to the crowd. He looked so in control and completely suited for the stage. No videos could do his performance justice.

Track after track coursed through the room, until the tempo slowed and Cain brought out a stool, sitting in the centre of the stage. I recognised the track immediately, and leant against the wall, unsure I'd be able to stand steadily. Cain sang about chasing the lonely ghost of summer and the whiskey chasing, and I found it hard to believe it was the same song from just a few weeks ago. Polished and honed, this song would be another number one for him. When it finished, the crowd erupted, confirming my suspicions. He held his hand over his heart, and pointed in the general direction we were standing. Elle squealed, tapping away on her phone that Cain had just sung new music, practically to her.

I joined the crowd exiting the venue and text Cain.

22

Cain

My eyes scanned the crowd more than they usually did. Where was she? I'd expected to see her in the front, as I'd arranged, but Lucy definitely wasn't there.

Christmas shows were a wild time, anyway, Santa hats throughout the venue. This was my last gig and then I was heading to Jason's for Christmas, before flying out for New York shows, and a day of back to back meetings in Nashville.

Just another quiet holiday.

I now wouldn't get to see Lucy until the new year, when I had a couple of night's free mid-January.

Mid-January; literally next year.

'There you are.' Sarah cornered me, usual clipboard in her hand and headset on top of her grey top knot. 'Need you for a few radio sound bites before you head outside with your Sharpie. Say something Christmassy.'

'Ho ho-'

'Not to me, you goose. Into the mic.'

'Anyone ask for me?' I asked.

She pointed to the crush of women behind a velvet rope and security. 'Could you be more specific?'

'The woman I'm going to marry.'

'Oh, she said to tell you not to – hell. You're serious.' Sarah stopped walking, shouted shush in her ear piece and pulled it off her head, before leaning against the wall.

'Talk to me, Cain.'

And I told her how Lucy's love of stories equalled my own, how she was the only woman in a long time I couldn't wait to get back to. How I carried my grandmother's engagement ring in my guitar case.

'Then how come we haven't seen her?'

'I left passes for her and her sister tonight. Thought she'd be backstage.'

'Hmm-hmm.'

'Lucy's not like that.'

'I know – she didn't rush to get backstage.'

I smiled then. Maybe it wasn't me she was rejecting.

'She does prefer her own company.' I turned to the waiting crowd of fans. Waved. Lowered my hand. What was I thinking, expecting Lucy to walk through a crowd of strangers to an unknown destination?

Sarah smiled and got back to work, marching down a corridor to awaiting media. As I was about to walk in, my phone pinged.

A message from Lucy: **Amazing. The beach song had people next to me silent for the first time in the whole show. Elle is hysterical. In a good way, I think x**

And just like that my heart soared again.

Missed you earlier. I replied.

I thought you'd be working. Didn't want to disturb you. Or get mugged for the passes at the box office! I've never done anything like this before.

When can I call you? I text, trying to concentrate on the assistant talking to me. I could feel Sarah glaring at me, but when I looked up to apologise she was just smiling.

I put my phone away.

'Sorry about that everyone – have to work with inspiration when it strikes, you know. Did you all enjoy the show?' I grinned my way through the next half an hour, gave the sound bites of my career, to be played on special Christmas shows, and headed off, wishing everyone a merry Christmas.

I slipped through a side door, to the awaiting fans, and signed photos, some body parts, Santa hats and even found room for my squiggle on the canvas bag of a fan that clearly enjoyed her live shows.

Sarah came out at the pre-arranged half hour mark to tell me we had to go, which meant I had another twenty minutes before she sent out security. Thankfully it was a cold night so the crowd were happy to return to their own parties and beds.

Eighteen minutes later I was in the dressing room, on my phone to Lucy.

'You liked the show?' I asked.

'It was unlike anything I'd ever seen. Think it'll take Elle a while to calm down.'

'Are you alone now?'

'Yeah, we've stopped for something to eat. Elle's in the bathroom, probably on Snappychat or something.'

I roared at the same ambivalence towards chatting online that Lucy showed. It would be much better to talk in person.

'What are your plans? Are you heading back to Cornwall?'

'Normally, yes, but my flight to New York on Boxing Day is an early one. In a few hours I'm likely going to be woken by my gorgeous niece and nephew, demanding to know if I saw Santa from my spot on the sofa.'

'Does your brother live near?'

'Yeah, South Manchester. How are you feeling about going back to your parents?' I was careful not to ask about going home. I knew that meant something different to both of us.

'I'll be okay. I haven't spoken to them in so long, so they may have mellowed with old age.'

Neither one of us believed that.

23

Lucy

Once I had begun working full-time, I invited Elle to live with me, to transfer schools, and complete her studies in London. I had the money to support us both. But she had a great group of friends, a good part-time job in a local Italian restaurant - and earned great tips, which had paid for her small car - and would support her scholarship to Boston to study Business. And she handles our parents better than I ever did. I'd been the parent for Elle during her first ten years, and the bond had only grown stronger, as had her confidence.

'So, how's Bryan?' I asked Elle, as we walked through the streets of Manchester, delaying my return home. 'I haven't heard you mention him much?'

'Bryan is Bryan. He's a cute boy who works with me and is my lab partner in science. But he's not going to distract me from America. Too many of my friends are so hung up on boys, on prom. I can't even think about that until exams are done'.

I patted my sister's arm. 'I know how important this year is. But you have a great group of friends. Enjoy those experiences, too. Although I'm with you on the boy issue. You don't want to go to Boston a Mum, do you?'

'Ewww, gross. No way. There's no way I want children.'

'You don't know what love has in store for you. But perhaps his name isn't Bryan.'

We continued the walk. 'Sis. How have you been since Tim? I was too young to know what really happened. But has there been anyone since? You really loved him, didn't you? Not like Danny – I had no idea what you saw in that loser.'

My seventeen year old self certainly had seen something in Danny. Attention.

And Tim. He'd been the first boy I'd started to like, far too briefly. The first person who might have also liked me.

I shook my head, unable to speak. She hugged me close to her. So close to understanding love, and so far away from it. I hoped she'd never get her heart broken, but it was probably as inevitable as the tide rolling along a Cornish beach.

The red brick terraced house looked smaller as we approached. The overgrown garden, once such a source of misery, seemed to warn us against entry.

'Look who I found?' Elle sang out, turning her key in the lock. I had to smile at her optimism that we would receive anything other than an icy welcome.

'What time do you call this? We could have been asleep.' Mother rattled, like something out of a gothic horror film, turning her back to the lounge where Dad no doubt sprawled on the sofa, watching who-knew-what skewed historical documentary. They hadn't gone to bed before two or three in the morning their whole lives.

I inhaled and poked my head into the dark living room. 'Hi' I whispered.

'Close the fucking door, girl. We're not heating streets.' I didn't know if they meant I should be on the inside or the outside and tears sprang to my eyes. So much for a decade apart; only a minute in the house and I'm a nervous wreck. Elle pulled me back, and closed the door.

'I'm going up now. See you in the morning.' I whispered.

'Not too early, we need our rest, y'know.' They didn't even glance up from the TV show.
I climbed the stairs quietly, reaching the room I escaped to every night for almost twenty years. I opened the door on my childhood. Revision posters still on the walls, my escapist eighties films collection, a map of the United States, with pen marks for likely colleges I could have applied to.

But it had been more practical to stay in the UK, in case Elle needed me.

I sank onto the bed, and drew a short vertical line on the whiteboard in front of me; only one more day to survive and then I could legitimately leave.

The following morning, Elle and I exchanged our gifts.

'A key? Just what I've always wanted, Sis. she sang, waving the key in front of me.

'There's a new -red - car waiting in a showroom in Boston. All you have to do is get out there'.

'WHAT?!' Elle squealed as quietly as she could, so as not to disturb our parents, and wrapped her arms around me. 'I love Lucy! Here, open mine. She handed me a small cardboard box.

Taking the lid off, I gasped at the tickets to Disneyland, and a tour of several film studios.

'I know you always wanted to do this trip as a child, so I thought we could both do it next summer?'

'Absolutely, Elle. You're the best sister ever.'

'Er, you are – shiny red car buyer! Can't believe I'll leave Dorothy behind'.

'Maybe great for one of your friend's little brothers or sisters?'

We chatted quietly for a while and then she went for a shower.

I text Cain a Merry Christmas, not wanting to disturb his family time, and he rang back immediately.

'Merry Christmas, Sweetheart.'

'Merry Christmas, Cain. What time did the children wake you for evidence?'

'About five something, I think. All I know is I'm ready for a nap. Wish you were here. How is it?'

'Elle's good.' I smiled. 'We're about to make lunch. Wanted to say hello, though.'

'In just a few weeks we'll be together again, Luce. Call me if you just want to talk, though.'

I nodded, and rang off, hearing shrieks of laughter in the background. Then I dressed and headed downstairs, to prepare lunch.

Our parents came down about eleven and switched the TV on, cursing the holidays and rubbish television. But they would sit in front of the box all day.

The day didn't much improve, and I planned an escape to my room in the afternoon, while Elle headed out to see Bryan and his parents. I had an open invitation, but declined politely.

I made three mugs of coffee and took two into the lounge.

'Still single, then, eh?' Mum called out. 'Yer should have stayed with Danny. You'd have had kids be now. You're selfish denying us grandkids. A career won't keep you warm at night.'

Bitten, I backed away, body trembling, stumbling upstairs.

Had I put my career ahead of everything else? Was that why I was fixated on a musician? Living some stupid teenage fantasy as an almost thirty year old? What kind of example was that setting for Elle?

I waited for the inevitable ragged breaths and sought my phone for the blues.

But there was nothing. I was breathing normally.

And tomorrow I'd be on the train back to London. Back home.

And next Christmas I'd be in Boston with Elle.

When I thought of my aged parents, only a few feet away, entombed in their dim lounge, their self-made cave, I really I hadn't had a choice but to sever the pain of being their child.

I opened my laptop and searched for a film. I opted for the Michael J. Fox classic Secrets of my Success. TV had been my constant friend throughout my childhood, which had never let me down, and I could still watch and re-watch any film made in the eighties.

Halfway through the film, just as I was lost in Michael's ability to up sell his career, my phone rang.

Cain.

I paused the film and I answered with what I hoped was a cheery voice.

'Hey, you.'

'Hey, pretty girl. Merry Christmas. Again.'

I paused myself this time, before eventually finding my vocal chords.

'Merry Christmas to you, too, Cain.'

'What's wrong?' I could almost hear him spring forward.

I blinked back tears, stared at the ceiling. I exhaled as slowly and quietly as I was used to doing.

'Nothing. It's all good.'

'Then how come you don't sound like it's good? Want me to come get you?'

'What? No. I'm fine. It's only a few more hours – everyone feels like this at some point over Christmas.'

'Ahhh, Luce, I wish you were in my arms.'

I smiled my response, words evading me again, my throat caught between heaven and hell.

'Let me sing you something I'm working on'. I was grateful just to listen.

Eventually he rang off, and I curled up on my bed and fell asleep, just as I had for most of my teenage years, my face sticky with tears against a poly-cotton floral pillowcase.

When I woke, my room was in darkness, but I saw Cain in front of me, knelt down, felt his fingers brushing my hair back from my forehead.

Elle hovered excitedly in the doorway.

Without saying a word, I got up, hugged Elle and grabbed my packed bag. I followed Cain out to his truck.

What the hell was I doing?

I'd waited so long for someone to come and rescue me, and here he was, right?

Except, I'd rescued myself from my family a long time ago.

Here was a man worth following; Cain was more than an eighties hero in some teenage girl's fantasy.

As he drove me home, I listened, but didn't really respond to his conversation – my head throbbed where past hurts collided with the present.

I was lulled by his voice, something about the gigs in and around New York, and I was going to stay with him – if that was okay. I'd nodded, unwilling to go back to an empty house except to retrieve my passport.

'Are you okay, Luce?' He eventually asked.

I turned to face him, the man who had slowly helped me to find my trust again, and suddenly I had a real glimpse into the emotions of Heathcliffe and Rochester.

My face broadened into a smile that seemed to warm me through from my stomach, and I absolutely knew the truth with arrow-like certainty.

'I love you.'

He almost swerved the car, but jammed to a stop on the hard shoulder of a motorway.

There in the middle of nowhere, on a deserted road, I knew what I was feeling. No matter how fleeting, how long I would have with Cain, this was love.

My heart was his.

He unclipped and reached for me, his arms crushing around me.

'I love you, too, Lucy.'

Like a couple of crazed kids in the first throes of Something Big, we clung on to each other; our heads pressed together, breathing in our revelations.

Realisation dawned that we'd have to restart the car and continue on, I settled back into my seat, occasionally stealing furtive glances at his frame, like I'd just joined a secret society that half the world knew about. And now it really was my turn. I felt my eyes drift close. I was safe.

I felt the car slow and opened my eyes, glancing around me. We'd made it to my house.

Cain reached for my hand and I fell into his kiss, which I really didn't want to end.

But I was shattered. Cain pulled away and
opened the truck door for me. I rummaged in
drawers packing an overnight bag, storing my
passport in my hand bag. In just a few hours we'd
be flying off to New York. Together.

  As we re-seated ourselves in his truck, I
messaged Elle to let her know I was okay, that I'd
met Cain in Plymouth, that we were heading to
New York, and I'd call her when I could. I had no
idea what was happening, but I knew I needed to
sleep.

24

Cain

Springsteen lyrics dove in and out of my head, as we travelled across Jersey, not just for the destination, but for the feelings burning me up.

During the cab ride to the midtown hotel, I'd watched Lucy's awe at the backdrop of Manhattan and discovered it was possible to be jealous of a city.

She reached for my hand, and I wrapped my fingers over hers, craving her touch. She was tougher than anyone I'd ever known.

And I really needed to do things to this woman that no one should witness.

In the hotel lobby I was painfully aware of every millimetre of her body pressed up against mine, deadening my left side in the most magnificent way. Her chin rested on my shoulder, and I somehow signed us in and followed instructions in the elevator and to the suite. I fumbled with the key lock a few times, trying to control my breathing as I waited for the beep and click and the green light. I pushed the door open and pulled us in, dropping our bags to the floor.

I managed a glance at her before her kiss landed on my lips.

To think this incredible woman loved me, too.

Limbs and teeth and clothing clashing we sank to the floor.

But it couldn't be like this.

Fighting with physics I pulled away, positioning my arms around her waist and knees, grateful the bed was close by. She was under me, clawing my back, tasting my chest, and I vowed to make up for the brief loss of contact these last few months.

I was ruined, in a way I'd never known.

So, this was love.

I roared out her name, my chest tightening when I heard my own sung on her beautiful lips.

'Fuuuuuck.' I finally exhaled.

I collapsed on her, careful not to crush her, if she was feeling half as satisfied as I was.

I turned her so I could stare into her pale blue eyes, and we both knew.

We dissolved into laughter as our stomachs rumbled, and my face discovered a new happiness as I buried my nose in the crook of her breast and shoulder, a hiding spot fit just for me.

'Room service.' I whispered, knowing there was no way I could be in public with her just yet.

'Yeah, in a minute.' She replied, dragging me closer than close to her.

Sometime later, I stirred awake in a hotel bed. A Manhattan hotel bed. With the woman I loved. Who loved me back.

'Hey.' Lucy whispered, lying on her stomach, her fingers lightly stroking my chest.

I growled and pulled her on top of me, drinking in her lips, my hands burying in her hair.

'I want to kiss you forever.' I rasped.

'What, until we get it right?' Her laughs turned to groans as we rediscovered our bodies.

When I woke again, Lucy was reading a menu.

'Breakfast? Lunch? What meal are we on?' she asked.

I checked my phone.

'Dinner. I think. It's five o'clock somewhere. Let's actually order the room service.'

'Five! Well, that's the best way to get over jet lag, ever. Do you need to be at sound check soon?'

I shook my head, stroking her back, delighting at the shudders I induced.

'No, I need to be in Nashville tomorrow, just for the day, then the gig's here. I'm not doing a large venue. Each Christmas I go to the shelters, play a few songs, help out with meals, conversation. Anything I can, really'.

'As if I wasn't already in love with you, eh?'

I grinned. 'We don't normally ask for anything in return, but if you're willing to give....'

'Wait, no....we have to order dinner first...but tell them not to rush.

After a quick pasta recharge, Lucy insisted on showering – alone, so she could sing like Julia Roberts in her tub - while I rustled up something for us to see in the city. She was running on New York time now, the last few horrendous days behind her.

After she'd told me she loved me she'd crashed out for the remainder of the journey to her flat for her passport. She'd slept on me in the airport lounge, and crashed out on the bed on the flight. She hadn't even responded to the fact that films were showing from Bratpack stalwart Emilio Estevez. I'd worried that the fight had gone from my wonderful, in-the-moment Lucy.

'All yours, Sunshine.' She sauntered out of the bathroom, naked and tormenting, her eyes now very much present.

'I am, Sweetheart, I am.' I retorted, walking my naked backside into the shower.

Lucy stood on the 70th floor observatory of the Rockefeller Plaza, her eyes scanning midtown and the iconic buildings laid out before us. I stood behind her, my arms wrapped around her to keep her warm, to keep me sane.

'It's so beautiful, Cain. Thank you for inviting me.'

I pressed us closer together.

'This moment is all we deserve, and so much more.'

'Like dinner? And dessert?' She whispered in my ear, turning away from the Empire State Building and kissing me like we both needed.

We had a late dinner in the restaurant just a few floors below the observation deck, the Empire State lit up red and green in front of us.

'You know you have cinematic history to share.' I stated.

She nodded. 'The Empire State Building is indeed synonymous with New York. Mainly because of the multitude of films and TV shows it features in. Sleepless in Seattle, released in 1993, so clearly born in the eighties, is the obvious romantic film. As is the 1957 Cary Grant and Deborah Kerr film that is referenced throughout Sleepless: An Affair to Remember. But the iconic film for me? Involves a pig and a frog. Second only to the only twentieth century film I really love, and the best

Christmas film – although it is based on a nineteenth century novel - The Muppet Christmas Carol. And, as it was released in 1992, it is also clearly another eighties film.'

I pulled her in close to kiss her smug grin, just before the waiter appeared with our steaks. We shared more stories of New York, New York; we'd both travelled here, but Lucy only used the city as a stopover, in her search for quiet.

'What's the best song to celebrate New York?' She asked.

'No hesitation, the best song to appreciate New York is Billy Joel's wistful love song to the city, New York State of Mind. The song is from his 1976 Turnstiles album, but he never released it as a single, though he plays it at his – incredible - live shows'.

'Will you play the song for me when we get back to the hotel? I mean, on your phone or whatever you play music on when you don't have a CD player.'

'Even though the song is piano based, from the original Piano Man, I'll play it on my guitar for you later, if you like.'

'Thank you, I would. I love hearing you play.'

'Ahh, it's time for dessert and the bill, right?'

After, of course, New York Cheesecake, we headed back to the hotel, wrapped in each others' arms.

I couldn't wait to get all Harry to her real Sally.

25

Lucy

On the short flight to Nashville I'd dozed, holding onto Cain's arm, as he read on his tablet.

I would love this man forever, I thought, for however long the feelings were reciprocated.

We were adults and having fun, but once term started again, I knew Cain's life would take him away from London, from the UK. I'd see him when he could visit.

As we walked through the arrivals gate, a driver greeted Cain with easy familiarity and they quickly engrossed themselves in a previous conversation. We drove through the city to the hotel and I messaged Elle to let her know I was safe, and now in Nashville. Her texts were full of heart emoticons and guitars and big eyes. I would deal with her questions next year.

We checked into the hotel room and I sank onto the bed.

Cain kissed me as I needed him to, but slowly pulled away.

'I have meetings all day.'

'That's okay, I'm sure I'll find something to do.'

'I wish I could be with you.'

'Yup, but your people need you.'

'Are you my people?' He asked, his fingers twirling upwards through my hair.

I answered by pulling him onto me, and we thoroughly checked in to Nashville.

We showered, and then headed to the car.

Ok, we were adults having a lot of fun.

Cain was dropped off first, outside the record label's office, and Ty was to be my driver for the day. A veteran of the city, and Cain, he drove me to the must-see sights of the Grand Ol' Opry and the Ryman Auditorium. The undisputed history of country music lay before me, hardwood floors holding must-hear stories of heartbreak and determination.

We shared some hot chicken in a honky tonk bar owned by a country artist Ty couldn't believe I'd never heard of. He asked me about life in England, told me how he lived for live music, but couldn't play a note. He was, he said, very good at getting to gigs on time and navigating a tour bus away from lively fans.

'Really?'

'Really. Girls, grown women, hang around the bus waiting for Cain and the guys to leave. They're desperate for him to sign an arm – or other body parts – so they can have it inked.'

'Have it what?' I asked.

'Inked. Get a new tattoo.'

'Of Cain's signature?'

He nodded, heading towards nostalgia.

'One time, these girls approached the bus just before the gig finished. They didn't think anyone was on it, so I unlocked the door and waited to see what they'd do. Their faces when they pushed the button and the doors opened. Well, I was upstairs and heard them giggling. Asking each other the best place they should hang out and wait for Cain – like I was gonna let that happen.

'Anyways, up the stairs they came, heels clicking, cameras going, and as soon as they reached the top, my 250lb frame appeared. I just gave them a look, like the parent who's caught their child eating candy before dinner. I ain't even got chance to ask what they were doing, they ran out of the bus squealing like they was on a Scooby Doo cartoon.'

There was so much about this life that I didn't know about.

'Where's the best place for me to see live music? I'd like to see what else is out there.'

'Ah, well, you have the big shows over at Bridgestone or Nissan Stadium. Or you have the hard-to-get-shows at The Ryman or Bluebird. But I expect you'll be catching up with Cain shortly. So y'all gonna need another honky tonk. With more emphasis on the music.'

'Ok, lead the way, Ty.'

'My pleasure, Miss Rawcliffe.'

'Oh, Lucy is absolutely fine. Umm, actually do you know where I could get some boots?' I suddenly had an urge to understand Cain from the bottom up.

At my insistence, Ty dropped me off further along on Broadway for boot shopping while he parked the car. The street was so neon it was brighter than Times Square in places. Everyone I met was so friendly, welcoming me to Music City.

I went into a double-fronted boot store, where a woman was dallying over several pairs of boots, stalled at which pair to buy. I asked her why she didn't buy all four pairs of boots in front of her, so she did.

The store owner came from the back of the store, hugged me and introduced herself as Rita, before going into a series of questions about my boot size, preferred colour and accessories. I told her I had no idea, this was my first time foray into country. She disappeared down an aisle, returning a few minutes later with three pairs. I discreetly passed over the white leather rhinestone pair –

they wouldn't last an hour on my London commute. Neither would my feet.

I picked up a tan suede pair, with several layers of fringing, but the London rain would put paid to those dreams.

The final pair was a gorgeous buttery tan leather ankle pair, with a punched out pattern of swirls. And they'd be cute enough to wear with jeans or maybe I'd wear a summer dress again. And I'd probably stride across London in my usual time. I bought a pair for Elle, too.

'Oh, yeah, those are the classics. I can see you walking out after midnight in those.'
When she asked what plans I had for the afternoon, I told her the name of the bar I was supposed to meet Ty in, at just the same time he entered the store. I was ever so thankful I wasn't about to get lost in another city. Although with the live music pouring out of every bar, my distraction would feel like entertainment.

The three of us headed to the bar together, and pitchers were brought to our table, as Rita asked me about life in England. My phone rang and she caught Cain's photo as it flashed up. I assured him I was having a fantastic day, that Ty had been brilliant, and we were now in a bar. He apologised for meetings running over, but I couldn't really hear him, so he rang off.

'Now, did I see that right, honey? Was that Cain Adams you were talking to?' Rita asked.

I nodded and she shared with me stories of his playing in Nashville all hours of the day until his big break arrived.

Ty had rung Cain, checking in for driving duties, and caught him up on where we were. From the conversation I could see Ty both visibly relax and stand to attention, throwing a glance towards me.

More margaritas arrived. Ty returned to the table and grabbed a glass, almost downing it in one.

'That hit the spot; Ty is off-duty!' We raised and cheered to that, downing the frosted liquid. The lime rinsed my mouth, in a good way. I'd forgotten how much I like a cocktail.

My phone buzzed and a message appeared from Cain, assuring me he'd join me as soon as he could.

The band began to play and I was whisked out of my seat and on to the dance floor. Sandwiched between Rita and Ty I think I followed their sequence of steps to the electric guitar infused music, but whatever my feet were doing, the rest of my body enjoyed itself. When one song finished another took its place, and as long as I followed Rita I was okay. Ty was right there with me, too, a natural born dancer, his large frame handled the steps with Gene Kelly flair.

In need of a drink, though, I motioned that I was heading to the bar for the next round.

Suddenly, arms were around my waist, stroking my hips. I breathed in a familiar scent.

The bartender arrived and I ordered four drinks of something fruity. Then slowly turned around in Cain's arms, and pulled him in for a long overdue kiss. About ten years overdue.

My arms reached up around his neck, deepening the kiss, until I heard a not-so-subtle cough near us. I drew myself back, my arms resting on Cain's shoulders.

'Evening, boss.' Ty said, taking the tray of drinks back to the table.

Cain and I followed, arms interlocked.

Then Rita hauled Cain in for a hug, and we were all on the dance floor again. But there was only one partner for me this time.

At one point in the evening Cain was handed a guitar and persuaded to play a couple of cover songs, and Rita twirled me faster around the room. All I wanted to do was absorb every moment of Cain, locking in the memories of his voice, his electrifying playing, his eyes on me. I wanted to stave off reality for as long as I could.

But when Cain returned to the table and whispered in my ear that he wanted me naked on the bed, I was ready for the night to end. A cab was found from somewhere and we said a thorough goodbye to Nashville. I pretty much loved Music City.

26

Cain

I had three meetings booked whilst I was in Nashville, one with my label, one with an act who wanted me to write on their next album, and a sound engineer for my new album. In between we had meetings with PR, video directors and social media analysts.

All I wanted to do was spend time with the woman who loved me.

When the option for more work in Nashville arose, I toned things down. It was enough of a frustration to try to work with Lucy in the same city; I didn't have a clue how I'd concentrate when we're in separate countries. And there was no way I was dragging her across the world with me, away from her career.

I called her in the afternoon, and she was in a rowdy bar. She sounded so happy that I wrapped up the final meeting in as brusque and polite a way as I could, before heading to her.

Kip Moore was playing a sold out show at the Bridgestone Arena so traffic was at a standstill. I couldn't wait to introduce Lucy to his Springsteen-inspired stories.

I turned up just after nine and found Lucy at the bar. Wrapping my arms around her while she ordered, I waited for her to turn around. When she did, she kissed me like a lime-soaked hurricane, her deep blue eyes staring holes through me.

We danced to a few songs, but when we returned to the table I was handed a guitar by a writer I know and within a few minutes other guitarists joined us.

But Lucy was the centre of attention at the table. I was so glad I knew half the writers there, so that I could temper down the protective jealousy that bubbled when I saw Lucy's rapt attention on their performances.

We'd had a good night.

But I needed more.

I needed Lucy all to myself.

I nodded goodbye to Ty as we fumbled out of the door towards our hotel.

We woke just in time for the car to take us back to the airport, back to New York, back to bed.

Inter-State flying can be weary on a body, but Lucy's eyes shone as bright as if she was in her own apartment, without having crossed time zones.

I took my guitar case from the corner of the messy hotel room and slung it over my shoulder. I pulled my cap down and held out my hand for Lucy.
   She cuddled up to me, wrapping her arms around my waist, until our lips were almost touching.
   'I love you, Mr Adams.' She whispered.
   'I love you, too, Miss Rawcliffe'.
We kissed and swayed out of the room, our bodies needing to be connected to each other.

27

Lucy

The cold blast of New York air whipped our faces, and I pulled my hat lower, to cover my ears, and wound my scarf once more around my neck. Cain wrapped me to him and together we somehow walked the ten blocks or so through downtown Manhattan in December, nestled amongst tourists and Christmas music.

'Here we are.' Cain pulled us through a front door and we were hit by a blast of warm air and bright lights. A stout man in a padded checked shirt approached us with a smile and his hands held out.

'Hey, Man, thank you for coming.'

'Jed. Every chance I get, man. How are you?'

'Could complain, man, but ain't gonna help no one.'

When they'd hugged, Cain introduced me.

'Jed here runs the Veterans' shelter. Organising people to bring in food and supplies, be on hand, everything. This is Lucy. She came with me from London.'

'Wow, you're also from England, eh?' Jed grinned, hugging me to him as I nodded.

'That where you want me, man?' Cain, shrugging out of his guitar and coat, nodded to a corner with varying chairs set up around it. A few people sat huddled in coats, clutching steaming cups of coffee and tea.

'Absolutely – help yourself to refreshments, guys – Marie brought in cakes and cookies, too.'

As Cain headed to the make shift stage, I shrugged out of my coat and headed to the warming flasks of coffee, preparing one for myself and one for Cain.

'Hey. Welcome to the best coffee in town.' A man approached, reaching for a cup.
I turned and smiled at the stranger, his vivid blue eyes searching across my face.

'Hey. It sure smells amazing.'

'Try the French Vanilla creamer, too. And be sure to have one of these cookies.'

'Thank you. I'm Lucy.'

I held out my hand and after a second or two, he shook it vigorously.

'David. You here with him?' He nodded in the direction of Cain, his tune up settling down, and I smiled.

'Yes. I hear he plays the best guitar in town.'

David chuckled and carried our cups on a tray to the now crowded area.

'Make way for the lady.' David growled at another man whose sprawled legs unintentionally blocked our access.

The man moved and I smiled, again, following David to the end of the front row, where we could watch Cain. David handed his coffee over and raised his chin to Cain, calling out,

'Thanks for playing tonight. Wouldn't be Christmas if you didn't show your damn ugly face around here. Learned any Bob Seger tunes yet?'

Cain placed his cup on a nearby table and answered by opening with the stripped down version of Hollywood Nights, the one he'd played in Newquay a lifetime ago. I wasn't the only one transfixed.

Over the next forty minutes, Cain played covers, including, David said, a song by Springsteen, Tougher than the Rest. The delivery almost sank me to my knees.

Cain also played his own material, followed by a few Christmas songs. Some people stood up and moved closer, but mostly people were as transfixed as I was.

'I'll play one more song, and then take a little break, if that's okay, but I'll be back with requests. And if anyone else would like to sing, you'd be very welcome.' Cain played O Holy Night, and I felt my heart contract and still. My favourite carol would never be heard any other way again.

During the break, Cain chatted with a few people, including Jed.

I remained on my seat, next to David.

'That boy sure is talented. And has as big a heart as I have ever known.' David said.

'You're not wrong.' I said, looking around at everyone crammed into the space, huddled together to keep out of the cold, sharing stories and spending time together.

And, if the work top area was extended, they could fit in a microwave, maybe seats around the coffee bar. An idea formed in my mind, and I hoped Cain wasn't in a rush to disappear later.

'Excuse me, Miss', David said. 'I'm just going to say hello.'

'Of course.' I buried in closer into my scarf and looked around the room. People chatted quietly by the coffee, sharing smiles and exchanges. A few women sat in a corner to the stage, whispering, and laughing, looking over at Cain frequently, and he grinned at them occasionally. One of them mimed fainting and her friends burst out laughing. More chairs had been added to the room, and people stood where they couldn't sit.

'Okay, folks, time for round two. And David is our first volunteer singer.' Cain announced.

'No, no way, man.' David stuttered, trying to return to his seat. A gentle round of applause went round the room, and suddenly David froze. Cain began playing Hollywood Nights, and David's creased forehead visibly settled. When he opened his mouth to sing, I was the only one who didn't expect the soulful power. For the next three minutes David was another person, as he responded the instinctive call to obviously much-loved lyrics.

When the song ended the room applauded instantly, and loudly, to show their appreciation.

One person after another stepped forward to offer their vocals, and Cain played everything, even nursery rhymes when requested.

At the end of the second hour, he stood up, to rapturous applause, and walked over to me.

'You okay?' He asked, bending to brush our lips together, his hand reaching around to the back of my neck. It took me a few seconds to reply.

'Are you kidding? You're amazing.'

He grinned but shook his head. All I do is play guitar. These guys sacrificed so much more for their country.

He sat next to me, his arm wrapped around my shoulder.

'Ever played outside for spare change?' I asked.

He shook his head. 'I don't ask for anything.'

I nudged his arm. 'I meant for donations. If you could handle a little more playing, I think New York could show their appreciation on this cold, cold evening.'

He turned my face to his and kissed me again.

'I like it. '

'If David was up for a repeat performance, you guys would draw people in with your reworking of Hollywood Nights. I'm in love with that song all over again.'

Cain called Jed and David over, discussed their plans, and donation buckets were quickly found. Coats and scarves were pulled tighter, as they made their way to the cold. They found a spot just off the sidewalk, and I offered buckets to a few of the assembled, positioning myself at the entrance, and throwing some change into the bucket to start proceedings.

Cain began with O Holy Night again, and we didn't have long to wait before people stopped to listen.

I approached them with a smile, and held the bucket out for them, as Cain's voice tore the night air open.

The group managed half an hour in the cold, before heading back inside. A couple of the women staggered in with full buckets and counted out the change. Altogether, almost five hundred dollars collected in notes and coins.

David bounded up to me and enveloped me in a bear hug.

'Thank you for being here tonight, don't be strangers, guys, come on back any time.'

'I wouldn't have missed your Seeger covers for anything'. I said, hugging him close.

Cain shook his hand, wished him a good new year, and we walked the journey back to the hotel in comfortable silence. I'd had a perfect trip away, had the luxury of seeing Cain working. It didn't matter that soon the trip would be over and we'd go our separate ways - his life was in Nashville, my life was in London - I loved him so much that I could let him go, I told myself.

I'd always be grateful that he taught me to love unconditionally.

28

Cain

The cold was killing my vocal chords, but I always kept on playing if I was needed.

Especially with my woman staring right at me, from the corner of her eyes, when she didn't think I was looking. But I was always looking.

It felt so good to have played such an intimate setting with her in the room.

I watched her warmth draw people in, her eyes sparkling thanks each time a bucket received a donation, and my heart grew ever closer to hers.

I had no idea how we were going to make it work. Perhaps it was time for me to settle down in London; I needed Lucy by my side.

I said goodbye to Jed and David, reminded them I was only ever a phone call away if they needed anything, and walked into the night with Lucy, hailing a cab as we rounded the corner and a gust of chill wind rose to greet us.

Lucy sat on the bed and within minutes was flat out like a starfish. Jet lag kicking in.

I removed her boots and coat, inched her up towards the bed to tuck her in, then removed my

own outer clothes and curled up next to her, my
arm across her beautiful body.

29

Lucy

'Are you sure you'll be okay in New York by yourself?' Cain asked. Again.

Again I rolled my eyes, and sipped my caramel latte as baristas and customers worked in time to the holiday music. 'One huge city full of museums and coffee shops is a lot like another. Go to your meeting.'

'But it's New Years' Eve.'

'Yes. A day just like any other. Bit of a party in Times Square later, so I hear.'

'We'll go. Definitely.'

'Definitely not. But anyway, we can sort plans out later. Now go.'

He finished his Americano and leaned over the table to kiss me goodbye.

I watched him leave Starbucks and caught sight of the wide pavements crammed full of people heading somewhere. I needed to join them.

I downed the last of my drink and waved goodbye to the barista who'd upgraded us when they heard our accents.

Outside the crisp air felt … good. I turned right and headed south, away from Central Park. I couldn't believe I'd never appreciated New York so much before. I'd been, of course I had – every student exchange programme starts in Manhattan. But I'd never been here just wandering before. I had a vague familiarity with everything, perhaps from watching so many films.

I spotted signs for MoMA, and opted to step through the doors to see what modern art could offer; I was truly on a break from work.

I pushed myself through the revolving doors that were *so New York*, and into another world.

Several hours, and possibly miles later, it was time for lunch, and more coffee. I stepped outside into the early afternoon, and walked east, away from the Midtown madness of party goers. I found a diner for a sandwich and coffee refill, absorbed myself with watching New Yorkers going about their last day of the year, with family, with friends, with intentions.

I had something to celebrate this year, too, as well as turning 30 tomorrow. While I wasn't in the mood for midtown tonight, we should definitely go out for dinner.

I looked down at my clothes and realised how drab they looked. Maybe a little shopping trip was in order?

I paid the bill, left a tip and left the warm coffee shop to enter a wide, windy pavement.
I took Bloomingdales being on the opposite street as a good sign, and hurried in through one of the doorways, my feet sinking into the lushest carpet I'd ever walked on. I found the escalator, escaping the ground floor crowds, and climbed through the building to their women's section.

The fashionable and over-priced clothing did not appeal to me, but there was a seemingly endless array of rails to choose from. I'd be ready for another coffee at this rate.

Or cocktails, maybe, as I eyed up the party wear. I didn't feel comfortable in dresses, nor heels. But I was learning to trust my heart, and when it lined me up in front of a black jersey halter neck jumpsuit, I should pay attention. I selected a few sizes to try on, and a cute silver, glittery faux fur jacket as I walked past. The changing room was empty, and I wandered into a large cubicle to change.

I've never appreciated shopping for clothes. I know what I look professional in, what's suitable for work, for speaking engagements. I am extremely comfortable in relaxed wear, and even have a pair of jeans or two that aren't embarrassing.

But I felt incredible in this jumpsuit.

I didn't even want to remove it to buy it. In fact, as soon as I bought it I was coming right back into the fitting rooms to change. And it had pockets in. I hoped they had other colours.

I turned every which way I could in the confined space, liking every angle. I stepped outside to the larger mirrors, to be greeted enthusiastically by a sales assistant.

'Wow. Just wow. '

'I know, right?' I agreed, smiling. 'You should be able to buy this kind of feeling.'

'Oh, honey you can, it's called Visa. That jacket is just cute as, too. What footwear you have?'

I faltered. I couldn't walk around Manhattan barefooted, and my trainers had seen much better days. I guess the tan boots would work?

'Hold up, lemme get something for you. What size are you?' I told her the UK size and she disappeared. I rotated a few more times, trying to find fault with the outfit, and I couldn't. I was in no hurry to remove it, so sat in a chair and texted Cain to find out where he was.

Is it cocktail hour yet? I asked. Almost immediately he replied.

Back at the hotel. Where are you?

Heaven. I think New Yorkers call it Bloomingdales. Meet up soon?

Yes, I'll come to you. Be about half an hour?

'Here you go, doll. Try these. Anything else you need?'

'Do you have this suit in any other colours?'

She shook her head, sadly. I retrieved the shoes she'd handed to me. The skyscraper heels would be given a miss. But the fur boots with the block heel had potential. I put them on and didn't think it was possible to feel any better than I did. But those shoes had it.

'I'll have all of it, please!' I giggled. 'I barely want to change.'

'Hell, it is New Years'. Give me the tags at the register and I'll zap you through. You're my last customer of the year, I guess'.

I thanked her and she snipped the tags, putting them in my bag with my other clothes. I wandered through the accessories department, and picked up a black leather rucksack, a bit more of a party bag than a huge paper carrier bag. I paid for my new bag, and then wandered down the escalator.

As I walked through the beauty department I slowed, looking for a helpful, and non-threatening, assistant. I spotted someone by a counter and headed over to her.

'Hey, honey, can I help you?'

'Do you think you could give me a makeover?'

'Of course. I love that jumpsuit.'

'Thank you. I just bought it here.' I sat in the high backed chair she motioned to, grateful for the heels so that I didn't have to clamber into the chair like a toddler.

She chatted as she worked, and I've no idea what she was talking about really when it came to the products. But she worked on me with ease, complimenting my skin and eyes.

'There you go.' She offered a mirror and I had to blink a few times at the reflection. I peered closer into the mirror to see my eyes.

'I love the purple!' I gushed. 'So unexpected.'

'In the light you'll really notice it. Still subtle. But it'll draw the eyes.'

I paid for the products and fluffed up my hair.

'Want me to fix that for you?' she asked, smiling as I bit my lip. 'That outfit is begging for height.' I returned to the chair and from who knows where she produced products and clips. Then she handed me a mirror again.

I mirrored her smile. The top knot was amazing.

I checked my watch and headed for the door. Cain was on his phone, his thumbs swiping across the screen. He only looked up when my phone beeped from his message.

I wish I could have recorded his expression. I marvelled at the slow smile that spread across his face as he drank in my outfit.

'You sure you don't just want to head straight back to the hotel?'

'Absolutely not. This outfit needs cocktails. Lead the way.'

He shook his head, and pulled me in towards him, his hand at my neck.

When his lips landed on mine I was already eager for midnight.

Then he wrapped our arms, hands and fingers together and held his hand up for a cab.

I have waited too long to enjoy the last day of the year. And to celebrate my birthday.   Here I am, in New York City, with a man who I've only known for a few months. This is the city of possibilities, just like all the films have ever declared.

Meg Ryan and Tom Hanks finally make sense.

I turned to look at him and Cain was right there, his gaze on me.

When a cab pulled up I opened the door for him.

'You first, I'm not hauling over to the other side and ruffling my outfit.' I winked at him and he pulled me into the back straight after him.

'Margaritaville, driver.' I stated.

Cain laughed and told the driver an actual address. His hands never once left mine.

I sat back and watched the lights of the city blaze past, soaking in the energy.

Cain whispered in my ear.

'This city can't compete with you. I love you, Luce.'

When my lips met his, not for the last time this evening, hopefully, I felt like I was home.

No matter where this evening took us, I would remember every moment.

Somewhere just before midnight, I dragged Cain to a corner of the noisy bar.

'Got something to say?' He smiled, leaning over me.

I shook my head and reached out, pulling his face towards mine.

I was starting the new year already.

30

Cain

I didn't see Lucy until she stood in front of me.

Even then I didn't recognise her, even though she was in my personal space. It was only when our phones beeped that I looked up.

And I was torn between making a public nuisance of myself with her, and cancelling the night out.

'You look incredible.' I managed, as I took in the perfect hug of her curves in the black material, the light sparkle on the jacket that shimmered. She'd even worn make up, which I don't think I'd ever seen her in. I loved the natural look about her, but when she wore it, she knew how to wear it.

I hadn't ever seen her in heels, either. I loved the additional height, which enabled us to entwine limbs as we walked. It also gave me an excuse to hold her close in case she teetered in the boots.

Her eyes, though. I didn't think it was possible for them to be any more hypnotic.

I managed to hail us a cab, and my Lucy, telling me to haul in first, and drinking in all that Manhattan displayed, told me this was going to be a good night. And I believed her.

I knew a great Caribbean bar to start a new year in, too.

A band played in the back room, and the bar was packed with revellers. I nodded to the owner, Charlie, and he came out from behind the bar to say hello. He held onto Lucy a little longer than either of us were comfortable with, and I was glad I was holding her hand. When he pulled away, Lucy snuggled up to me and Charlie handed us a margarita pitcher and a couple of glasses, waving my money away.

'You've done enough to help with trade over the years, man, go have fun with your beautiful woman'.

I nodded my thanks, and steered our way to one side of the bar. Lucy sourced a stool, and I found another one. The noise was incredible, but this wasn't a night for conversation. I poured our drinks, we downed them, and I had her up dancing. I wanted her body next to mine forever, but especially in this outfit.

After another cocktail, another party came through the doors, and made their way over to our side of the bar. Lucy clung tighter to me wrapping her arms around my neck.

Was it midnight yet?

Eventually we needed more drinks, and Lucy followed me to the bar. We lost contact and when I turned to find her, she was dancing with two of the girls who'd just walked in. I held up the pitcher and she nodded at me, her body cutting perfect time with the music. Shakira's hips had nothing on tipsy-Lucy's hips.

I joined the group, and pulled her closer to me. She looked up, smiling and danced with me until our thirst cut in.

More cocktails arrived, and shots. Before I knew it the band was counting down.

I had the best woman I'd ever known in my arms.

And she was so very tipsy.

I took us outside for the burst of cold air that would come from the short walk back to the hotel.

Once we were outside, Lucy realised her limbs weren't working as they should.

We stumbled out into the streets of Manhattan, somewhere north of Times Square, just in time to welcome in the New Year. I wrapped my arms around a giddy Lucy, to keep her upright. She was like an octopus, all flailing limbs, as she celebrated with the streets and kissed me.

She was perhaps going to feel a little sore headed tomorrow. Our last day together, before flying back to London.

'Happy New Year, Sweetheart.' I whispered, cupping her face in my hands and kissing her gently on the lips. The fruity cocktails began to take effect and she groaned on my name, her lips parting easily for me. She tasted of lemon and salt. I pulled away, smiling at her grumpy protestations, and tucked her under my arm, guiding her through the streets back to the hotel.

When we arrived back into the room, I brought Lucy a glass of water and a Tylenol.

'My sweet girl,' I whispered, sweeping her hair back across her shoulder.

We danced around the room, and I loved watching the happiness in her eyes. She was the most relaxed I'd ever seen her. All I wanted was to take her back to England and spend forever, making her as happy.

I saw her fade, and lifted her towards the bathroom. I gently placed her into a warm shower that she hadn't even been aware was running.

'Come on, Luce. Let's get you ready for bed.'

I stripped her clothes, needing to take care of her more than she was turning me on.

It was a quick shower.

I wrapped her in a robe and placed her in bed, kissing her forehead. Right before she passed out, I heard her whisper 'Happy Birthday, Me.'

Her birthday? I had just the gift.

'Happy New Year, Gorgeous,' I whispered the next morning.

She groaned and sank further under the duvet.

'How're you feeling?'

She waved her hand slowly, indicating full sentences were too much for her right now. I placed another glass of water and a black coffee on the table beside the bed. She emerged to sip the water.

'Did I hear you tell me it's your birthday, last night?'

She nodded once, her mouth to her glass. 'Thirty today.' She drank gratefully, and replaced the glass on the table. Before she could dive back under the covers, I pulled her towards me, so our foreheads were touching. I reached under my pillow and held my gift out to her.

'Then I'm glad I've been carrying this around with me.'

I retrieved the small red box, and she stilled.

I mean she didn't move.

I tried to place it into her hand, but she refused to open her palm, or even look at me.

'Luce?'

Suddenly she bolted from the bed and headed for the bathroom, locking the door.

'Luce. Are you okay? Do you need anything?' I called out, a split second behind her. There was no answer and I knocked again.

'Are you sick? Shall I call a Doctor?'

That kick drum went off in my heart again. I realised I was pounding on the door like a madman, but she had me scared. Seconds away from bursting the door open in case she was hurt, had knocked her head on the sink or anything, I heard the shower start.

I banged louder, trying to compete with running water, and my fear.

Still no response, but I calmed a little, certain she hadn't passed out.

I sat on the bed for a good half an hour, waiting for her to emerge, but still the water ran.

I grabbed my wallet and key, and left the room, needing to walk off my energy so that we could talk.

31

Lucy

My stomach rolled.

I'd had so much to drink. The cocktails had been so pretty, and everywhere I turned. And I hadn't had that buzz in so long. We'd danced all night. In the Caribbean. Well, a bar, not the sea. I was so happy.

I'd thought I was safe with Cain. But he wanted to control me, own me, too.

He slipped the box back on the table and tried to reach for my hands.

I stumbled to the bathroom, locking the door. I couldn't face him right now. My head pounded with his knocking, but I didn't know what to say. We'd known each other, what, months? Who the hell carries a jewellery box with them?

Oh, God, what if it was a gimmick, or a pin or charm, or something? And I went and expected it was a ring?

I was such a fool.

Mortified, I still couldn't bring myself to tell him I wasn't sick. Not when my stomach was churning and my head splitting. If I ignored the situation, then it wasn't happening. That had carried me through with dealing with parents who didn't want me, and though an abusive relationship, right on out to being by myself.

I switched on the shower but didn't get in. Eventually he stopped pounding, and I sat there waiting for the nausea to fade. I climbed under the steam and stayed there until I wrinkled. When I heard the door slam I turned off the water.

I wrapped myself in a towel and opened the bathroom door.

He had gone.

The red velvet box lay in front of me, still.

Of course it did, it was only a box.

My feet directed me to the table.

I slowly lifted the lid on the box, snapping it closed again as the diamond ring shouted at me.

My legs buckled, and I sank to the floor. Ugly tears rolled down my face until I dry heaved with emptiness.

Then I stood up, dressed, and packed up my week, my eyes stinging and head cramping.

At the last minute I launched the box into the bottom of my backpack. I would hate for it to go missing because I left it visible. I'd send it to his label.

I caught the first cab outside the hotel, and the first flight back to London.

32

Cain

I unlocked the door, balancing the pastries and coffee, expecting Lucy would still be in the bathroom.

I hadn't expected that she'd left.

'Luce?' I called out, already knowing there'd be no answer.

My eyes went straight to the table. The box had gone.

I was vaguely aware of coffee falling and my knees hitting the carpet. A dark fear spread through me, from the realisation that had just pierced my heart.

I yelled out her name again, hoping she'd just appear and tell me off for shouting. Her case had gone, the bathroom door was open, the bed still unmade. I could read the signs.

Just not the signs from the woman I loved, the signs that told me she'd skip out on me. At the first sign of trouble.

Trouble that I'd caused.

What the hell was I thinking?

I thought most women loved romance?

She was the nineteenth century addict - that proposal should have been just what she needed.
I cackled then, muffling a guttural scream.
The proposal was just what *I'd* needed.
I'd thought I had everything. Then I met Lucy.
It wasn't her fault I was a self-absorbed prick.

33

Lucy

The flight was eight hours of hell.

My eyes burned with exhaustion, every noise amplified from the endless sock shuffling to the toilets to the crinkling of airline food packaging. Nausea threatened my every move, so I'd thrown the blanket over my head and searched for an oblivion that didn't appear as much as the shiny stone that cut through every image in my screwed up eyes.

When we landed, and I'd endured the immigration queue, I climbed into a black cab, blinking through the early morning sun rise as we travelled through the silent city.

I opened the door to my flat, double-locked, climbed the stairs, opened my front door, dropped the bag and crawled onto the bed, fully clothed, and waited for sleep to claim me.

The last thing I heard was the empty silence of the hotel room as it echoed around the space where my heart used to lie.

I woke up to roaring traffic outside my window, and hated that people were living their lives.

I scrambled into my comfy sweats and a hooded top and brought coffee and my laptop back to bed. I was due to meet students the next day, but I called in sick to work for the first time in my life; each time I tried to walk my head spun.

I delegated an undergraduate elective class on the short story to Tallie, and replied to a couple of emails from Moira, asking if I was okay and if I needed anything. I cancelled the rest of my classes. Then I closed the laptop down. Exerted, I lay back down on the bed, the sunset streaming through the windows. The studiously unanswered message burned in my phone. Just one text:

> *I'm sorry. I didn't mean*
> *to cause you any pain,*
> *Luce – I love you so, so*
> *much. I have no idea*
> *what the future holds,*
> *for either of us, but I*
> *hope I can be in yours.*
> *If that's just as a co-*
> *writer, from a distance,*
> *then that's what I'll be*
> *– though we're so*
> *much better in the*
> *same room. Happy*

Birthday, Sweetheart.
Forever, Cain.

I couldn't sleep. Every time I closed my eyes, my mind ran a silent movie. A cornflower blue pierced every scene. I lay with my eyes open, lights off, staring at nothing. At some point I went into the kitchen, thinking I should eat. But I could only stomach salty crackers.

Every muscle and bone ached within me, like my body was reacting, badly, apocalyptically, to his absence. It hurt to sit, never mind stand. The only way I could breathe was lying down, curled on my side. Why had I ever gone to that ridiculous conference? What had happened that I had trusted someone so easily?

Why had I run away from him in that hotel room?

My head needed to stop spinning.

I might as well wish the sky away that lay above me, taunting my inertia.

Maybe I'd read so much nineteenth century literature that I'd become a doomed heroine, destined to crack apart, let loose the hysteria which bubbles beneath us all at some point in our lives.

London would no longer look the same.

In only a few short weeks – a semester – my home and my favourite city were hell.

I should have taken him to other places in London, not the places I used to call home.

Then my life wouldn't have been tainted.

No. He had been in it.

Life was tainted.

Again.

Maybe it was time to relocate? Somewhere they had never heard of Cain Adams.

Was Mars taking mortgages yet?

Hell, my own body would never be the same again. I felt him everywhere. The withdrawal was something out of a Danny Boyle film.

I'd promised myself that no man would ever affect me this way again.

Though I would never be repulsed by Cain.

I would never be terrified of him.

For the first time in months I'd missed back-to-back Dinner Club screenings, which had included John Hughes triple-bills.

Ash text me to see if I was okay, and then Kelly. When Rich, the man who hates technology, messaged me to ask if I was okay, I threw the phone across the room. What the hell was okay anyway?

Still a churning wreck of guilt and anguish, by the end of the week common sense fought through and I went to work. Sleep hadn't found me apart from short bursts of losing unconsciousness. But after a shower and fresh air I felt ok. Fissured, but I'd be able to teach. I'd be able to function.

I willed students to try to comment on their own inquiries, ignoring their obvious stares and questions about my sudden absence. I blamed the flu and proceeded to drill them on the Poe collection I'd asked Tallie to go through with them. They answered well, and comprehensively, and quickly paired off to discuss the themes I'd given them. I gave them twenty minutes to prepare their presentations and worked through emails whilst they studied.

Mindy approached me at my desk.

'Dr. Rawcliffe. It's good to see you back.'

'Thank you.' I replied automatically, and waited for her request.

'Is there any way you could hear our presentation first?'

I nodded and she walked back, clapping briefly. I couldn't quite place it, but there was an edge to that student.

When the class ended, Tallie approached me as I packed away papers.

'Is there anything more enjoyable than a good horror story?' She stated her preamble.

Welcome to my life, I thought, enjoyment aside.

'I just wanted to say that I loved teaching the sessions on gothic horror. I found a great article to open up the debate of horror and psychotic behaviour in Poe's work. I'd be happy to teach any other classes you'd like me to?' She asked hopefully.

'And what about your own research?'

'Well, I live alone, so have no annoying flatmates dragging me out and away from gender and conformity in nineteenth century America. It might be a welcome change reading outside of my field. I've read a few books on education, too, as the drama class is going very well.'

I closed my bag and turned to answer her.

'I was very pleased with the class progress, whilst I was away. And your enthusiasm for the teaching side of your research tells me this could be a pathway for you. But life isn't all about research. It must be dived into. Distractions and all.

'Having said that. If you would like to continue the sessions on gothic horror, I'm happy for you to do so until Easter.'

Her face lit up and I couldn't help but return her smile. Briefly.

I returned to the office and sank onto the sofa, my bags falling to the floor. I had a couple of hours before my next class, on early twentieth century playwrights. I could find lunch, but I wasn't in the mood for noisy cafeterias. Or eating, really. Maybe I'd just rest my eyes a while.

When I woke up, Moira was stood in the doorway, leaning on the frame, her hands in her trouser pockets.

'I would have woken you in time for your class. Looks like you needed that REM cycle.'

Did she put the blanket over me, too? Had I said anything in my sleep I shouldn't have?

Done anything I shouldn't have? I didn't feel damp.

'Give yourself a few minutes to wake up, and then we'll go for coffee. Something to eat.' She walked to her office down the corridor and I leant back against the sofa again, blinking my eyes awake. Checking my watch I saw I had half an hour before class, and stood reluctantly. Maybe I'd try sleeping here tonight?

I called for Moira and we walked across to a small cafe just off campus. She ordered our black coffees and a chicken sandwich for me.

'How are things with you and Cain?' She asked. I'd always appreciated her bluntness until now. 'I read the article a few months ago. Anyone coming out of your apartment had to be serious. Am I wrong?' I shook my head. 'Something has happened – you don't need to tell me what.' I couldn't even tell myself what had happened. 'If you need more time off we can work on something. But - and I speak from personal experience here – work can be heaven sent at a time of personal---'

'Crisis. Anguish. Torment.' I finished, lightly. It was certainly good for sleep. 'I'm sorry for disappearing.'

'No need to apologise. It's not just our bodies that become ill, we know this. 'But nobody is worth losing sleep over.'

I'd like to think she was right. But I just smiled and ate my chicken sandwich, grateful when she talked about a museum exhibition she'd just visited, and off the topic of Cain.

34

Cain

One more song left in me. Two left in the set.
  I'd worked harder; I could do this.
  Twelve shows down, three more left.
  Then Bali or Portugal or Costa Rica; rock hard
waves numbing my days, tequila drowning my
nights.
  Sweat rolled off my back as I prowled the stage,
toward Jam's beat, heading for Seb's bass to pull
me through. I was worn and torn, like I'd been
overturned by a perfect ten.
  Or the woman I loved had walked away from
me.
  Muscle memory knew the routine of the songs
perfectly. In minutes I'd be done.
  I craved.
  Something.
  My eyes scanned the jumping audience.
Sparkles and shouts and smiles and flashes.
  And nothing.
  No wide-eyed, long-lashed, beautiful-smile Lucy
looking at me.

Why did this gig have to be in London? Lucy wasn't answering her phone, wasn't replying to messages. She hadn't even answered the unknown numbers when I rang from Jam and Seb's phones.

She was done with me.

And I was done for the night.

I threw my hands up as I walked off stage to screams, but headed directly for the exit. The lights went up, no encore again tonight.

In the dressing room I tore off my vest, pulled on a nearby t-shirt, grabbed my jacket and a cap and stormed out of the building.

I followed the street lights of the city, needing distraction, needing neon. I looked up and found myself near Leicester Square Tube station. I remembered walking around here with Lucy on that perfect weekend when she'd shown me her city.

She was so close.

But I would respect her wishes, and willed my feet away from her apartment.

The hardest part was wondering if she was hurting, too.

Why had I been so fucking presumptuous about our future?

Why hadn't I just accepted, for whatever reason, that she loved me, and just enjoyed us?

A queue of people had formed in front of me and I stopped walking whilst I looked for a way around or through them.

I wasn't ready to throw myself into traffic; three more shows.

I looked up while a family walked, crocodile file, towards me. Dad, Mum, three children of perfect sizes.

My imagined life literally about to walk on by.

I threw my head back to avoid seeing what believing in fate had done to me. Above me was a sign for The Dinner Club. The doting Dad was so close to me.

I ducked through the doorway and entered the foyer. It was busier than last time, people everywhere. I pulled my cap lower.

The owner – Ash? – was stood by the till, with a queue of customers. When he saw me he waved me through and I nodded my head in appreciation as I entered the darkened screening room.

I had no idea what was playing, but the cinema looked fuller than the previous time I'd visited. I chose a seat near the front and stared at the adverts on screen. A couple sat next to me, a huge bucket of popcorn and even larger drinks balanced on thighs and in cup holders. Through their conversation I picked up that there was a horror film on.

Art might as well reflect life.

The screen darkened and text flooded the screen with a familiar sound track from Kenny Loggins. Not that soundtrack from the Kevin Bacon film, but the one accompanying fighter jets.

I didn't know as much about films as Lucy, or Ash, but even I didn't think Top Gun was a horror.

Mumbles started in a few rows, but it seemed like the volume increased on an already loud film, and there was nothing quite like an air show for distracting noise.

I settled in to the commotion and allowed myself to enjoy the alpha male competition between Tom Cruise and Val Kilmer. A few people left, but I was already embroiled in the film. Where else was I going to be?

Twenty minutes later, when the opening bars of the Righteous Brothers' You've Lost That Loving Feeling played, I didn't know whether to stay or run. Kelly McGillis looked a little different to the woman I remembered previously on screen. I hadn't realised how authoritative she was. The scene passed and I remained. I knew this film was in Lucy's collection, but we'd never watched it together. This almost felt like a connection, even if it was only for two hours. I was helpless to move.

35

Lucy

For weeks I'd gone to work, I'd come home, I'd read and planned and graded. I was averaging two hours sleep at a time. I'd given up going to bed anymore, just waited for sleep to take me where I was, and hoped I was sitting down.

January was almost over. Then we'd only have eleven months left in the year.

Sometime after midnight, I was dragged back to the twenty first century by a savage phone that wouldn't stop ringing. Finally, a message: **Lucy, let me in. It's Luke**.

If I didn't answer, he'd call the police.

I shuffled downstairs and when he pushed open the door the horror on his face was evident. Luke, who always looked stylish, verses me, the end of the world.

'Upstairs now.'

I led the way, collapsing on the sofa.

'Fair enough you're too busy for Pretty in Pink, which we haven't shown for ages, but missing the annual Nineties Night of Goodfellas, Pretty

Woman and Home Alone? I should have known something was up.'

I started sobbing, and trying to explain. Luke translated back to me through the mess.

'You were seeing Cain. Sort of. Yes, we know - you brought him onto hallowed cinematic ground. You haven't brought anyone ever. You went to New York together? So very Ryan and Hanks. AND Nashville? Well, lookit you. Oh. He did what? A ring? Wow. An actual ring. Of course it's lunacy to think he wanted to control you – he loves you. Where is it? Okay, okay. Why's it lunacy? Because the proposal should have been at a showing of The Breakfast Club. Or at the very least Dirty Dancing. What? He clearly loves you. Who cares that you've only known each other five minutes? Why? Because, snot aside, you're gorgeous. Why wouldn't you have the right to love anyone? Yours isn't the only past to mess you up, Buttercup. I know, I know.'

Luke gently pushed me away from him, so he could look into my eyes. My achy, crimson eyes. His hands held my wrists lightly.   'Yes, It hurts. But you have to let go of that fear if you're going to take a chance on love.' He brushed my greasy hair back from my face, and we nodded in synchronisation. 'No one knows if we're with the holy grail of The One until you can look back on a twenty year relationship. I didn't know Ash was my one at the beginning. All I knew was that he made me laugh, and we have excellent taste in films.

'When did you last sleep? Or shower? I'll make more tea. You shower. Yes, I'm serious.'

A shower and a cup of tea later, I was down to just being a bit of a hiccupping state.

'Cain was in The Dinner Club tonight.'

I struggled to focus.

'He looked like shit. Ash swapped the movie. We were due to show Halloween, but he put on Top Gun instead.'

Now I just looked confused.

'A few people left, but it's a classic film. With a terrific romantic thread.'

I wiped my nose.

'Have you been online?' He asked, scrolling through his ever-present phone.

I shook my head, my arms wrapped around my knees.

He held the device in front of my eyes and I moved forward.

Cain.

But not the Cain I knew.

I took the phone from him and read the article.

A sold-out arena show. Exorcising demons on stage. No after-show appearances. No interviews about his album.

I zoomed in on his eyes, their misty morning grey drawing me in. He looked exhausted.

I returned to resting my chin on my knees.

It shouldn't be like this.

I didn't care what I was feeling, but pain shredded through me to see him so empty. Why wasn't anyone taking care of him?

'Call him, Lucy. Your man needs you.'

I shook my head. 'It's almost five in the morning. I ran out of the country on him. I don't know what to say.' I croaked.

'Can anything *more* worse already happen?' He asked.

I shook my head again, then hugged him, and vaguely heard him close the door behind him.

I swiped slowly through the apps on my phone, trying to engage my brain to perform the simple task of making a phone call, scrolling through to find the function.

My fingers rested on his number.

I clicked the green button, before I could change my mind. He answered on the second ring.

'Luce.' My heart tore at the sound of my name on his voice.

Throat cracking, it took me a moment or two to find sound.

'Luce?'

'I'm here.' I whispered, dry sobbing. 'I'm so sorry.'

'Sssh, you have nothing to apologise for. I'm sorry I hurt you. I've missed you.'

'Can we meet?'

'I can come over now, if that's okay?'

'Yes.' I nodded and hung up, lying down again.

I must have drifted into a semi-sleep, because I woke to the sound of my phone vibrating.

Let me in, Luce, I'm outside.

I stumbled down the stairs, gripping hold of the door to face him, sunlight stabbing my eyes.

He held his arms out for me and I fell into them, his grip holding me up as I sank into him.

I pulled back and stared at his eyes, shocked by the reality of their dullness.

'I'm sorry.' I cracked. 'I didn't know what I was supposed to do.'

'No, I'm sorry. I didn't mean to hurt you.' He repeated, pulling me closer.

My axis spun; I was in Cain's arms again. Breathing his scent.

'It was the best birthday present I've ever had.' My head pounded from the proximity, from the honesty. 'I want to be more than a co-writer, but I don't know how to be. I don't know how to be with someone else, properly. I can't be controlled again. '

'Ssssh, it's okay, Luce. Do you trust me?'

Did I trust the man who had taken this separation thing as lightly as I had?

Did I trust the man who'd come running as soon as I called?

I nodded easily. He still had my heart, even if it was in tatters.

Could I now earn his trust? I absolutely hoped so.

'Thank you, Sweetheart, for calling me. I want you in my life, too. I need you. And I don't know what forever is either. Perhaps we could start over again? One day at a time.'

I nodded furiously.

'Maybe we could actually go on some regular dates, instead of spending days and weekends holed up together? We've sort of been connected without maybe understanding why.'

'I would love that. One date at a time.' I burst out, my tears sticky on my face, and on his shirt. 'Coffee date?' I asked.

He nodded, and followed me up the stairs.

I somehow prepared coffee in my suddenly too-small kitchen, aware of his eyes on my every move as he stood holding onto the worktop behind him. As the kettle boiled, I glanced up and he reached out for me. I moved the step towards him.

'I've missed you Luce.' He entwined his fingers with mine and pulled me in slowly. I gladly followed, relieved when our lips finally met, his hands at the base of my head as the last month faded into insignificance.

Breathing took over, our foreheads resting against each other, his hands wrapped around my waist.

'I've missed me, too.' I whispered, sighing at the feel of his laugh against my body. 'I'd hoped you hadn't forgotten me'.

'I had everything, except you, Luce, so nothing mattered.' His fingers traced my jaw line.

'Cain.'

'Luce.'

All thoughts of breathing and coffee were forgotten.

36

Cain

I've been alone many times; the only seat in a row on flights, alone in a room awaiting shows, driving myself to gigs across the country.

But I'd never felt the emptiness since I'd returned to the hotel room in New York, expecting to talk about my insane proposal. I'd simply never imagined she wouldn't be there.

Hadn't she always been there?

And finally she was again. On that tiny screen in front of me, asking to see me. I'd turned off the road to Newquay and driven straight to her.

But I was terrified of taking things too far again; clearly, I couldn't see clearly when it came to Lucy.

I would follow her lead exactly from now on.

Which might have explained how we'd ended up on her sofa, her body resting on mine.

I was exhausted from the last few weeks of shows and insomnia. And Lucy must have been just as tired, because we fell asleep together without needing a film.

I'd woken first, hardly daring to move.

It was like November all over again, when we frequently fell asleep on each other.   Her clock had said it was after twelve, and from the light in the room I guessed midday and not midnight. But we could have slept for days.

Lucy woke up, startled, panic in her soft blue eyes, but she didn't move from me.

'Hello, Sweetheart'. I whispered. 'Any idea what day it is?'

'Pizza.' She declared, and I chuckled under her. 'Thank you for not forgetting me.' She whispered, her sleepy eyes awakening me.

'I could as soon forget you as I forget my own existence.'

'Oh, hello, been spending time with Heathcliffe?' She smiled.

'Well, the films. And Wikipedia. That book is big. It made me feel closer to you, though.'

'Be with me always – in any form – drive me mad. Do not leave me in this abyss where I cannot find you.' She quoted, as my lips sought out hers again.

'As we're doing the regular dating thing, now.' She said, sitting up on the sofa and rolling her eyes. 'Maybe we could meet for our date this evening?'

I nodded. 'The Dinner Club?'

'Yes, and then dinner. They show films at 5 pm on a ... Sunday.' She checked her phone to confirm the day; we had only slept a morning.

'It's a ---'

'Don't say it.' She finished, drawing me to her before I left her apartment, closing the door softly behind me. Four hours until our first official date.

We sat at the back of the almost empty Dinner Club cinema screen and light-heartedly pulled the script and the character's relationship apart.

'No girl should spend that much money on her appearance.' Lucy had started. 'Much better on a college education.'

'They'll be together for five minutes after the closing credits and then he'll realise how vacuous she really is. Much better to be with an educated woman. A Dr. if you can.'

'And he's far too boring. She needs herself a musician.'

I placed my hand over hers on the arm of the chair.

I would go as slowly as she needed me to. But I would always let her know I was here.

'Oh, look, here comes the well-meaning friend who'll tell her to get her act together.'

'She'll end up with the guy's geeky best friend, right? Got this narrative thing nailed. Maybe I could do a Literature class.' I said.

'Maybe you would be a distraction to your Lecturer.'

'Good.' I squeezed her hand lightly.

'Maybe the guy will turn to the girl now.' Lucy began. I turned to face her. 'And the girl will bite her delicious, salty, sweet popcorn lips.'

The tip of her tongue darted across her bottom lip, 'in anticipation of a humdinger of a smacker.' I added.

'And the guy will count to three in his head' she whispered. 'Then lean in for the biggest kiss since Gone with the Wind's Rhett and Scarlet.'

'And the girl will also count three, but the kiss will be more reminiscent of Springsteen and Scialfa, or Ringo and Barbara, or Dolly and Carl, or Jon and Dorothea...'

'Three.' Lucy declared, and her lips sought out mine, popcorn tumbling to the floor, as the final credits rolled.

When we eventually pulled apart, the lights flicked on; Ash and Luke stood at the bottom of the stairs, grinning up at us and cheering.

I strode out of the cinema, Lucy giggling behind me.

'Time for dinner?' I suggested. My heart swelled when she nodded. My life was complete, just having this woman near me. We had to make it work.

We walked to a nearby pizza chain and sat across from each other in a booth.

When we'd ordered I reached for her hand, connecting our fingers, tracing soft circles on her palm.

'I do love you, Cain. My heart's yours.' She whispered. I nodded.

'And you *are* my heart, Luce. My home. Nothing changed that.'

'But our lives are so different.' Her fingers trembled within mine.

'They are.' I acknowledged.

'And I don't know what this means.'

'Nope.' I stated.

She let out a beautiful laugh, deep and heart warming. 'There are no answers, you're telling me?'

'What's the question?' I asked.

'What are we doing?'

We were interrupted by pizza and parmesan.

'Figuring things out. Want to swap a slice?' She nodded and I cut up a slice of my spicy chicken and traded it for her double pepperoni. I was on the cusp of a career that was going to take me around the world for half a year; Lucy was a well-respected academic offering stability to her students in London.

I had no idea what we were doing.

We ordered dessert and coffee, and were the last customers in the restaurant. As we left she huddled close to me, away from the cold air, and I eagerly wrapped us up as we walked the short walk to her apartment. Just like I had done in New York, a life time ago.

At her door I intended to kiss her goodnight.

As I went to turn away, she pulled me close.

'A first date should end at the door, Luce.'

'Not a first date this good.'

After the slightest hesitation I followed her in to the building. We had a unique approach to regular dating.

Lucy brought out a bottle of red wine and two glasses.

I reached for the radio, tuning in to a country station, and sprawled out on the floor, drawing her to me.

She settled into my arms and I reached for her lips with mine, my hands reaching up to sink into her hair.

'We work together instinctively.' I breathed, and felt her nod. 'And now we're figuring out things.'

'We are.' She whispered. 'I'm glad your blue is back.'

I threw my leg over hers and felt her relax into me.

'Luce.'

'Cain.'

This woman was my everything, and my undoing.

'We're not sleeping together tonight.'

'Absolutely not.' She declared, wriggling in dangerously closer.

'I'm not kidding.'

'I'm not scared of right now, Cain. Its tomorrow and next week and whatever *after* is.'

'Oh, me too, me too.' I agreed.

But the taste of her, and the scent of her. I couldn't move away like I knew I should.

'How is this regular dating, Lucy?'

'This is our regular, Cain', she whispered. 'Cain, Cain, Cain'.

And just like that I was undone all over again.

37

Lucy

Moira peered her head around my office door.

'You're looking good, Lucy. Did you do something with your hair?'

I smiled. The follicles were certainly enjoying their workouts when they could.

'Anyway. Just wanted to let you know you're the new Digital Officer for the department. That won't be a problem, will it?

Oh, it absolutely would.

But Moira had always been a tell-don't-ask leader. Her faith in me, and my technical abilities, was possibly misplaced this time.

'Not at all.' I replied. Even if I didn't know which direction work was heading in, I could figure it out. It was personal stuff that confused me.

'Carry on the good work.' She wisped past the door like she hadn't ever been there. Except to tell me to tech-up.

How long would it take me to grapple with two hundred years of technology?

I turned back to my computer and composed an email to Elle, telling her my modern day news.

She immediately sent back a picture of a laughing cat.

I got the message.

But she was happy to help me. She sent me some coded message in the email, but even I knew if it was underlined I'd be taken to more information, which, like Johnny Five, I craved. So off I waded into the Internet, playing the eighties country compilation CD that Cain had put together for me.

An hour later I forced myself away from my screen and stretched out my back and neck.

And I needed more coffee; I'd rather read War and Peace in its native Russian, than have to spend more time than necessary on a computer.

I poured the hot water into the machine and waited for the coffee to brew. Reaching for a sheet of paper from my printer and a pen, I made a list of tasks that the department would need to achieve. Number one was going to have to be that lovely social media I kept hearing about. I'd need to find students to share their thoughts of studying English online.

Okay, second on the list: how could I get out of the role of Digital Officer?

Delegation; Tallie had been very helpful stepping in to cover classes in January. Perhaps she was ready for a spot of CV building?

She would be. And the funds could support her studies in Connecticut.

Third point: a blog would be required for the department. I was on board with any opportunity to share student writing, so the print magazine could advise and guide there.

I poured the coffee and reflected on a marvellous To Do list. Cain would roar when I told him of my new responsibility, and how I'd successfully achieved all my targets in the first day.

Cain.

In a few short weeks he'd be back in London again. Maybe I'd need the distraction of technology to support me through the tornado of desolation heading my way? But seeing him was as necessary as existing.

However long I had with him.

I turned back to the screen and emailed Tallie and Mindy to see if they would like to share content online. I was impressed with my new vocabulary.

A little box popped up on the bottom right of the screen. Mindy replied immediately with an underlined message. When I clicked on that it took me to her own blog, where she wrote about, of all things, Cain Adams.

She was certainly knowledgeable.

I was taken back to a certain Sunday not so long ago. Reporters on my doorstep.

I typed in the box and asked her to come to my office.

'I was trying to advance my writing skills. That's what you told us to do in the Journalism class.' Mindy sat in front of me, her hands folded in her lap, but her face belied her supposed apology.

'And your blog is very good – apart from your inattention to detail – you write engaging narrative.'

She blinked up at me. How was she to know I was so connected with her subject?

'Have you spoken to Cain, as you state?'

'I found things he's said online. And merged them in my articles. A news agency brought your name into it, as my tutor – I didn't mention you at all.'

'I'm sure I don't need to explain the importance of integrity as a writer; you only have your words and you must be able to stand by them. If you want to be a successful writer, you can't be lazy; you must fact-check or thoroughly investigate your story, this is what happens – people are hurt.'

I waited. And then the tears came.

'I was just walking through campus last year and he was right there. And not everyone knows who he is, so I thought it would be a creative exercise, sending out information, to see how much traction I could create. If I could go viral.'

Ah, the twenty-first century had a lot to answer for. I could at least see she was genuine.

'The question is, what are you going to do now?'

'I'll write a retraction, I promise.'

'I don't think this story needs any further mileage.'

'Tell me what to do.'

'There's only one thing that will make a story go away. Think about the Professional Journalism class that I ran last year.'

'A new story?'

'Exactly.'

'About what?'

'Exactly; that's for you to tell me.'

'Do you think there any other stories I can write about Cain?'

My look suggested that if she was asking that maybe she shouldn't. The story would come to her.

I thought back to Christmas with Cain.

Before my world imploded.

Voices soaring in community in the crisp night air.

'Why don't you look into the local Armed Forces centres? Cain might possibly help you with some fundraising.'

Mindy's eyes lit up, grateful for a lead. And for not being thrown off the course in the final semester, I expect.

'I will. Thank you, Dr. Rawcliffe.'

'I would like you to think about the professionalism – and the potential consequences - of your actions. In the meantime, how would you feel writing some authentic social media posts for the English department? And reflecting on this experience as part of your final year thesis?'

'Oh, absolutely. I won't let you down again. I'm so sorry for any trouble I caused Cain, too. I really admire him as a writer.'

'I am looking forward to your insights; you develop a good story.' I stood up and walked her to the door. 'Use the power of your words as your strength, Mindy. See you in class next week.'

I continued research for the rest of the afternoon, stunned at how much salary digital careers could command. I worked some digital activities into my lessons, aware that a strong grasp of the English language for career advancement might hold more appeal with some members of the classes who weren't quite as into gothic romances as the majority were. A love for nineteenth century novelists is why a lot of students study an English degree, but some characters do plan on coasting through three years of watching film versions of books until the elusive graduate job rolls around.

I logged off around five and headed for a cheer up burger at Sam's. Cain was doing a run of shows and appearances in New England, and wasn't due back into the UK for another month. It felt cruel that we'd just reconnected again, and I couldn't rush home to see him every night after work.

But, then that wasn't the life we'd ever have.

He'd always be travelling; Nashville was a second home, and his first home of Newquay wasn't much closer to London.

I could look for another job, but what kind of base would I need? I couldn't start at the bottom again. I had too much invested in my current role – digital skills aside. Moira was due to announce her retirement soon, and I was in a good place to become the youngest Head of Department.

I couldn't imagine a life without Cain.

The last month had been visceral.

I'd just have to accept whatever time we had together, and keep busy in between. See what other roles Moira could find for me.

I walked through the familiar doors of Sam's and approached the mahogany bar. A few people huddled in corners, but there were plenty of free tables against the far wall, my favoured spot.

'Cheeseburger, please, Sam, extra bacon. Sweet potato fries. And have one of those chocolate caramel sundaes started for me, too, yeah?'

It was that kind of night.

Sam nodded, pouring a large Pinot; he knew.

38

Cain

Man, album promotion was intense.

Over the last two weeks days and nights merged as time zones were crossed and re-crossed. This was the sacrifice I had chosen, and I turned up to every gig, every interview and every meet and greet as if it was the first one. I had almost always given everything, even when I had nothing, not even sleep, in January. For the hard working people who saved and saved for a show, coordinating work and childcare, for a night out with friends, sometimes travelling a day to get to a venue, then waiting in line from breakfast time, just to hear my songs. I was forever grateful.

Now, I was between interviews just before a show, walking around the corridors of the arena towards lunch. All I wanted was Lucy walking beside me.

More than I wanted the music?

I could always play shows in London.

In another two weeks I'd be back with her. Perhaps it was time I developed my talents on home ground. Country music was rapidly growing in the UK.

I spotted a woman walking towards me, along the deserted corridor, her heels clacking on the concrete, hair long and loose, eyes concentrating on me.

I knew trouble when she looked like that.

I slipped through the next doorway, praying it led somewhere, and found myself in the rehearsal room. Lots of musical equipment and no escape route. Not even an inside lock on the door.

From the outside came a confident knock and a call of my name, before a release of the handle.

The woman's head peered around the room and I picked up a pair of drumsticks, quickly seating myself, grinning my trademark grin as I hit the cymbals and hoped to hell I had some natural drumming talent.

'Hey there, handsome.' She tried to speak against a back drop of clashes and kick drumming, and I was thankful she couldn't make her way through the kit. Though it didn't stop her from trying to squeeze through the gap between the drums and the piano.

I cranked up the volume, just waiting for Jam to come in and demand to know why I was wrecking his kit.

The woman whipped out her phone and tried to capture a selfie.

I groaned when I realised she was talking into the camera; she was recording my inaugural drumming, for the whole wide Internet to enjoy this afternoon.

A few minutes later Sarah and her clipboard walked in and escorted the roving reporter out of the room, and possibly the building.

When Sarah returned I was still sat by the drums.

'Talk to me, Cain.'

'I want to buy a house in London.'

'Should the label be worried?'

'You don't need to be worried. Or Seb or Jam.'

She nodded, writing notes on her phone.

'I'll make enquiries. Come on, you have a press interview before dinner.'

39

Lucy

I had explored more of London in the last fortnight than I had in all my time living in Bloomsbury.

I was doing anything to stay away from the house, and the expectations of my door opening to that fatal smile.

I was at The Dinner Club, indulging in a daytime showing of When Harry met Sally. The lively dialogue between Billy Crystal and Meg Ryan, as they balanced friendship, was pure delight.

My phone beeped to life, and a few people's heads suddenly turn towards me.

I quickly silenced the device, seeing a friend request on Facebook notification from somebody I didn't know. And an entertainment website I followed on Twitter had sent out a new video featuring Cain Adams.

I slipped out of the screen, plugged in my earphones, and played the video in the corridor.

A vivacious and curvaceous woman, her long blonde hair cascading around exposed shoulders, was talking about her one-on-one interview with

Cain as he rehearsed the drums on the Massachusetts leg of his tour.

My eyes and mind smarting from her access, that I had been denied for the last fourteen days, I shut down the video and tapped out a message before thought intervened: **Swap the drumming for a pedal steel guitar**.

Then I hit send and left the cinema, no longer interested in Ryan's romantic entanglement.

I walked to the nearest TGI Friday's and ordered ice-cream.

A reply beeped into my chocolate sundae reverie: *I don't think Jam needs to worry*.

Always good to be outside your comfort zone, though. I replied.

You have no idea. What are you doing?

At TGI's, eating the biggest ice-cream I've ever seen. I need two hands.

I haven't had ice-cream in so long. We have a Denny's around here. I'm joining you.

Virtually, at least.

In a few minutes my phone began ringing, Cain's face appeared on screen.

'Hello?' I whispered, inserting my earphones.

'I wondered if you'd pick up.'

'Always. I couldn't not, to you.'

He stopped walking across the car park, and placed his hand over his heart.

'Thank you, Luce, you are truly a beautiful person. I miss you. You also have a little sauce on your chin.'

I rubbed away at the spot with my thumb then licked the thumb clean.

'All better?'

'Not at all. I want to be right there in that booth with you.'

'My quiet afternoon would be wrecked then, wouldn't it?' I smiled,

'I can cause unintentional chaos. Okay, I'm in. Ma'am, I need to order this ice-cream, to go.' He told the assistant. 'Sally, meet Lucy. She's in London. What is that you're eating?'

'You're nuts. Sally, he'll have a Brownie Sundae, thanks, with caramel sauce.'

Sally nodded, and walked away, uninspired by the international phone call, or the country music star in her restaurant. Cain hopped into a booth and continued to chat with me.

'I've been writing. Different to how I used to. The lyrics are fragments. But I'm only writing the good stuff down. I'm not trying to connect anything yet.'

I nodded, tears threatening, and popped a spoonful of ice-cream into my mouth. All twenty thousand of my nerve endings were actively seeking his.

'I may take up the pedal guitar, too. I've been meaning to.'

'Natural extension of your skill set. ' I managed. I could only imagine the music he'd create.

Without me.

He nodded. Sally returned with his dessert and a pen.

'There you go, Mr Adams. And could you sign my apron?' Sally held out the skirt of her white apron and a black Sharpie. Cain smiled and signed away, but wrote on his arm before handing the pen back. He took his ice-cream and left.

'What on earth did you write on your arm – in permanent marker?' I asked.
He held the phone over his arm so that I could read.

'Always. I couldn't not, to you.' I read aloud.

'Lyric potential. Uh-oh, gotta run. Love you, Lucy.'

Cain switched off the video and I sent another message: **Thanks for interrupting my afternoon with your chaos. Always.**

Twenty thousand nerve endings had only one thought. Cain.

I booked a flight to Boston.

And hired a car so that I could drive to his next gig.

Quite possibly the biggest contribution towards acknowledging St. Valentine that I had ever undertaken.

Or medical research, depending on the driving.

40

Cain

I'd just stepped out of the shower, when my phone rang.

Lucy was video-calling me.

I picked up on the second ring,

She faltered in her greeting, and I grinned.

'Like what you see, Darlin'?' I drawled. She nodded. Slowly. Deliberately?

Then she hovered her phone over the menu's location of the restaurant and asked me the same question.

I have never dressed so quickly.

Moments later, in a baseball cap and questionable clothes, I barrelled into the restaurant.

She stood up from her seat, offering a spoon out to me. I pulled her to me, my hands cupping the back of her head as I kissed her. Like I hadn't kissed her in sixteen days.

When I sat down, I held my hand in hers as I scooped up the cold vanilla from our shared sundae into my mouth. I couldn't believe she was really here. She'd flown to see me.

Somehow we made it through ice cream and reconnections, our limbs tangled, as much as decency permitted in public. We had just the night together.

'I need to ask a favour.' She asked, as our spoons collided when we both scraped the dish for the chocolate sauce.

'Anything, my gorgeous Lucy.'

'Are there any spare tickets for tonight? You went and sold out on me, and I'd love to watch you on stage, not-drumming.'

I pulled her into a hug, and laughed.

'There will always be a ticket for you. Side stage is my best angle.'

'Now there's a three minute song waiting to happen – the view from the sidelines. You have a Sharpie?!'

'Even better, I have a notebook in my dressing room.'

'Oh, that old line, hey?'

'Only for you, sweet Luce.'

She kissed me then. Hard.

'I only have twenty minutes before my Meet and Greets begin.' I ground out.

'We only need ten.' She whispered, standing.

I didn't intend to waste any of them.

Every time I looked to my left, Lucy was there, watching me.

I put that smile on her face.

It took all my remaining strength to concentrate on the set list on the floor.

Lucy. Dancing in the sidelines. Her eyes on me.

My performance was for the thousand in front of me, for the hundreds of times I'd done this.

But I could change the energy.

I controlled us from front and centre.

Desire charged through me as I realised Lucy had to wait until I was ready to come off stage.

To stop playing, to stop talking, to stop working.

That could take an hour, or most of the night.

What state would she be in then?

I took to the piano to play a new ballad.

Sweet torment; I would make up to her after the show.

I drove Lucy to the airport early the next morning.

Neither of us had slept, but I knew American roads better than she did. We were at the airport sooner than I'd expected, but I joined her for coffee inside the building.

'We're doing that elongated goodbye at the airport that lovers do, aren't we?' She said, absently stirring a spoon in the black liquid in her cup. With fingers that had trailed along my body only hours earlier.

'Lovers. I love the sound of that.'

'How bad is the jet lag on fourteen hours of flying, for a no-regrets twenty-four hour trip, going to be?' She asked.

'Want me to lie?' I smiled as she groaned, pressing her head on the table. I stroked her hair. 'Ditch the films. Even if there's an eighties choice. Eye mask, ear buds, lots of water. Then some more.' I advised. 'Oh, and I've bumped you up to First, so curl up under that duvet as you stretch out on the bed. Think of me?'

Her head shot up, hair falling over her eyes. She shoved the strands aside.
'First? That's ridiculous. I mean, it's incredible. And generous and lovely and I mean. I don't know what I mean.'

'Your body will thank me when you land. Sarah's arranged a cab to take you home.'

'Cain.'

'Luce.'

'Cain, Cain, Cain.'

We stood as her last call was announced. As I held her and kissed her goodbye, I knew I couldn't spend half the year in the States an ymore.

Two days later I was talking to Jam and Seb about a set list change for that night's show, when my phone rang and an image of Lucy popped up onto my screen.

'Hey, Sweetheart' I answered, sitting on the arm of a sofa, rubbing my eyes.

'Hope I'm not interrupting?'

I shook my head.

'Bye Lucy!' Jam hollered, as he and Seb left the room.

Lucy waved at the screen.

'What's up?'

'Promise not to be mad?'

I nodded. 'Never at you.'

'I found the culprit of the co-writing song story.'

'What? Give me the name.'

'Oh, you're so funny – I won't do that. But we have an idea of how we can make the experience worthwhile.'

'Go on.'

'It would mean an extra gig.'

I groaned and rubbed my forehead. 'I have such a tight show schedule.' And only nine more days until Lucy was back in my arms.

'It's okay, Sarah and I found a night. And the gig would be in Cornwall.'

'I'm in. Tell me more'.

'A benefit concert for the Armed Forces and their families. Good press beats bad press any day. And no one thinks I wrote those songs – far too few nineteenth century references for starters – but I saw firsthand the impact your songs had on listeners in New York – and I saw how much money was raised spontaneously. Sarah thinks it's a good idea.'

 'Listen, I'm in – a worthwhile event AND I get to see my Luce? Rhetorical, right?'

 Lucy nodded, laughing. 'The student who sold the stupid story is organising the event. With me supervising her – and your team supervising me. She'll write up the piece and work with Sarah on promoting the event and the stories.'

 'I'll make it an annual event, and then we'll always have one night together during show season.   I'll rustle up some other performers, too. Thanks, Luce.'

 'The student needed to see how misplaced she'd been, going for the wrong story.
Okay, back to work. Love you.'

 'Before you, go, Luce...'

 She nodded. I took a deep breath. 'My Sister, Cassie, is on her way back from Hong Kong in a couple of weeks. Hasn't been back to the UK in a year, but her contract has finished, so she's heading back for spring. She'll probably only be here a fortnight before setting off again.' I smiled; my Sister definitely had itchy feet. She loved people and learning, and took her heart and her art with her wherever she went.

 'No problems – I'll be up to my ears in planning for next term.'

 'Come with me.'

She hesitated. Not an outright no. Was this moving us too fast again?

'The Lizard is lovely this time of year, with just a few tourists around. Stunning coastal scenery. Could you work in the car?'

Lucy fixed her eyes on me, deciding which direction she should go.

One simple nod.

'I'd like to.'

'But?'

'I'll come with you. I just wanted to be sure that I gave you my honest answer. It would be good to see how you were put together.'

'I have to warn you that my Mum is very excited to have Cassie back home. She's going to invite Jason and his family, if not the neighbours.'

I saw her gulp and exhale.

'In for a penny, right?'

'I love you, Lucy.'

I stared at the screen long after she'd gone. I knew what I had to do.

41

Lucy

The whole of London's 02 Arena swarmed with checked shirts, denim, Stetsons and boots, for the annual Country to Country festival held each March. Free stages were set up for a steady flow of artists, every bar and restaurant was filled with fans, stalls selling American-themed merchandise were crammed with eager shoppers. Twenty thousand fans had a ticket for the main show tonight.

Everywhere I turned I heard people enjoying country music.

Acts that even I've heard of – Lady Antebellum, Carrie Underwood and Brad Paisley – have headlined since the first performances in March 2013. Which I didn't know until Elle sent me the links, once she realised where I was spending the weekend, and knew I struggled with the twentieth century sometimes, never mind present day people.

Cain told me there were over a hundred performances, across the three days, at smaller stages and venues, although we're only here for the Friday, opening night.

I haven't seen a bad act yet. The quality of the storytelling is phenomenal, both within and around the three minutes.

He was shortly playing in a smaller room called Indigo, just before lunch, though according to Elle people have been queuing since just after breakfast, as, apparently it's where the important people perform. I showed Cain and he told me our sisters would get on. I can't quite imagine beyond this weekend yet.

I sat in a coffee shop, reading about universities in Tennessee. Especially any university with an interest in British Victorian literature. Cain was due to meet me in a few minutes, and we'd walk to his gig together. Did I know anyone at any US universities? I was suddenly back in Plymouth, surrounded by bodies on a dance floor. Gill. Where did she work? I scrolled through my conference report and there was her email. Chicago. I checked Google. It was a two hour flight from Nashville.

Two hours.

But still a lot closer than Camden.

I sent her a general enquiry, thinking it wouldn't hurt to ask about any opportunities she might be aware of.

Then I saw Cain rounding the corner, slowed down by fans, I took a screenshot of the research page of a school to read later. It had been handy becoming digital.

I stood as he approached my table and we arrived at the venue a few minutes before the doors were due to open. Cain walked along the crowd, chatting, smiling for cameras and signing, before security called him in for his show.

People's faces lit up when he came by, and he had a hug for anyone who reached out. Some stunning women lined themselves up for a shot, and I may have just been a teensy bit satisfied when he smiled briefly for the selfie, before crouching down to high five and chat to children and their parents.

He took my hand when it was time to go in, and I waited back stage. He was the third performer on, with a forty minute slot, and then he was meeting fans until the next act began.

I don't think I'd ever tire of hearing him sing his stories. He was one man on a stool with his guitar, and the audience was enraptured. There was a perfect silence as he played each song, and wild applause between the songs, as he tuned up and talked about their origins.

When he played the beach song, and he turned around to wink at me, energy fizzed through me and I bit my lip from squealing as loud as the crowd did at the end.

When he came off stage, he headed straight for my arms.

'How was it?' he asked.

'Completely different to your other shows. You could hear a pin drop when you were singing.'

'Yeah, there's no room for error here.'

'You could mess up every song and the crowd wouldn't care.'

He chuckled and hugged me once more. 'Speaking of which, time to meet and greet. You wanna head out with me?'

I shook my head.

'I'll watch from a safe distance.'

We kissed and he was greeted by a long queue. I watched him work, spending a sincere few minutes with each fan, thanking them for coming, laughing, signing, smiling.

I couldn't believe I was a part of his life.

This was the only thing he was meant to do.

Could I do what I had to do?

He had two more appearances that day, in between interviews, and I'm sure the crowd got bigger with each one. How could he do this week after week?

On the final appearance he was on a smaller stage in the main arena, just after an artist called Ashley McBryde nearly caused an earthquake with her two songs. We stood near the press room, waiting for Cain's cue to perform. A crowd milled around buying beers and chatting. For my first experience of a music festival the bar had been set high. Indoors and in the capital? The beast from the east wasn't a factor here, nor was Storm Emma.

Cain would perform two songs and then we were done, and on our way to Cornwall tonight.

To finally meet his family.

A performer had one more song to play on the main stage, but already I could see a crowd around the smaller, satellite stage, waiting for Cain.

I loved watching him work. It was so far removed from my own career. Nineteenth century characters tended to be quieter, too.

Sarah had the nod from security and he was escorted to the stage. I followed this time, and had a front row view of his acoustic slot, flanked by staff in neon high visibility jackets. Elle wouldn't believe me when I told her. I turned and took a few photos of the packed crowd to show her when she came down to see me at Easter.

A man in front of me offered to take my photo with Cain in the background and after only a

moment's hesitation I gave him the camera. He
snapped a few images and handed it back to me
with a thumbs up.

42

Cain

This was only my second time appearing at the C2C weekend, held simultaneously in London, Glasgow and Dublin each March. I was only in London this time, and just for the Friday.   Already I could see that people were singing to all the songs on the set list, not just the singles.

And Lucy was with me to share these memories.

As well as the opportunity to show off, I wanted her to see that fans could be wild, but most were respectful, listening to the stories, in love with the music and the atmosphere. And they understood that US artists travelled away from family, thousands of miles, to sing their guts out, not expecting that people will actually listen to their words.

There are plenty of opportunities for UK-based singer-songwriters.

And I would go home to Lucy each night. If that's what she wanted.

While I performed and interviewed, she had gone to see other shows, and I desperately wanted to see her reaction to the artists.

On our way to the Lizard tonight I'd talk through the acts and book up shows when they next played the UK. I couldn't wait to see which kind of music she was moved by. I knew the country genre had widened in recent years, not only including blues and pop but R 'n'B and rap. I had a hunch which stories she would prefer.

It was my final performance now.

I knew Lucy was to the left of me, watching the 20,000 strong arena crowd as much as she was watching me; this was truly a remarkable weekend of live music. I saw her hand over her phone to a man nearby so that he could take her picture, and I crouched down to wink behind Lucy for the camera, which she couldn't see, but when I caught his thumbs up, I knew he had.

It was just after nine when Lucy and I climbed into the car.

I'd just shared my favourite, UK-based, country music weekend, with my favourite woman.

'Are you sure you don't want to stay at mine tonight?' she asked. I had contemplated it, but the journey home was quieter at night.

'We'll arrive around three in the morning, at my parents' guest house, but we could stop over somewhere?'

She shook her head. 'It'll be good to visit the south west again. I really liked Plymouth.' She said. 'I remember a really helpful guide last time, who knew all about the city and its origins.'

I laughed; 'You'll have to tell my Mum that tomorrow, she'll howl that her interests in furthering my cultural pursuits eventually paid off. I had no idea I'd retained quite so much information. I was desperate to keep talking to you.'

'You were?'

I nodded. 'Absolutely, Luce.' I hit sixth gear as the M4 stretched out before us. 'I, er, may have taken the long route back to the hotel, too.'

'What?'

I laughed at her exclamation. I would never regret that decision.

'I didn't think it took me as long to find the conference as it did to walk to the lighthouse that night.' But she smiled as she berated me.

'The university only uses a couple of hotels for visitors, and when you mentioned Smeaton's Tower I knew which way I was taking you back.'

'I didn't feel unsafe with you at all.'

'That was a gamble I took, walking you around by the seafront at nearly midnight.'

'I'm glad you did.'
'Oh, me too, me too.'

43

Lucy

Families were alien to me, with their habits and in-jokes and expectations and observations.

I was used to being left alone.

I'd made room for Cain in my life, but two siblings, two loving parents, nieces and nephews and neighbours?

I needed a sit down just thinking about the complications.

But these were the people who'd grown Cain. I needed to see them. He was a part of me, and he was a part of them. When it came down to that simple equation, a nod was all it took. I'd just take things one hour at a time. And if they didn't like me, because I'd hurt him, or because my family was a shambles, or because I lived so far away, then that was that.

I would probably appreciate meeting just one person at a time, but at least the pressure wouldn't be wholly on me. I'd be able to disappear should I need to.

And Cain had grown up in spectacular settings.

When I'd Googled his parents' guest house, I'd been stunned. The Victorian style property had unforgettable sea views, and, because it was Victorian, that meant plenty of hiding space.

I woke to spectacular views of the ocean staring back at me through balcony doors.

'Cain. Is that the Atlantic?'

'What?' He murmured, failing to keep me in bed.

I got up and pressed up against the windows. Cain stood and pressed against me. Our reflection in the glass paled next to the vivid blue in front of us. I didn't know what the day held for us, but I'd found my first hiding place.

We'd dressed and were on our way to the patio where his parents were normally to be found.

'They'll love you, Lucy.'

I held on tight to the gift bag.

'Son.' His father said, reaching him first and gripping him into a bear hug. Then he turned to me and swooped me into a hug immediately after.

'You call me Joe.' He said, 'None of this Mr Adams crap.'

'Joe.' Mrs Adams admonished, although both their eyes twinkled. 'I'm Nancy. So lovely to meet you at last.' She hugged me, then Cain.

I held out the wine for her. 'I appreciate it's a little early.'

'Never too early. I did raise a Cain.' She had a warm laugh, full of the life of a big family.

   Forget the fear of them not liking me – how was I going to hold back the tears this weekend? Two strangers had shown me more love in minutes than my family had in a lifetime.

In their house, attached to the accommodation for guests, where we had stayed last night, Nancy showed me to Cain's room, where I would stay tonight, so that the children could have the room we'd shared. Cain was due to sleep on a sofa.

   In the room Cain had first learned about music in, an acoustic guitar stood in one corner, the strap well worn from travelling. On the walls were framed photos and tickets to gigs – Willie Nelson, Merle Haggard, Trisha Yearwood, Reba McEntire, Kip Moore, Bruce Springsteen, Bob Seger. Amongst these were shelves of surf trophies and medals.

   'I've made room for your things on the dresser next to the bed, and popped some flowers in here to sweeten up the place – Cain had bundles of rock magazines and tour information just piled everywhere. Not to worry, son, I've boxed them up and they're in your wardrobe.

   'Now, you guys can catch up here and we'll start breakfast. You just come down when you're ready.'

'Thank you – Nancy – the flowers are lovely.'

'Thanks, Mum, I'll be down shortly.' Cain hugged Nancy and she left humming a tune I recognised as one of Cain's. Something about a truck, I think.

'I don't think I was ever in a boy's bedroom.' I smiled, looking around. 'Bet there are all sorts of stories in here.'

Cain reached for me, pulling me into his arms, his fingers wrapping around my hair. 'Not too many – all my adventures took place outside.' He grinned, and brought our lips together, then murmuring, 'Wish I'd have known you as a teenager. You'd have enjoyed the stories from the artists I saw perform.'

I settled into his arms, lazily drawing circles across his chest, 'I wouldn't have had a clue what to say to someone like you at sixteen. Perhaps not even twenty.'

'If you'd have grown up in this town, my reputation would have warned you off.'

'Maybe we'd have met in the library? I could have helped you with your English homework; you could have helped me make friends.'

'Sweet Luce, you bring me to my knees. Course, I'd have cancelled all my friends, to spend all my time with you - I'd have clashed with your parents so much.'

'I wouldn't have brought you home – they'd have put you off me.'

'Never. We'd have hung out all night in my truck, switching radio stations to find the best songs.'

'You'd bring your guitar and play me cover songs.'

He reached behind me for his guitar, and settled it on one knee. I was trapped between his legs. A quick tune up and he began to sing one of his songs for me. I recognised the young love he sang about, and then laughed as he switched the lyrics to include meeting a girl called Lucy who would make him a better man.

'I wrote that when I was fifteen.' He revealed. 'Last bit a little more recently.' He returned the guitar to the stand, his body pressing against me. His hands reached up to run his fingers through my hair, as he kissed me again, his tongue teasing my lower lip, eliciting that familiar groan I knew so well. My hands reached around to his back jeans' pockets, pulling him even closer to me, so that it was his turn to moan. Reluctantly we pulled away, aware of the sudden smallness of the room, and the house.

'Let's go help your Mum.'

'Yes, Ma'am.'

Over a beautiful breakfast, of pastries, fresh fruit, pancakes, bacon and lots of tea, Nancy regaled me of childhood memories of Cain, Jason and Cassie always outside, often up to no good, but light-hearted capers – the boys teasing their sister, Cassie learning how to fight better than her brothers. Other boys discovering Cassie, and her brothers. They hadn't stood a hope, Nancy laughed.

I was mesmerised by the warmth and sincerity of Nancy and Joe, their fondness for each other and their family.

'What do you do, Lucy?'

I finished my water and pressed the napkin against my mouth, nodding,

'I teach English literature in a university, mainly the nineteenth century romantics.'

'Well, now, isn't that something! We tried to convince Cain he needed to go to university, but as soon as he turned eighteen he took off with that guitar – the one in his room.'

'Aww, Mum. You know I wrote to you regularly.'

'Yes, you did, and not always to ask for money, either.'

'It was actually Lucy's job that brought her to Plymouth, last September, which caused us to meet. In a bar, of all places.'

'Oh, were you playing a small gig?' Nancy asked, beginning to clear the plates, which Lucy helped her with.

'I didn't even know who Cain was. He stopped a bit of bother for me, then, after helping me find my hotel, invited me on a tour of the city. I was so impressed with his knowledge of Drake and the Pilgrims.'

'You hadn't heard of Cain before you met him?' Nancy almost dropped the plates as she carried them to the counter.

'Well, I do spend a lot of time in the nineteenth century, so a lot of things pass me by. Cain kept up when he came to one of my classes.'

'You got Cain into a classroom again?'

'See, I told you my parents would love you.' Cain grinned, guiding his Mum back to the table.

Joe shared stories as the father of three successful children, how proud they all were with Cain's first number one song, for a country artist I'd never heard of. They'd driven around town with their radio on, like a couple of teenagers, just waiting for their favourite song to be played.

Shortly after breakfast, Nancy shooed us outside, while she prepared lunch. Jason and Shelly were driving down from Chester, just south of Manchester, so would be here later today, with two hungry children.

We sat on a patio swing, Cain pushing us back and forth, back and forth. Seagulls squawked all around us.

'I'm so happy right now.' I said. I should have known that his family would be just as relaxed as he was. That's how it should be.

He nodded, his hand wrapped around mine. A gentle breeze blew through the garden, bringing the taste of salt to my lips.

'That sky is perfect.' I said. 'A perfect shade of blue.'

'It's bluetiful. That's what Cassie used to call it when she was little.'

'Bluetiful. I like it.'

He leaned in and whispered, 'I can find my way back to my room in the dark. Quietly.'

I snuggled further into him as he rocked us backwards and forwards.

44

Cain

Waking up to seeing Lucy, naked, staring out over the waves was a sight I needed to see every day in my life.

Of course, London didn't have the views, but we'd be able to head back to Cornwall every weekend we could. And she'd be with me at every family event down here. The sadness I heard in her voice over Christmas at her parent's house was something I never wanted to hear in her again. Elle would be welcome down any time she was on a break from studies, too. Although from what I've heard, she planned to stay in America as long as she could and return ridiculously rich. I'd ask Jam and Seb to keep an eye on her; no doubt they'd be touring the East coast a few times a year.

I joined Lucy by the window, leaning against her body, watching her drink in the views. She is as magnetised by the ocean as I am. I'd have to teach her to swim to fully appreciate the marine beauty.

All too soon she turned around and we dressed to go in search of Mum and Dad, and coffee.

I hadn't told Mum about the proposal over New Year. I hoped she didn't expect anything this weekend – having all of us together might not scare Lucy off, but I couldn't cope if she disappeared again.

I knew Mum wouldn't make any ridiculous suggestions about the future. She'd be too preoccupied having all of us in the same place. The last time we'd all been together was for Cassie's farewell party.

I was desperate to take Lucy down to Kynance Cove later. The incredible turquoise rivals any Indian Ocean dip. But the steep trail needs more than an hour or so, and I knew Jase was on his way. I couldn't wait for him to meet Lucy. She was so similar to Shelly, I knew he'd understand.

Dad had excelled himself with breakfast duties. Literally hadn't eaten that much, well, probably since Cassie's farewell. I always forgot how the salt in the air brought on an appetite.

We'd manage to waddle to the swing in the back garden that had been here forever. I first learned to play guitar here, tilting the seat so I could find the most comfortable spot for my gangly frame to hold the instrument.

I rocked us gently, now, my arm around Lucy's, as gulls played all around us. Perfect Bluetiful Monday.

Seconds later I heard a car pull up and peels of laughter from my adorable, if loud, niece and nephew.   I pulled Lucy towards me and we met more of my family.

45

Lucy

The sun was lowering over the headland, and I was glad I'd brought a jumper and scarf to wear under my coat as the temperature had cooled. I spent more time outdoors when I was with Cain than I probably had most of my life.

I looked over at him and he reached his hand out for mine, gently squeezing my fingers and pulling me closer to him.

His parents sat at the top of the biggest wooden table I'd ever seen, while Jason and his family occupied the bench across from us. The two children were very cute, and loved the space to run around. No one seemed worried that they would run off, or that danger would approach. No one was concerned about their yells and squeals either. Great way to burn off the energy of the best fish and chips I've ever tasted. If I could move, I'd probably pretend I was a gull or unicorn, too. My lips tasted of sea salt and Pepsi.

I could get used to this kind of contentedness.

Cassie was due in tomorrow morning, and Cain had assured me that would mean his Dad would be in the kitchen most of the day, working on the roast chicken dinner that she'd craved almost as soon as she'd arrived in Asia.

I remembered my own food experiences, travelling around Hong Kong and Thailand one summer, and the dishes were outstanding, but like nothing I recognised sometimes. I can imagine how a Sunday roast would be devoured by an expat.

'Right, who's for a nice pot of tea?' Nancy asked.

Absolutely. I thought. Instead I made the polite murmurings and smiles that everyone else did and wandered back into the guest house with them. Jason took the two kids upstairs, their limbs flailing against play being stopped, to get them ready for bed. Cain followed his Dad through to the lounge to start the fire, and I joined Nancy, reaching for cups.

'Thank you, honey.'

I smiled and enjoyed her casual chatter as we prepared pots of tea and sourced chocolate biscuits.

In the lounge someone had brought out a Monopoly board game, near the corner sofa. Cain was setting up the pieces with Jason. Shelly sat on a sofa with dressing gown clad children and was reading The Cat in the Hat to them. I sometimes taught Dr. Seuss in my classes, encouraging the students to think about how imagining and imagery in Children's literature extends beyond children.

I placed the tray on a nearby table and handed out mugs of tea while Nancy offered the biscuits.

She found a plain digestive biscuit each for the children and I handed them two small cups of milk. Thing One and Thing Two were temporarily forgotten.

Cain moved up so I could sit next to him at the board.

Nancy and Joe sat on the other side of the sofa, pulling up the storage seat to square off the table; evidently we were playing doubles.

'So, there are Monopoly rules, and then there's the Adams Family Monopoly rules.' Cain announced.

'Yeah, the best cheater wins.' Shelly called out, as she passed the table, a child under each of her arms.

'She's not kidding.' Jason said, at my bemused expression.

'That's why you double up. I acknowledged.'

Cain chuckled and handed over the money, nodding.

An hour later and the competition was definitely on between Cain and Jason. Nancy and Joe were clearly losing, and enjoying it. Cain and I had adopted distraction techniques to try to win; when Jason thought he was about to earn some money I brought out my arsenal of facts of Victorian evening past times, whilst Cain took our turn. Shelly was a gonner for the information, every time.

'Wait until Cassie hears about this.' Jason argued good naturedly. 'She'll demand a rematch tomorrow and nothing will catch her out.'

'Granted, we taught her well.'

Nancy brought wine and crisps out at some point, and said good night at another. The playing eventually slowed down until Jason declared the game a draw. After I gently nudged Cain, he agreed and the game was packed away.

'I can't believe how many useless facts you know about Victorian home entertainment.' Shelly said, curling her legs up on the sofa.

'You should ask her about eighties films.' Cain said, wrapping his arm around my shoulder.

'Oh, not another eighties enthusiast.' Jason drawled. 'What is it with that decade? They had no smart phones, no apps, no GPS...'

'The films were even on videos.' Shelly joined in.

'Yes, huge machines that would try to take your fingers off each time you switched tapes.' I sighed, 'Exactly. You can't put a price on that nostalgia. You had to actually get off the sofa every two hours to switch films.'

'Oh, that's true, that's true; I've lost track of how much time I spend just watching *one more episode*.'

I lost track of how much time we talked. Another bottle of wine was opened, perhaps. I yawned, but didn't want to leave. It was a long time since I was so comfortable in the presence of, essentially, strangers. But Jason and Shelly were a part of Cain, and not at all shy in revealing a life that I suspected, and really enjoyed hearing. Adventure ran through Cain's blood, apparently. And the wilds of the Cornish Atlantic coast were his playground. Until he discovered music, and how it drew the girls to him; I couldn't deny I was drawn to his storytelling.

Eventually the night had to end. With Jason threatening to send Ben and Olivia over to the sofa first thing.

Cain walked with me to my room, but as we passed Shelly I caught her grin. We all knew he wasn't staying on a sofa tonight.

I followed Cain to his room and properly ended the night.

When I woke the next morning, Cain had already left. I checked my phone and, as the digits declared it was only just after nine, snuggled back under the duvet. A moment later Cain opened the door, a mug of coffee in his hand.

'Good morning, Gorgeous.' He whispered, leaning over the bed to hand me my drink, and kiss me awake.

'How long have you been up?'

'An hour or so. Breakfast is almost ready.'

'Have you been swimming?' I asked, yelping, as he placed his cold hands on my thigh.

'Every chance I get.'

I groaned as I sipped my drink. He may be energetic, but he knew just how I liked my coffee.

'How's Shelly this morning?'

'Well, Jason got up with the children.' He grinned.

I finished my drink and reluctantly left the warmth of Cain's bed, to shower, after another *very* good morning kiss.

The breakfast room was a burst of the best kind of food and laughter, and I joined the table easily.

We were halfway through breakfast when a tall brunette woman appeared in the doorway, Starbucks travel mug in her hand.

'Auntie Caaaaaaasss!' Squealed Olivia as she cannon-balled into her. The woman reached down to hug her niece, but not until her eyes sought me out. There was a familiar steel behind her blue eyes, that lost some of the edge only when her niece was in her arms.

A chair was found and a plate brought out for Cassie. During her reunion she kept glancing over at me, her expression unreadable. I felt like I'd been called into the office, for something I wasn't aware of.

After breakfast a walk was suggested down to Lizard Point. A wind had kicked up, and I reached for my bobble hat, to keep my hair out of my eyes more than anything else. My hair was so thick, that it acted as protector in all but the most severe rain. But my usual top knot wasn't fit for the Atlantic coast line.

Cassie, Jason and Cain led the group, acting as unofficial safety monitors for the children. Neither one would pass them, no matter how much they tried; there was always a limb barrier blocking their way from the road, from stinging nettles, from the tremendous cliff face coastline.

Shelly walked with Nancy, and I remained at the back, taking out my phone to photograph views I knew I'd see again. I caught the family in unexpected moments of affection, too, like Cain holding the hand of Ben and Olivia. Jason with his arm around Shelly. Nancy between her boys.

As the pathway narrowed, Nancy and I opted to sit on a bench overlooking the Atlantic swell whilst the others scampered down what I could easily describe as a sheer drop, towards Kynance Cove, apparently to tire the children out.

'I can't believe Cain swims in that.' I said, watching the gulls fly off balance in the wind. Nancy nodded, smiling. 'He's drawn to the water alright. I'm so grateful Joe taught them to swim at an early age, and enrolled the children onto lifeguarding and life boat courses when they were old enough. Only Cain keeps hitting the waves though – Cassie and Jason prefer indoor pools and spas.'

'Yeah, I can't see Cain keen on that restriction.'

'Oh, you're right, you're right. You know him quite well.'

I nodded, even though it was posed as an observation not a question.

'We were surprised when he showed a talent for music. Honestly thought he'd end up working

outside. Well, I suppose he does sing at festivals.'
She chuckled. 'But he is set on an entirely
different course. Do you like to sing?'

'Oh, no, I have no ear, or voice, for music.' I
replied. 'Give me a book over a CD any day.'

'Now, Jason, he always had his nose in a book,
when Cain let him dry out. He read all these
biographies and autobiographies, of people who
brought us into the technology era. Cassie had no
time for reading or swimming, unless it was
because she was waiting for a flight. Travel is in
her blood. She never liked the idea of settling in
one place for long. I hear you've travelled?'

'Yes, I like to explore when the summer arrives.
I've been to Hong Kong. Because I live in London
though, I need to see blue horizons when I'm on
holiday. I can only imagine how this place looks on
a sunny day.'

'You come on back whenever you feel like you
can. Even if Cain is off with his music somewhere,
you're always welcome here.'

I gulped on the wind and smiled at her.

We set off back for the guest house, messaging
Cain and Cassie to say lunch would be ready in an
hour. I couldn't believe we'd only just had
breakfast, but I was ravenous already.

I sat between Cain and Jason at the dinner table,
and Cassie sat opposite me. When I could, I asked
her about her travels, but everybody wanted a

piece of her. After the gorgeous roast chicken lunch had been devoured, she turned her attention to me, whilst Joe and Nancy were sorting out the berry crumble dessert and coffee.

'So, what do you think of our little house by the sea? Bit different to London, isn't it?'

Before I could reply, the challenge in her tone notched up.

'What would you want to come all this way to Cornwall for, when you have everything on your doorstep?'

'Except Cornwall.' Was out of my mouth before I had a chance to think.

'We're well used to holidaymakers here, aren't we? Arrive for the week and then go back to their lives with empty promises to return.'

Cain stopped talking with Ben and looked across at Cassie.

I hadn't imagined her challenging tone.

'It was good luck that brought me to the West Country for the first time a few months ago.'

'And what are your plans now? Are you moving here?'

'Cass.' Cain warned. I reached for his fingers under the table.

'Come on, you two, let's go play in the garden, shall we?' Shelly took the children outside.

'I usually can't think much beyond the current term. My students have finals coming up, so it's rare that I can travel this far.'

'Oh, then I guess America is out of the equation then?'

'Cassie.' His sharpness turned her head.

'I'm just looking out for your best interests, Cain.'

'Why don't you tell us about your travels, Cass.' Jason interrupted, but she wasn't for slowing down. I had no idea if she knew about New York at all. How would she feel if she knew I'd hurt her brother?

I glanced at Cain and his face was murderous.

Cassie averted her eyes from mine, to meet her brother's glare. Then she was back to me.

'Long distance relationships are notoriously tricky. It's why I never get serious with anyone in another country.'

'Cut it out, Cassie.' Jason said, at the same time that Cain scraped his chair back and left the room.

Joe and Nancy returned, oblivious.

'Who's for crumble then?'

'A bit later, Mum.' Jason said, kissing her cheek as he left the room.

Cassie got up, too. 'Think I'm suffering from jet lag, I'm going to head out for a walk.'

If there was one thing I'd read enough about, it was to never get involved between siblings.

'I'd love some crumble, Nancy, thank you.' I said, smiling. She shrugged her shoulders and we chatted until I felt it was okay to leave.

But I didn't go back to my room, to my laptop and my films. I needed to take in more of these stunning surroundings, where sky and sea became one.

I climbed into my shoes and coat, wrapping my scarf twice around me, and headed towards the lighthouse. It stood white and majestic, overlooking the most southerly point in England. I hoped I'd have time to climb it, if not on this trip, when I returned. I felt more welcome here than I did in my own home. Even the one I'd created for myself.

As I clambered down the natural stone steps to the seal spotting area, I saw Cassie sat on one of the benches. Her eyes challenged me, but she didn't block the seat or move away. I sat down next to her, the wind whipping my hair all around. Cassie's was hidden under her hat.

'I love your brother, Cassie. You don't need to be worried about that.'

'I'm not worried about you.'

'I can't say I won't hurt him, because I have no idea what's around the corner, any more than you do. We could both be wiped out by a seagull tomorrow.' She didn't seem to appreciate my attempt at light-heartedness. I leaned back into the bench.

'You know, I didn't know Cain was a musician before I met him. And even when I found out he was, I had no idea who he was.'

'You're kidding?'

I shook my head. 'I spend more time in the nineteenth century than the twenty-first. And I would choose a book over music every time. But, when I heard Cain's stories, I needed to find out more.'

'I didn't mean to be a bitch.'

'Yes you did.' Her laugh was as spontaneous and as deep as Cain's. I turned to face her then. 'He's your little brother. If you don't look out for him, who will? I will say one thing though - he's worth the unknown.'

She relaxed her shoulders, her expression one of seemingly wondering what it was about me that was different. 'You are the first woman he's brought home.'

'And your family is incredible. I've had such a warm welcome. Almost.'

'Sorry about that.'

'I never apologise when I'm in the right.'

She laughed again and stood up, 'Come on, it's freezing, and I need to hear more from you. And I now need Mum's blackberry crumble with a gallon of custard.'

We walked arm in arm back to the house. She
roared when I said I'd only been to a few of gigs,
sitting right at the back at my first one.

She told me how Jamie had almost broken him
when their relationship ended, although in
hindsight, he didn't end up wallowing and writing
maudlin songs like everyone thought. She did try
to come back into Cain's life, but Cassie had
overheard her anticipating all the benefits of being
married to the career, not the man. And she'd
stepped in to warn her. Jamie, apparently, hadn't
tracked her down to demand an apology. Strictly,
neither had I.

But I hadn't backed down from her challenge.

When we returned to the guest house, neither
Cain nor Jason appeared. Shelly was visibly
relieved that Cassie and I were on friendlier terms.

We tucked into crumble, and I found it easy to
devour my second portion. I swapped travel
stories with Cass while the children watched a
Disney film.

It was almost dark when Cain thundered through
the door, soaking from presumably either a
shower or a wild Atlantic swim. I couldn't be sure.

Cassie brought her arm around my shoulder and
gave him the thumbs up.

Somewhere behind me I heard Shelly release a
sigh.

But all I could see was Cain's indigo eyes, switching between me and Cassie, as he registered the softer countenance of his sister.

46

Cain

I couldn't stay in the room any longer, for fear of what I'd do or say - to Cassie or Lucy, I wasn't sure.

I couldn't believe the gall of my Sister, interrogating Lucy even when I'd warned her that she should stop.

I'd only just got Lucy back, I couldn't lose her again. I'd told her we're taking things as slow as we need, and then suddenly there's Cassie, demanding that Lucy buys a house in Cornwall, or doesn't darken our doorstep again.

I found myself walking towards the cove, and was so focused on putting one foot in front of the other that I didn't hear Jason until he'd fallen into step with me.

We said nothing as we made our way to the hiding place of our childhood, when Jason wanted freedom from parents, and I needed freedom from myself. Or to convince Jason he needed to be part of my next dare.

Eventually I slowed my pace.

'I can't believe Cassie.'

'She's always been direct.'

'She had no right.'

'It's no less than what we've done to her potential boyfriends. It's why she keeps her men well away from us now.'

I stopped then, wiped my hand across my upper lip. She had just been in protective mode.

I sank to the grass beneath me, and Jason followed.

'I nearly lost Lucy. I can't lose her again.'

'From what I've seen, that is unlikely.'

'You don't understand.'

'So tell me.'

'I proposed and she turned me down.'

'What?!'

'I've known she's the only woman for me, probably since our second day together. Since we wrote together. Since we spent the whole day with each other and I knew I couldn't walk away.'

'Oh, man, that's Shelly-serious.'

I nodded, agreeing with my brother's love for his wife.

'I rushed Lucy, though. I got caught up in what I wanted, and I never appreciated what she wanted. She didn't just turn me down, she locked herself in the bathroom and refused to talk to me. Then when I went out for coffee, she caught the next plane, and didn't speak to me for a month.'

'Ah, that was January, then.' He said, referring to the only time he's been scared for me.

'I'm perfectly capable of breaking this by myself; I don't need Cass' help.'

'Wanna go for a swim?' Jason asked.

When I returned home I had no idea what I'd find.

I did not expect to see Lucy and Cass giggling over dessert, nor for Cass to give me a mighty thumbs up. In front of Lucy.

Lucy. She was still here. Her smile spread through me like the appearance of sun after a summer's downpour.

When she went to her room later, to lend a book to Shelly, I followed her.

'Everything alright, Cain?' she asked, facing me, her palm pressing lightly against my chest.

Although the pressure felt like a perfect ten wave.

I nodded, placing my hand over hers as I caught my breath.

'You tell me.'

'You mean earlier? Cassie was just looking out for her brother.'

'I'm sorry for the way she was with you.'

'I told her not to apologise, so I don't expect you to.' She said.

'I should have stayed.'

'I get it.'

'I don't know if you do.' I whispered, holding tighter on to her hand. 'I didn't know if you'd be here when I came back.'

She pressed her body up against me.

'You can't be scared every time there's a problem. That's just not practical.'

'What I feel for you isn't very practical.' I ground out, as her hand smoothed hair from my face.

I couldn't wait for us to return to London tomorrow, so that I could keep on with my search. Time to buy that apartment in London I've never known I needed.

47

Lucy

The last two weeks of long hours at the office, gearing up for the Easter break, and working with Mindy on her press releases for the show, had caused too many sleepless nights.

Tonight, Elle was arriving, for a well-earned study break, and she had a full-time itinerary planned; I'd explained that Cain was working, especially with the upcoming Cornish gig so it wasn't possible to spend every minute with him, which I knew from painful experience.

But he had suggested we drive down to his parents for a few days before the gig, and I couldn't wait to see Elle's face when she saw the wide blue expanses.

As I was leaving a delivery man arrived with a bouquet of red roses. There was no card, so I didn't know why Cain had sent them, but they were beautiful. I hurriedly placed them on the kitchen table before locking up.

I was a few minutes late for Elle's train, by the time I arrived at Euston, and I searched for her amongst the passengers pouring onto the platforms.

She flew out of the carriage, straight into me, and then glanced behind me.

'Good to see you again, Sis. You're looking well; Cain will meet us at the restaurant in an hour.'

Realisation dawned on Elle that Cain really wasn't with me, but she linked her arm through mine and chatted all the way home about teachers, visas, accommodation in the States and her friends.

When we arrived at my apartment she took the stairs two at a time and threw her case into the room, heading to the bathroom to reapply make-up. I caught up with some messages from Mindy, and told Cain we were on our way.

As we opened my front door, a car pulled up and a driver stepped out, opening the door for us.

'Lucy, Elle? With compliments of Cain Adams.'

I rolled my eyes at the extravagance, but Elle squealed, diving into the open door. I joined her on the back seat, and she already had her eye on the bottles.

'Don't you think we should eat first?' I asked.

But Elle nodded confidently as she opened the mini bottles of wine. 'I ate sandwiches on the train.'

Cain stood from his seat at the table as we arrived, and thankfully he has a strong core, seeing that Elle bowled into him.

I pulled her arm to settle her back down, and reached in to kiss Cain. He'd just showered, and after the six days apart I craved him. He tasted of Merlot and promises. I settled down into my chair quickly.

Elle had somehow ordered a bottle of wine in the few seconds embrace, and I hastily picked up a menu, searching for the most carbohydrate heavy meal I could find. I ordered us cheeseburgers and Cain ordered a burger, too.

As Elle gushed over Cain's songs, in between more sips of wine than mouthfuls of food, I was feeling mortified. Cain was being so patient with her enthusiasm. I had no idea how she'd survive in the States all by herself. At least she'd have to be older to be served alcohol.

When the bottle was finished I delivered the look that said that was enough, and both Cain and I successfully avoided her drinking anything other than water.

By the time we got outside, it was obvious she got drunk quickly. Before I knew what was happening, Cain had steered her to the bushes. Where my almost eighteen year old sister reminded the streets of what she'd just attempted to eat, and had definitely drunk. I swapped places with Cain and he sourced a car for us.

Thankfully Elle was slumped over me, and in no fit state to do anything other than snore lightly.

When the car pulled up, Cain paid the driver, and took Elle from me. While I opened doors he carried her to the bathroom.

Mumbling something like an apology to me, I managed to clean Elle up and tuck her up into bed, after encouraging her to drinking water and replenishing her glass for the early-morning drought she'd no doubt experience.

When I went through to the lounge, Cain had made coffee and was poised with the remote.

'Drunk scene in *St Elmo's Fire* gonna be okay?' He asked, laughing as he held out his arm and I sank into him. 'Or we could watch drunk ET?' He suggested.

'We're setting off nice and early tomorrow morning, right?' I was already looking forward to dragging Elle out of her bed.

To my amazement, when I woke the next morning, Elle was sat at the kitchen table. Looking like she didn't have a care in the world. She flew into my arms, though.

'I did not get that drunk last night, did I, Sis?' She asked.

'That drunk? You've been like that before?'

'Never that bad – I'm the one who holds people's hair back, and calls cabs. Was I a complete ---?'

She didn't complete her sentence, as Cain walked into the room, dropping a kiss on my forehead and hugging Elle.

'HOW'S THE HEAD?' He yelled.

'Nowhere near as bad as the guilt. I am so sorry about last night. Both of you. Was there singing?'

He nodded, laughing.

'We did a duet. Islands in the Stream. You were a perfect Kenny.'

'We did not!' Elle looked at me and somehow I kept my face straight.

'It went viral online.' I said, turning my back as she scrambled through her phone.

'You absolute fibbers.' She finally declared, dropping her head on the table when she realised there was no online evidence of her adventures.

'Big breakfast, anyone? Scrambled egg and bacon?'

Elle ran out of the room and I settled into Cain for a proper good morning kiss, before going to check on Elle.

She slept most of the day in the back of the truck as we wound our way the six hours down to the Lizard, stocking up on Pringles and Diet Pepsi when we stopped at the service stations. I caught up with Cain's week and listened to the nineties country play list he had compiled, enjoying the revenge stories of the Dixie Chicks he'd chosen, and the Garth Brooks albums he played. It was understandable how he was one of the biggest country artists.

'Oh, thank you for the flowers, too, they're lovely.'

'Flowers?' Cain asked.

'Yes, they arrived just before the car you sent.'

'I didn't send flowers. I completely should. Maybe they're from a secret admirer?'

I snorted. 'They're probably from Mindy, or Moira.' Funny that there had been no card, though. I continued to stare out of the window at the gorgeous Devonshire countryside, on our way into the last western county of England, Cornwall, as the music played, and Elle slept.

'Elle.' I whispered, reaching around in my seat to stir her awake. She opened her eyes slowly and looked around her. 'Isn't that just the most bluetiful sea colour you've ever seen? I asked.

She nodded, leaning out of the window to take a closer look and breathe in the sea air.

'Fish and chips? On me.' She whispered sleepily, clearly capable of food again, instead of the sugar rush.

We sat outside at one of the wooden picnic tables in the garden, tucking into the best fish supper I'd eaten, just as good as the last time we were here.

'It's the Cornish sea salt they use.' Cain declared at our very satisfied sounds, as dinner disappeared.

After Elle had disposed of the rubbish, and made a pot of tea, she watered the plants in the garden. Cain and I went in to the lounge and curled up next to each other with a book; he was tucking into the Twain novel A Connecticut Yankee at King Arthur's Court, and I was devouring the Springsteen autobiography, Born to Run. Elle popped her head around the door shortly after nine to wish us good night, and it wasn't long before we headed upstairs. Travelling was exhausting. I had no idea how Cain regularly flew between countries.

'Let's go to the beach.' Elle declared, as she arrived at the breakfast table the next morning.

Cain looked up at my pink-bombshell of a sister, who had grown even more beautiful since I'd seen her at Christmas. Her long limbs were already beach-ready in cut off denim shorts and a t-shirt.

'It's still spring out there, the Atlantic water will be cold.'

'That's okay, I'll swim faster to warm up.'

He looked at me, then.

'Yes, Elle is the sister who swims.' I said, swiping a strawberry from his plate.

'I'll see if Jam's arrived yet.' Cain sent a message and reached over for my peaches.

'Oooh, yay. More people to play with.' Elle folded her legs under her and sat on the bench, pouring herself coffee and reaching for an almond croissant.

Cain wandered off in search of Jam and I sighed, refilling my own mug.

'You're happy, Sis, aren't you?' Elle suddenly asked. I smiled at her and nodded.

'Absolutely.'

'You really deserve it. Cain is besotted with you, and so hot it's unreal.'

I still couldn't get used to being in a relationship, but I couldn't deny the warmth that swam through me whenever I thought of him. Which was frequently, now that I knew it was okay to. Now that I knew we were...together. In our own sort of way.

He appeared in the doorway again.

'Jam got here last night, and he's up for the beach, too. Shall we head off in half an hour?' I nodded, 'I'll read, you guys can swim and I'll look after our things.'

Cain joined me on the bench again, his body leaning into mine.

'I'd be happy to teach you to swim.'

'Sure. When we're in much warmer weather. And possibly the Caribbean.'

'Deal.' He whispered.

Elle downed her coffee and bounded upstairs to get ready.

Which left me and Cain alone again. My new favourite place.

The walk down from the headland to Kynance Cove was ridiculously steep. Elle was piggybacking on Jam, and I insisted Cain walked in front of me on the rocky incline, so he could stop my stumbles. I stopped periodically to admire the turquoise waters, and azure sky, my arms wrapped around his waist.

I could only imagine what the area looked like at the height of summer, in complete contrast to the few people around today. Well, probably full of people.

'Almost there.' Cain looked up at me, grinning. He had offered his back, too, but I preferred the ground under my feet.

I knew I was going to sleep well tonight.

Eventually.

I was glad I brought a picnic with us, too, the memory of breakfast quickly dissipating at the thought of the energy I was using just to remain upright.

And, despite everyone moaning we'd just eaten, I knew the extra snacks I'd packed would soon go.

Elle and Jam made it to the bottom first, racing ahead to the soft white sand and splashing into the bluetiful ocean.

I sprawled out on a towel, loving the feel of Cain alongside me, as he reached over to ask if I wanted to go into the water with him. I shook my head, no, but pulled him in for a goodbye kiss. Then he pulled off his t-shirt and tore into the water.

Jam and Elle were already out swimming. I'd paddle in later, once the midday sun had helped me out a little, by warming the water. For now I enjoyed watching the three of them confidently own this beautiful piece of the Atlantic.

Before I fell asleep I opened my book and began reading. I was a few chapters in when Cain returned, shaking water everywhere.

'God, that is cold.' I shrieked.

'You get used to it after a while. What sandwiches did you make?'

I pushed the back pack towards him and he devoured a ham bap before he spoke again.

'So good.'

'The sandwich?'

'The day.'

I nodded and closed my book, tucking into a tuna roll.

Jam turned up a few minutes later; clearly he'd smelt the food.

'Where's Elle?' I asked.

'She's doing a few more lengths he said, reaching his hand into the bag to retrieve sustenance.

I went back to my book, as Cain and Jam talked surf and music.

Another chapter later I realised Elle was still out in the water. We were the only ones around and I quickly spotted her pink hair in the sea. She seemed further out than I expected. I looked to Jam and Cain, who were also looking out to sea.

Silently.

I willed her to turn around; the sky had gone grey and it would already take a while for her to return to the shore. Rocky areas surrounded the coast.

I was aware of Jam standing, stretching, his eyes trained on the sea.

Then things happened so quickly.

Jam took off at a run and dived in to the water.

Then Cain was up and tearing off for the waves that seemed to hold my sister hostage as she disappeared from sight.

I ran to the surf, unable to go further and certainly no match for two surfers. I was desperate to see a glimpse of pink. I lost both men as the greys darkened.

Hours seemed to go by, but my pragmatism knew, hoped, it was only seconds.

Then there she was, under Jam's arms. Cain swam back with them.

I ran in to my knees - I needed to see her face.

Her eyes were closed.

A wave caught me and I tumbled in, quickly righting myself, as Cain's arm found mine.

Jam reached the sand first, and laid Elle out, her body unusually still.

He began performing CPR as Cain reached for his phone.

I could have saved us time by calling for help. But I was frozen to the spot, I couldn't take my eyes off her. I couldn't lose her.

Elle coughed and I sank to my knees, clutching at the sand. She groaned and looked up at both of us, seemingly wondering what we were doing. Jam was checking her eyes, until she slapped him away, struggling to sit up. Cain was back, holding her up as he spoke with a medic on the phone. Jam collapsed face down on the sand, his breathing ragged, presumably from the incredibly fast swim.

She groaned and reached down to rub her calf. 'Cramp.' She offered weakly.

Cain was next to Jam, whispering something to him.

I hugged my sister, right before I wanted to launch into a tirade about safety. Except, I couldn't. I would have had no idea what to do.

Cain was back with us, while Jam lay on the floor, stiller now.

Elle sat up shivering and I moved to action then, reaching for the towels. Cain came with me and found my flask.

'So glad you have a coffee obsession, Sweetheart.' He poured a cup for Elle, while I surrounded her with towels. I helped her out of her costume, and wrapped her up, pulling her into another hug. She couldn't go to America alone.

Cain bent down to Jam, sat him up and they whispered quietly to each other. Jam nodded then stared on the sea, once more. He looked like a man in search of his own horizon.

'We need to get back.' I said, helping Elle into whatever clothes we had available – my jumper and an extra pair of her shorts, a dry towel tied around her waist.

'There's a longer way around to the top that isn't as steep.' Cain offered.

'Throw us up to the top if you have to, but I want to get back now.'

He nodded, and helped to pack everything away, pulling the bags onto his shoulders. Jam pulled on his jeans and joined us.

The incline conversation was quiet, but provided the necessary warmth from the effort as well as the afternoon sun on our backs. One foot in front of the other we made it back. Elle sank down onto a rock. I urged her to keep moving so that her legs wouldn't seize up again, and reluctantly she followed me.

Cain suddenly held a hand up to a turning jeep, running over to talk to the driver. Then he waved us all over.

'Hop in; Mr Davis will give us a lift back.'

Grateful for the small village where everyone knew each other, I opened the door for Elle and Jam, and climbed in after them. Cain sat up at the front, talking quietly with Mr Davis, occasionally turning around to us. I offered a sombre smile, thankful and exhausted.

Once back inside the guest house, I took Elle upstairs to help her shower and dress. I stood by the window, the sky a betrayal of cobalt blue that belied the dangers lurking in the depths of the coast.

I turned when Elle reappeared in leggings and a band hooded top and joined me at the window.

'I am never swimming in the ocean again.'

I smiled then, glad to have her teenage self back again.

'There is something to be said for a nice paddle' I agreed.

I would have died had I lost her.

Elle went for a nap and, after insisting I didn't watch her sleep, I went downstairs to the kitchen. Cain was already making coffee. I wrapped my arms around his waist and rested my cheek on his back.

'Thank you, so, so much.'

He turned around and brought me into his arms.

'Jam reacted so fast. It was like he'd understood she was in trouble before Elle did. Where is he?'

'He's gone for a walk. He'll be okay. Just needs to clear his head. Is Elle resting?'

'Yep, and I'm going to check on her every five minutes.'

My body started to tremble, like the San Andreas was letting rip within me.

I sensed Cain by my side, but I couldn't move, as the terror took over again.

It had been so long since I'd had an episode, I thought I was ok.

I closed my eyes, tried to regulate my breathing, before the dark spiral returned.

Before I woke up on the floor wondering where I was and why I was soaking through again.

I sucked in air, released it, picturing blue. I knew my gasps were ragged. I was trying to slow them down, honest.

In, out, in out.

Sounded like in, in, in, out, out, out, like a knife cut the air at my lips.

I felt Cain's hand on my back. Steadying. I couldn't hear what he was saying.

In in, out, out.

Blink.

Not enough.

The sea's gone.

I'm still drowning.

Glance up.

Grip my eyes closed.

Found my blue.

Shudder.

In. In. Out. Out.

Metallic taste in my mouth.

Try to prise my teeth from my lip.

Panic subsiding.

In out. In out.

Pins and needles in my fingers and toes.

In.

Out.

In.

Out.

Open my eyes.

Cain.

His hand still on my back.

Up and down.

'Welcome back.' He said.

I attempt a laugh. It sounds like a snort.

He offers me a handkerchief. I hold the white cloth to my mouth and nose.

I nod, thank you.

Breathe normally.

So, so, grateful I haven't lost control of my bladder this time.

'So, I have panic attacks.' I said.

'So does my brother. I may have possibly caused a few, encouraging him to dive into the Atlantic throughout our childhood.

'Ah.'

'Ah?'

'That's why you knew to keep quiet.'

'Jase couldn't handle information overload. Not when he was trying to remember how to breathe.'

I nod. Check the hanky. Clean. The metallic taste has gone, too.

'What?'

I shake my head.

'You're blushing.'

'I just had an episode.'

'Nope – you were thinking of something after that.'

'Your eyes. They were my blue.' I whispered.

I groaned and sank down into the chair at his baffled expression.

'A therapist suggested that I look for a horizon, a life raft to cling onto. It works for sea sickness.

So, I pictured the line where sky meets sea. Except that didn't work for me this time. I couldn't find my blue. Then I saw your eyes. That's why I suddenly gripped mine shut. Yours was the blue I needed.'

He lowered himself down, until our foreheads were touching. Until I could feel the warmth from his body slow down my thinking. Until I looked up and saw my blue again. The blue of the Atlantic Ocean. He didn't blink. He just let me look. So I did. Open for three, close for three. Committing this blue to my memory.

A smile began on one side of his mouth, and I mirrored it reflexively. Then he turned up the other side of his mouth, and I repeated his actions. Before I could laugh, his lips caught mine in a kiss, as he drank me in. Until the butterfly touch became an after-shock.

Until he pulled away.

And placed his hands over mine, before I pulled away.

I couldn't have gone anywhere.

'Tell me, Luce.'

And this time I did.

Of every panic attack. Since they'd first started. When I was 14.

'I'd returned home from school and no one was home. At all. I assumed they'd be back soon. It was late. I didn't know the neighbours, didn't have any grandparents or aunts to turn to. So I waited. I did my homework. I never strayed from that doorstep. I must have fallen asleep because I woke up to being kicked. Dad walked ahead of Mum, who was carrying Elle. I was clearly in the way.

As Mum walked past, I saw the cuts near her eye, on her lip. The shadows on her cheek. Her eyes dared me to say anything and I didn't. She dragged me inside, and gave Elle to me, while she went into the kitchen with Dad. I put Elle to bed and was desperate to eat something from the kitchen, but they stayed in there all night.

'As sun broke through, Elle stirred, and I quickly washed and dressed her. Then I brought her into my room while I made sense of my uniform and brushed my hair for another school day. I brought Elle downstairs – she was chattering along, oblivious, as toddlers are – and opened the kitchen door. Mum was sat there, dressed. She held out her arms for Elle and gave my baby sister her breakfast. I was stunned, terrified of the deep blues and purples on her face. Looking back I think it had happened before, but it was the first time I'd really noticed it.

'I must have found breakfast, and then was shooed out the door to school.

'From then on, I squirreled away food into my bag, my bedroom, just in case I was left outside again.'

All the time I'd been talking, Cain's thumbs brushed the tops of my white knuckles.

I continued.

'Life got back to normal around the house, on the surface at least. I was still responsible for Elle when I was there. There were no more lock outs. But I was asked one night if I could babysit a neighbour's child and was so happy when Dad said yes. I was to hand over the money, but I'd have a few hours by myself, and started to build up a network of houses I could go to, if I was ever locked out in the rain.

'I also started to clean, for extra money, which I kept for myself. When I was 18 I had a thousand pounds to deposit into my first bank account. Which bought my first six months' rent in Manchester. You know most of the rest.'

Then I cried into his arms, my body shaking as it dealt with the guilt. This was the first time I'd told anyone what had happened.

And while I gave the last piece of myself, the shameful truth that I was an unwanted child, an unwanted adult, he soothed my hair, holding me close. When I was dry inside he'd smiled,

'Most of the rest?'

Could I? I couldn't not.

'I need to tell you about Tim. He was the first boy I liked. We met at college, and he did all my accounting coursework, because I, y'know, was a reader.' I leant further in to Cain. I clung to him.

'We lost touch at uni. Danny made sure of that. But when I graduated we bumped into each other in Manchester. He was still the same kind boy I remembered. We went for dinner and I told him I'd had a crush on him, and he'd had feelings for me. It was the best night I'd had in ... probably ever.'

Tears poured down my face, Cain held me tighter.

'We walked to the station through a short cut. We shouldn't have. Two men approached, in hooded tops. Tim stood in front of me. They only wanted him. Five stab wounds he took. I have a scar on my left palm.' I showed Cain and he kissed along the line. I was almost done.

'As Tim lay dying in my arms, I looked up to see another man. He kept his hood up as he walked away, and he could have been anyone. But I suspected it was Danny. That was the night I left Manchester for good. The night I killed Tim.'

'Don't you ever think that again, Luce. You didn't do anything apart from love. It wasn't your fault.' Cain grasped at me through his words, kissing me through my tears, his thumbs brushing my cheeks dry as we held on to each other. When I could move again, I excused myself to the bathroom and cleaned my face up.

When I returned to the lounge, Cain held out his arms for me on the sofa.

'Do you think its film o'clock?' He asked.

'You know me so well. Or, in the words of Meg Ryan, yes, yes, yes.'

'I love you so much, Lucy.'

'Cain, Cain, Cain.' I whispered, nestling in to him, all thoughts of the comedy part of a romance temporarily forgotten.

We sat in the garden later that evening, stars illuminating the sky, drinking chilled white wine. I felt lighter than I had done in forever, the responsibility of doubt absent now that I'd shared it.

Cain held his guitar on his knee, his frame arched over the body as he shared notes of his favourite artists. He saved his vocal chords for tomorrow's gig, but I hadn't realised what a talented player he was. As I told him so, Jam rounded the corner.

'Now what did you need to tell him that for, Lucy? Cain doesn't need any more confidence.'

He brought out a harmonica from his pocket and he played alongside Cain's strings.

'I wish I'd brought my recorder'. Elle whispered, seating herself next to me and taking a sip of the wine, before wrinkling her nose and returning the glass to the table.

Song intros were played, Jam brought on his percussion skills on the table, and I silently thanked Moira for forcing me to go to that conference. I hoped she'd be okay with what I had to do.

48

Cain

Lucy twitched her leg beside me, as I perched on the edge of the bed on my phone, sorting out some equipment changes for the gig this afternoon. I stroked her leg softly and she snuggled in, wrapping her arms around my waist. The sun was bright this morning, which was always a good sign on the day of an outdoor gig.

'Game day. Welcome to the madness.' I said, kissing her fully awake, and then groaning as my phone beeped several times in quick succession. 'Interviews coming up.'

'Go. Elle and I will head over later. She's very excited.'

'Work it!' I hollered, dancing around the room.

Lucy swatted me with a pillow and ran into the bathroom squealing, only for those squeals to drop a tone or two when I caught her in the shower.

Eventually we dressed and I went out to meet the press. Mindy and Sarah joined me, and whilst I was initially prickly towards her, I could see her genuine remorse at trying to fast track her experience. She had nothing but respect for Dr. Rawcliffe, and was mortified that she'd lost sign of her writing integrity. Sarah had reviewed some early drafts that Mindy had written, promoting the event, and liked her sharp writing style.

Quite a crowd had formed, although it was only early afternoon. Lucy and Elle were sharing lunch with Jam and Seb in a catering truck. I picked at my lunch, distracted by calls and chatting to the crew. Elle followed my every move, equally distracted from her salad.

'You hungry, Jam?' Lucy asked, noting the speed his food disappeared.

He grinned as he held a handful of fries above his mouth.

'Once sound check starts and tune ups, there's a different energy on stage. In fact, I think you and Elle should be front and centre'.

Elle's eyes flew between us - a hundred questions in her eyes.

'I think there's a little queue forming already.'

He shook his head, wiping sauce from his mouth with a balled up napkin.

'That's okay, security will let you in before the crowd. You want to see Cain in his element.

Elle squealed, laying rest to any further questions.

I walked over to Lucy, absently rubbing her shoulders.

'Elle, come with me for the security wristbands, yeah?' Jam said, motioning with his arm for her to follow him.

Elle was up and out of the door so fast, that Lucy almost forgot that she was now alone with me. Until I buried my face in the crook of her neck. But I wasn't capable of starting anything right now.

'Going to be a good day, Luce; my woman by my side, lots of donations for families in need and good weather.'

'Mostly true, but I won't be side stage this afternoon – I have it on good authority we need to be front and centre today?'

'That sounds a great idea. Got any requests?'

'You were working on the set list all morning.'

'Can change that in a moment for you.'

'I've never been at the front row at a Cain Adams gig.'

'Keep your eyes on him at all times.'

'That shouldn't be a problem.'

Suddenly, Sarah came into the room, digital devices all around her.

'They're ready for you now, Cain.'

'That's my cue to join the queue, and see what Elle's up to. Have fun, Sweetheart.'

49

Lucy

Elle was beside herself, up against the metal barrier, eyes following every activity on the stage, camera in hand, recording The Truckers, a country duo with major beardage, on the cusp of a breakthrough, she informed me. And they were good, full of energy and stories.

A quick transition on stage and a female solo artist appeared before them for her forty-five minute set. I was mesmerised with her gorgeous, long-blonde hair, and the contemporary lyrics of heart break – with those similes and sensory images, there was definite lesson plan material in her set for the creative writing component of a course.

Elle called over a security guard and flashed her pass. Minutes later soft drinks arrived, which I downed gratefully.

'It's okay, they'll let us out and back in when we need the toilet, Jam's had a word. In fact I'm about to go.'

'Cain will be on next!' I cried.

'Relax, Sis, I'll be back before then.' And she disappeared as fast as a rabbit down a hole. The crowd shuffled up and Elle's place was lost.

I briefly thought about going after her, but the crowd had surged forward, and began shouting. I turned to the stage and saw Jam setting up. Trademark sunnies over his eyes he waved to everyone. Seb appeared to settle into his bass, then a couple of session guitarists.

The sun lowered in the sky. I leant on the barrier, fascinated with this up close opportunity, and how very different it was from the side of the stage. Chatter around me turned to much-anticipated songs, and previous gigs. A couple of younger girls, likely mid-teens, with possibly a Mum and an Aunt behind them, squealed and shouted for Jam. He checked his earpiece, cheekily shook his ass in time to a beat, throttling the volume from the young girls.

Suddenly there was a commotion behind her, and murmurs of disapproval. I heard the shout of my sister and turned around. At around 5' 8" Elle was more than capable of making herself visible, and never more so as she wedged her way to the front of a crowd. I reached out an arm to guide her through, and a t-shirt was thrust into my hand.

'Come on, Sis, you have to wear Cain's face when he's singing to you.'

I laughed and copied Elle's style.

Suddenly the crowd roared and I heard the opening bars of the field song as Cain strutted across the stage.

He was completely home.

The crowd sang every word and he played every song for every one. The kick drum of Jam's kit perfectly amplified the energy of the show in my body.

By the third track Cain had slowed the pace, and I recognised the beach song. My heart stilled as he edged to the front of the stage, crouching down in front of me. My nerve endings had never been so shot. And I'd never wanted to be in his arms so much.

As he walked away, he pressed his palm over his heart and pointed at me. Tears sprang into my eyes; I'd never been so proud of someone else. I hoped he didn't have any post-show interviews planned.

He played the rest of the song to a chorus from the crowd, holding the microphone out to us, his hand behind his ear. When the song ended, he perched on a stool and switched guitars, retrieving a battered acoustic. I recognised the memory from his bedroom of youth, but the track was unrecognisable.

As he tuned up, he smiled at the crowd, thanked everyone for coming, and supporting the armed forces and their families. When the applause and shouts died down he continued.   'Y'all ready for some new music?' The crowd went louder. 'Here's a first airing for you, so y'know, bear with me if I miss a lyric or two.'

  He was so natural right there, thousands of people watching him.

  'I've been touched by some beautiful souls this year, men and women who've fought tougher battles than I ever will. So this one is for you.'

  The next three minutes held me transfixed. The story that unfolded transcended his previous work. And the hush that fell on the sombre crowd, who erupted as soon as he finished, told me I wasn't alone in my thinking. I turned to face the crowd, and took out my phone to record their reaction. It took a good few minutes for the applause to settle, and then the beat went up tempo again, as the band played the more familiar part of their set list.

  I whooped, yelled, swayed and sang with everyone else. Before I knew it he was playing the final song, his first number one, and my body had been through the run of emotions.

  Suddenly he leapt off the stage, and hopped onto a box by the metal barrier, just in front of me. He scooped me into his arms, his lips finding mine. I was vaguely aware of camera flashes, but his engulfed arms were all I needed. He pulled away with a wink, and then ran through the crowd high fiving and hugging as much as he could while the band continued the song for as long as it took him to then return to the stage.

With a *see ya* he was off, and people suddenly grabbed me in amazement.

If it hadn't been for Elle waving over security, or them opening the barrier for us, as the crowd dispersed, I would have remained frozen to this spot. Yet equally I needed to see Cain.

50

Cain

Where was Lucy?

That was all I could think about as I tore off stage, amid congratulations and back slaps and high fives. I stalked through the dressing room, dismayed she wasn't there, and then engaged my head; she'd be in the throng of the crowd for a while yet, until she made her way back to me. I would wait for her. I always would.

Oh, but to see her watching me for the last two hours, to hear her scream for me? To see her dance and yell with everyone? I'd never wanted to peel off stage and into the crowd so much.

The adrenaline of performance would normally see me wound up after a gig, wired until I got into my truck and drove to Lucy.

I pulled off my shirt and quickly showered, spinning around when I sensed someone open the door.

Lucy.

'I've never been so proud of anyone in my life, Cain Adams. Is this what you've been hiding on me the whole time?'

'I've no idea what you mean.' I feigned innocence, holding my hand out to her, pulling her in close to me. I pulled the Cain Adams shirt over her head as she pressed her body up against mine.

My Lucy.

51

Lucy

When we returned from Cornwall together, Cain had been on an almost immediate flight out of Heathrow to Nashville for a week, for meetings with the label and songwriters. The emptiness around me had been harsh.

I stared at the email which had lain in my inbox for the last two days. Gill had reached out to colleagues in the US and "told them about this British academic they NEED on their team". Would I hold a Skype chat with a small college about a teaching post? In Tennessee.

I had no idea how to respond. Step back or step forward? How did Skype even work?

When all was confused in my life, I needed the beach.

I didn't think I could face going back to the West Country without Cain, so I pulled up a map of London on the screen and zoomed out until the southern coast lay before me. My eyes were drawn to the west. Bournemouth, it was believed, had the heart of Percy Bysshe Shelley, buried with his wife and Frankenstein-novelist, Mary Shelley.

That was a connection I couldn't turn down, although there might not be enough time to wander around graveyards on this quick visit.

I needed the expanse of sky, to figure things out. I didn't want to be without Cain, but could I give up the career I'd worked so hard for? The US college was only in need of an assistant head of department, of which there were several already. I'd teach Victorian Literature, but there was no early chance of promotion, and a lot more competition.

But I'd be with Cain.

As the train pulled to a stop at Bournemouth I collected my rucksack and stepped into the sun. The B&B wasn't far from the station. I reached into the front pocket of my bag to check the directions on my phone, but my fingers came up empty.

A small purse, compact mirror, a mint lip balm, even an old loyalty card, all found their way to my eyes, but none of them were the reassuring hard case of my phone. And I always put it in an inside pocket of the front pocket of my bag, despite being told off by both Cain and Elle. Too many times I'd lost the device in between papers and books. I hardly used my first generation smart phone, and I suspect any handbag thief would quickly return the relic.

I pushed instincts to one side and checked all the pockets in my bag. Twice.

I hadn't unplugged it from the wall where I'd been charging it.

No matter. I'd chosen a seafront hotel, and had read the directions at home before leaving, so it didn't take me long to find the building.

After checking in I unpacked my bag and headed out for dinner. The sea air already made me hungry for fish and chips.

I strolled along the wide, sandy beach, shoes in my hand, as the tide rushed to greet me, the water cool over my toes. There'd be no opportunities to do this in Tennessee. Maybe I'd be better at a college in Florida or Georgia? No, I shook my head, the wind playing with my hair. I couldn't be in the same country as Cain and still unable to see him every day. To wrap my arms around him, feel his chest beside mine.

He'd only been gone a few days and I missed him almost like January. These last few weeks of being together had been incredible.

I took a deep breath and watched the orange sun delve towards the sea.

We were both busy, and with Cain's upcoming US touring schedule it would still be weeks, if not months at a time, before we saw each other.

And could I leave Elle? She'd be in north eastern America for four years, and then have no one on her return to the UK.

But that was years away; I couldn't wait the three days for Cain to return.

I sat on a stone wall, drying my feet in the sun, before replacing my sandals. Ahead was a row of inviting tea rooms and eateries. I watched the sun sink over the sea, over the horizon that had served me so well. Blues and teals danced before me in the sunlight, the warmth caressing my face. Families walked past me, laden with beach supplies, wrapping up their day.

I wanted Cain by my side, to fill the loneliness I now felt.

I'd email the college tomorrow and accept their Skype invitation. Then ring Elle and ask her how Skype worked.

After a full fish and chip supper, complete with a pot of tea, I waddled back to the Victorian terraced B&B, quite full and satisfied.

I picked up a book from the lounge and turned in for an early night. Then I spotted a PC for guest access. I logged on to my emails and re-read the website of the college. I might not be able to advance my career, but there were some interesting research options for possible diversification. I sent a thank you email to Gill, and an acceptance email to Tennessee, and then climbed to the top floor for my bed.

I had one of the best sleeps that I'd had in a long time.

52

Cain

'So you're saying in three months, after the summer festivals, you'll both relocate to London?' I asked, as we sat around the wooden oval table. Label execs were due in shortly, to discuss future directions; I didn't think they expected this news.

Jam and Seb nodded.

'But there's no guarantee of work in the UK.'

Seb leaned across the table. 'I know we don't have much time before the meeting, but Sarah and I both believe in adventure, music and this cocky Brit who took a hold of Nashville'.

Jam nodded along.

'Until you say you don't want us we're your band'.

'And even then, if it's two-to-one-we-are, we'll over ride you'. Jam finished, just as the door opened and Sarah walked in with the record label executives.

My phone bounced around the table; I hadn't had a chance to shove it in my pocket or turn it off. I took it off the table and put it in my shirt pocket as greetings were exchanged. Three more months ... the phone vibrated against my chest again, interrupting my thoughts. As a graph of record sales projected in front of me, I took the phone out to check the call. A number from the UK I didn't recognise. By the time the fifth ring came through, in as many minutes, I had to excuse myself and left the room.

'Hello?'

'Oh, god, Cain, thank god you answered. I can't get hold of Lucy have you heard from her at all today?'

'Elle?'

'Yes, I'm shit, sorry, it's Elle have you heard from Lucy?'

'What's happened, slow down, tell me.'

I could hear her exhale and almost stop pacing, just as my gait was picking up. I'd said goodnight to Lucy last night, and was going to ring her after the meeting; her evening.

'It's Danny. He's out and he's on his way to London he saw that stupid news report apparently and he set off to see Lucy and I can't get hold of her.'

I stopped moving, my mouth suddenly dry.

'Okay. I'm coming over. It'll be okay, Elle. Lucy will probably be caught up in work or something. Where are you?'

'I'm with Bryan. He's keeping me calm.'

'Good. You have my number, call me any time. I'm on my way to the airport.'

'Thank you, Cain, thank you.'

I rang off and stalked into the room. 'I have to go back to London. I'm going to agree with anything you need; Sarah will act on my behalf.'

Jam stood up. 'Anything you need, Man?' Seb and Sarah nodded, too.

I shook their hands and backed out of the room, scheduling a cab.

In the few hours I had to wait for the flight to Chicago then to London's Heathrow, I had Lucy on redial but there was no answer. Her department said she was working from home. Ash and Luke hadn't seen her, neither had Rich or Kelly. Why had I not yet convinced her that social media could be a good thing?

The eleven hours in the air were the longest I'd ever survived immobility.

Since January.

I couldn't lose her again. But I couldn't concentrate on anything apart from trying to reason out why no one had seen or heard from Lucy since we spoke just before I went to bed; her breakfast time.

Without fearing the worst.

Damn my overactive imagination.

53

Lucy

My train wasn't due to depart for another half an hour, so I wandered into the newsagents to browse the magazines. Nothing appealed on most of the shelves, and I was just drifting towards the books when I spotted a country music magazine. The cover was emboldened with names I recognised from the Country to Country festival in London, and from Cain's playlists.

I ordered a large Americano coffee at the station's cafe, handing over my travel mug, and then walked to the platform for my train. The decision of last night had been a good one. The college had a research group on the work of TS Eliot, an early twentieth century poet born in the US who gained British citizenship in the late 1920s. I hadn't taught modern poetry for a few years but he would be a good starting point for a discussion. I could probably indulge in a library afternoon, nestled amongst archives and manuscripts.

I didn't want to stay home in an empty house trying not to think about Cain.

When the train arrived into London's Charing Cross station I joined the Northern Line towards home to drop off my bag, and collect my phone.

I jogged upstairs, swapped my rucksack for my work bag and unplugged my phone, shoving it into the front pocket of my bag. I made a sandwich and refilled my coffee cup then headed out into the lunch time traffic of workers and students to walk the half an hour to the British Library.

My stomach rumbled just after four o'clock, and I closed up the books for the evening, my head swimming with Eliot's free verse and iambic pentameters. I gathered up my bag and entered a disarming daylight as I walked towards the busy, and direct to my home, Euston Road.

I dug my phone out of my bag and it seemed to spring to life. I was so caught up in the hundreds of messages my phone had tried to send me that I didn't pay too much attention to the man blocking my path.

'Alright, Lucy?'

I froze at the voice I hadn't heard in almost a decade, my fingers poised over my phone.

Danny.

'Missed me?'

I fought down a retch as I took in his skeletal appearance, an oversized faded black hooded top covering blue jeans that had seen better days.

How had I once been terrified by this man? How had even his memory controlled my habits, years after last seeing him? I pressed the right-sided button on the phone in my pocket.

'What do you think you want, Danny?'

'I've missed you.'

'I've been busy.'

'Got a nice little set up here in the big city.' He shuffled side to side in his well-worn trainers, laces trailing the floor.

'I've worked hard.' This was surreal. Apparently, I had to manipulate him this time. 'When did you get out?'

'Been out a while. Took care of a few things. Then hopped on the train to see my girl. Did you like the flowers?'

Oh god, he had my address? The absolute bastard. I swallowed some saliva.

'You were always good at taking care of things, Danny.'

He stepped closer and I fought hard not to step back. Every instinct told me I was on the right path. I just had to hold my nerve.

'You missed me taking care of you?'

I smiled like a Stepford woman, ignoring the fires of hell swirling around my stomach.

'You always take care of business, don't you? Like that night in Manchester. It was you, wasn't it?' All around us London carried on about her business, as afternoon paved the way for evening.

'What do you mean?'

'You know.' This was the last game of cat and mouse I ever wanted to play.

'Awful business. Your friend dying like that.'

'What made you think he was my friend?' It'll be worth it, Tim, I promised.

'You were all over him.'

'I was so scared. I just needed someone's help. I thought I was next.'

'They would never have hurt you.'

'How do you know?' I held up my palm, with the scar. 'You weren't there, in that dark alley, the smell of blood and urine and canal in your nostrils.'

'No one should have moved on you. I made sure of that.'

'If you were nearby, why didn't you rescue me?' He was thrown. I kept my head slightly lowered, subservient, my voice low. Flatter the fucker until I had him.

'I, I.' He coughed. 'Well, you were with him.'

'Tim was never as strong as you.'   Not physically. Danny's strength was always in the pharmaceutical dose he was running on.

'I saw you holding hands. You were going off with 'im.'

'I was saying goodbye. I was coming home to Salford.' Don't even dare inhale, Luce. 'To you. If you'd have helped me up...'

'I thought you were going off with him. I saw red and the boys knew what they had to do. Saved me from bangin' him out and getting banged up for longer.'

'Did you order them to kill Tim, but not me?'

'All I needed to do was nod. He had to be out of the picture.'

My head flew up. I was done.

'You need to go, Danny. We were over a long time ago.'

I checked my phone, stopped the recording, and then held it up. 'Thank you for confirming what I always knew.'

He was heading to that dark place again, and he moved to grab my phone, but I stepped back and uppercut his jaw before either of us knew what had happened. The phone went back into my pocket and he raged at me again, but my hands exploded over his ears in a self-defence move I'd learned a long time ago. He crumbled to the pavement at the din he was now experiencing in his auditory canal.

Two of London's finest police officers were running towards us. I calmly explained what had happened, gave my details to their notebook and walked away as they dealt with a furious Danny.

I turned the corner, trembling, grabbing hold of a black wrought iron railing as my right hand exploded with pain.

54

Cain

I checked in with Ash again. No, no one had heard from Lucy. He would call me if he saw her or anyone else did.

Another wave of sickness surged through me as the time difference tinged the fear I'd been holding back all day. I'd struggled concentrating for the last hour, systematically calling Elle, Ash and Lucy's boss, Moira, without trying to alarm anyone.

I had Lucy's keys in my wallet and was on my way to her flat to look for signs of where she'd gone, if not a shower and to wake up. I regretted not having packed a bag in Nashville, but I had some joggers and a hoody at Lucy's.

I unlocked her front door and bounced up the steps, hoping to see her curled up under a blanket on the sofa, a book still in her hands. A quick look in every room revealed I was over-imagining again. Then I spotted a large travel bag at the foot of her bed. Was she going somewhere? I glanced in the bag. I didn't want to snoop, but she had disappeared. Small wash bag, dirty laundry. She'd been somewhere. And had been home to return her bag. She hadn't mentioned a trip.

I had the quickest shower and climbed gratefully into clean clothes, then headed out into the late afternoon. I would walk over all of London until I found Lucy again.

I'd done it once and I'd do it again.

I stood on the pavement, swarms of workers moving around me as they headed home or for trains. I closed my eyes and thought about the path Lucy would take. She hated crowds and chose a green space as often as she could. Russell Square was nearby, one of the scenes of the bus and Underground terrorist attack, what, almost 13 years ago now. I was just a kid with a guitar on my way to Nashville for the first time in 2005. But it was a green space that Lucy would walk through between work and home.

I waited for traffic lights to turn red, as London ebbed in front of us. Then a flash of blonde hair caught my eye on the other side of the road.

Lucy. With Police Officers.

Buses and taxis came out of nowhere to block my dart across the road. When I had a gap I ran around cycle couriers towards Lucy. The officers were walking away from where she had stood, a man between them. Where'd she gone? I turned a corner and there she was, doubled over, clinging onto a fence.

'Lucy.' I wrapped her around me, felt her crush her body against my rib cage. Her heart beat was only marginally faster than mine.

'Are you okay? Are you hurt?'

'Just my hand, but some Paracetamol and a hug will sort it.' She pulled away then, realisation on her face.

'You're in Nashville?'

'Yeah, no I'm not. Long story.'

'Elle.'

'Yeah. 'Are you ...'

'I'm fine. I can't believe you're here. How long until you go back?'

I shook my head. 'Luce, I'm not going back. Well, I am in June for the country music festival. But that's weeks away. I can't believe I almost lost you again.'

'What in the world did my Sister tell you?' She asked. Then followed it up with, 'Thai food at mine to sort out what's going on?'

I nodded quickly. Hunger now bounced to the top spot for my attention, ahead of jet lag and time difference. I reached down to kiss Lucy, my hands wrapped in her hair, only the two of us in the whole world.

My phone buzzed us apart; Elle.

'I'll call Elle, you call Seb.' Lucy said. 'Do I need to call Moira?'

I nodded. 'I'll message Ash, too.' Then I quickly left a message for Seb, and messaged Jam and asked him to bring over my guitar. I wasn't going anywhere until I absolutely had to.

55

Lucy

I'd had a whole fortnight of Cain pacing my small apartment, like a child in need of attention to relieve boredom.

Or somebody terrified of my past.

He prowled my office, picking up pens and putting them down, a book, a journal.

'This is no good' he declared, leaning his rather distracting frame against my desk.

'I still have a few more hours' work here.' I said. Preparing for yesterday's Skype interview had taken me away from grading, so I was now house-bound until all my papers were competed and I had final scores for Moira. Plus, having Cain around had been wonderfully distracting, certainly the first week.

I tilted my head at the caged animal in front of me. 'If you weren't on tour, what would you be doing?'

'Nothing. I don't know. I wanna be with you.'

'We're no use to each other like this. What would you be doing in Newquay?'

He shook his head, his arms folded across his chest. Feet crossed at the ankles.

'I wouldn't be in England. I'd be in Hawaii.'

'So, go to Hawaii.' I smiled.

'But you're working.'

'Yes. Go by yourself. Do what you'd normally do.' I smiled, and whispered 'then come back to me'.

He knelt down before me. 'Always. You're my home.'

'But you're scared witless I'll wind up lost again?' He nodded solemnly. 'Did I, or did I not, successfully use twenty-first century technology to avoid bother last time? Danny is awaiting trial for his part in Tim's murder, safely ensconced in Manchester. And, he doesn't scare me anymore'. I leaned over Cain, my body stirring awake at the thought of suddenly not having him around.

Slowly I crossed the room and locked my office door. He caught me in his arms, that delicious grin spreading all the way up to his eyes.

'Got something you need to tell me?' he twinkled.

I shook my head, 'to show you.' I whispered, pulling him towards the sofa. Our shirts were off and our bodies craving each other, damp skin on damp skin.

'What do you want, Luce?' He growled.

I reached for his belt loops and pulled him on top of me.

'A goodbye to remember.'

'You just call me and I'll be back with you before you miss me.'

I nodded and he understood.

56

Cain

I stepped off the plane and fell in love with Maui all over again.

I'd been coming here for years, since I first escaped university. The island's surf and hibiscus fragrances were so familiar.

My heart felt a little lighter, at the prospect of climbing the waves, submerging my body in the cool Pacific, again and again, until bone tiredness and the inevitable beach bar called me back ashore.

But this time felt different.

It was the first time I didn't want to be alone.

Lucy had made it wonderfully clear I was to enjoy myself, sort my head out, and then come back to her, and I couldn't wait.

I would bring her back to these shores as soon as school finished, watch her unfold tired limbs on the beach, stealing through the white sand barefooted, on her way to me. She'd likely have a stack of books to enjoy, or maybe I could persuade her to join me in the water?

I hopped in the hire truck, and rolled the windows down as I drove to the beach front lodge I'd bought off the back of my first album's platinum achievement.

The salty air relaxed my muscles on the short drive.
Jam and Seb were already out here, as were a few of the crew. The four bedrooms would be occupied, and there'd be a few tents dotted around the beach.

But the first time I brought Lucy out here it would just be the two of us.

I'd never wanted school to finish so badly.

I'd have to say no to the festivals next year, as they usually took up summer.

The only thing that mattered was Lucy wrapped in my arms, possibly wearing a lethal sundress.

'Hey, man, surf is outstanding today.' Jam yelled, high-fiving me as he parked, tearing off to beautiful waves, his board relaxed under his arms, as if it was a natural extension of him.

I knew exactly how he felt.

I breathed in a lungful of the air and exhaled slowly, taking in the blue and green surroundings. I video dialled Lucy, and chuckled as she answered on the second ring.

'You have your phone in your hand, sweetheart?'

'Well, I had a rough idea of your arrival time.'

I wished I could kiss the pink on her cheeks right now.

'So, here's Maui.' I rotated a slow three sixty, holding out my arm to the ocean.

'Wow.' She declared, sitting up. 'Why have I never been to Hawaii?'

'You'll be with me next time.' I grinned.

'Oh, I wasn't angling for an invite, and I don't even swim, plus I know you boys-'

I shook my head.

'Those boys will find their own place when you visit. And I'll teach you to swim. We'll swim and surf together. I might even read one of the books you'll bring along.'

She chuckled and pushed her hair behind her ears. 'Where are you now?'

'This is the kitchen, diner, lounge'. I whipped the phone around, and then climbed the stairs.

'And this is where you'll stay.' I spun in the room, holding the camera on the king sized bed and the view.'

'I've really lost the appetite for grading papers you know.' She sighed. Then, before I could answer, added, 'Or, y'know, you've motivated me to work a little faster.'

I angled my head to one side, and then set up my phone on the desk as I stripped off my t-shirt and grabbed the hem of my shorts. 'Anything else motivating you?'

'Yep, there may well be.' She laughed.   'You go shower and surf and have a great time. I love you, Cain.'

'Love you, too, Luce. Grade quickly.' I blew her a kiss and, after a wink and a quick shake of my naked butt, I switched off the call.

I'd probably need the big drink to cool me down.

For the next ten days I slipped easily into the routine of surfing before breakfast, then calling Lucy and catching up, before more surfing and lunch. I went to the store in the afternoons to load up the truck with beers and meat and fresh veggies, checked the estate agency in London about the development of the sale, then evening surf, before calling it a night with Lucy on the phone.

Once or twice things had ended spectacularly for both of us, and I'd drifted off sleep with the waves crashing around me and the image of a pink-tinged Lucy in my mind.

I couldn't wait to show her the house I'd bought, not far from hers. And to christen all three bedrooms with her.

Maui was surrounded by friends, from the island and the mainland, and most nights I heard Jam try his luck with a girl, but nothing seemed to go further. Usually Jam grabbed a board and headed for late night waves, a portable torch strapped to his head. He hadn't yet found a woman crazy enough to follow him. Seb was out purely for the surf and post-tour unwind, and he'd be back to Sarah and their family before the end of the week.

Over dinner one night I told them of my UK-based plans. I outlined the package I had put aside for them, in case they preferred to remain in the States, and reminded them that they'd be welcome to stay in my new London apartment soon.

At almost the same time the two of them had snorted.

'Where you are Cain, so will we be.' Seb started. 'We've already bought a house in Camden.'

'So have I. Well, Newquay and London. You're not getting rid of us that easily', Jam finished.

'You're – all - moving to the UK?' I stumbled.

They nodded, raising their glasses. Now all I had to do was tell Lucy.

I woke early on the final morning, all was dark and calm outside.

After a quick rinse, I pulled on a wet suit and padded with my board to the water's edge.

The salt had worked its way through my skin and into my hair, but my nostrils still flared and my toes buried into the sand as I stood watching the waves roll and break.

Semi-content for the first time since my arrival, I didn't hear Jam until he was right beside me.

'Fresh morning.' He acknowledged, stretching out the kinks in his neck and limbs.

'Another night in, huh?' I asked.

'Yup. Still haven't found the elusive Mrs Jam, yet.'

'Don't give up, man, she's out there. When you're at the top of your game, and you have everything, love will come calling.'

'That what you and Lucy have?' Jam asked.

'Absolutely. She knows me a split second before I know myself. Never had that before.'

'She coming out here?'

'Soon. Can't be without her.'

'I'll play wherever you are, but I need my own Hawaiian hideaway, huh?'

'Absolutely.' I grinned, slapping Jam on the back and racing across the sand into the sunrise.

I paddled out on my board into what felt like the middle of the Pacific. Surrounded by blue and white, I normally thrived off the physical exhaustion, but this time I was too wired.

One more set and it was time to head home, to Lucy.

57

Lucy

Finally finished with grading the papers in front of me, I resisted calling Cain; it was still dark o'clock on Maui.

We'd spoken several times a day since he'd arrived, and he had settled into a routine of surfing, climbing and hiking. My body physically missed him more than I'd anticipated.

Except, I didn't want to aimlessly follow him around, from city to city. I needed to teach. Education was all I'd known.

Then an email notification popped up on my screen and after reading the contents several times, I immediately booked a flight to Honolulu, leaving that night from LA.

I threw some clean clothes and my wash bag into my case, selecting a few sun dresses and laying them on the top. I only had one swimsuit, and I couldn't remember the last time I wore it, not wanting to draw attention to my body. But in it went. I was no longer the woman I had been last

May, so submerged in work I hadn't realised I was holding back my future.

I booked a cab to Heathrow and rang Elle to tell her I was off to Hawaii for half-term.

As I stepped into the warm breeze, some eighteen hours and two flights later, I switched my phone on.

It pinged to life immediately.

I stroked the red velvet box in my bag, as I waited for my final, island-hopper flight to Cain, before I looked at my phone.

I tried to read the screen again and a wave of nausea hit. I dialled Jam immediately.

'Cain's been hurt.'

I asked him to repeat what had happened before taking a cab to the hospital in Honolulu.

The ride down town was thirty minutes of horror. I couldn't not have Cain in my life. It didn't matter what state he was in, I loved him more than any stupid career. I should have joined him earlier. What if he could never surf again? What if he couldn't play music anymore?

When Cain woke in the hospital bed, I was right there, my hand covering his.

I smiled and licked tears from my lips.

Disoriented, he struggled to sit up. I supported his head as I adjusted his pillows, my fingers reaching out to caress his jaw, to brush the hair from his eyes when he was settled. A shock of purple and blue framed his face.

But bruises would heal.

'Hello, Gorgeous.' I whispered.

He wrinkled his eyes in a questioning confusion. My fingers trailed the little pathways to his temple, his hairline.

'A wave brought a board onto your head.' I croaked. 'You were under water for a few minutes, and unconscious when its surfer, and Jam, found you. Yesterday. Doctors say you're made of tough stuff. So, it seems, is my heart.'

He squeezed my fingers as I continued. 'You were kept in for observation, but nothing is broken. You'll have some black and blue tattoos for a while. I was terrified when Jam called and said you'd been in a surfing accident.'

'You thought I'd taken on a shark.' He rasped, searching for a drink. I handed him the cup of water and a straw, watched him sip. 'You got here fast.'

'I was already in Honolulu. On my way to Maui.'

His smile lightened the bruises, although momentarily, as the act clearly hurt his face.

'I was on my way to see you.' He said. 'To show you my new house in London.'

'What?' Now my eyes creased in confusion.

'Umm, we're all moving to London. I'm done with America. I need to be with you every day, Luce.'

'That's a little unfortunate. I've just accepted a new job.'

'What?' He narrowed his eyes.

'In Tennessee.'

He sat up, then, pulling me to his lips; neither of us minded the wincing.

'I couldn't give up my career, or my man, it turns out.' I murmured.

I placed the little velvet box I'd been clutching all day in his hand and nodded.

He opened the box and placed the platinum and diamond ring on my trembling finger.

'Your man. Man, I love the sound of that'.

We kissed.
The end.
(For now).

Hello!

As you read, the story of Lucy and Cain doesn't end just yet. I believe in the power of love above all else, but sometimes life can send us confused messages, about who we think we are and what we think we should do. It only takes a unique moment for everything to change.

Elle and Jam will search for their own everything, alongside the continued story of Lucy and Cain, in the second of the *Everything* trilogy, **Everything And Nothing**, due for publication in the summer of 2020.

Fancy a little peak into their lives?

Everything and Nothing

Elle

~ August ~

My Sister was going to kill me.

I was already an hour late to the launch party of the new writing retreat, but there was absolutely nothing to wear in either of these wardrobes.

No party started until I was there anyway.

I shoved the clothes to one side, again, in order to find something to wear that I could go shopping for a new dress in. The outfits I brought with me were definite night time attire.

Sparkle and glitter just didn't seem right for a lunch – maybe dinner by the time I arrived – affair in the middle of nowhere, Tennessee.

I mean. The only night life here actually hooted.

I rummaged in the back of the wardrobe – even after three years living in the States I still collated my outfits in the very European device. Of course, wardrobes were obviously fitted and plentiful. I just wish I'd maybe thought a little more about my outfit choices during packing.   But, I'd expected I'd be able to shop whilst I hung out with everyone over the summer.

I was fed up to my hind teeth of cowgirl boots and gingham. I missed Boston more than I realised. Oh, for a Donna Karen cashmere.

'Come in! Will just be two seconds!' I yelled to the knock on the door, as I grabbed a black pantsuit hanging in a Bloomingdales bag and turned around.

'Jam!' I yelled, wrapping my robe around me.

'Lucy is wearing a hole out downstairs.   I thought I'd see where you were.'

'Clearly here. Go on; I'll have a champagne waiting for me.'

When he left, eventually, I leant back against the wall. That man was almost too cute for words. I'd forgotten what strong arms a drummer needed.

I quickly climbed into the black jersey I'd found, marvelling at the halter neck design. This was far too modern for my sister. She probably wouldn't miss it. I slipped on my favourite zebra print heels and did a final retouch of my hair and make-up in the mirror, satisfied that the trousers at least made the ensemble daytime-suitable, and prepared to meet Lucy's wrath.

I made my way through the vast building which
Lucy and Cain called their home – each of the
eight bedrooms had an en-suite! I couldn't wait to
own a home like this, overlooking the Cape. I'd
swap the recording studio basement for a cinema,
though, and there would be moored boats, not
parked trucks, out back.

'Auntie Elle!' My adorable two year old niece
flew into my legs and I scooped her up. She
smelled gorgeous and chocolately.

'Who's a Chocolate Monster?' I whispered
against her shrieks, as she cuddled in to me.
'Where's your Mummy and Daddy?'

'Daddy panno.' Lottie said, pointing through the
house.

'I'll carry this in for you.' I turned and Jam stood
behind me, a glass of bubbles and a bottle of beer
in front of him. I nodded and walked through the
front of the house to the barn which was the
writing retreat.

I slowed my approach as I heard Cain playing a
familiar ballad, which I believe had paid for a wing
of their home. His playing was simply beautiful.
He could turn his hand to any instrument and
make it sound incredible. My Sister was such a
lucky woman.

Lottie wriggled out of my hands and flew
towards the door. I followed, and Lucy looked up

at our arrival, a perfect smile on her face. Guests stood around the ridiculously happy couple, or sat on sofas or exquisitely carved and equally comfortable chairs. This room was the main feature in the barn. A huge dining table, big enough for ten people, took up one side of the room, but it seemed small in the vast space.

I scanned the fifty or so people gathered, as Jam handed me my glass. I focused on the heads looking in my direction, but immediately disregarded anyone in a flannel shirt. I knew half of the scruffy guests were worth a fortune based on their album sales, but I was only here for the next few weeks and then I was back to Boston to begin work at an art gallery. Suits and Champagne were my cup of tea.

The song finished and I clapped on my thigh as others cheered. Lucy made her way to me, enveloping me in a warm hug.

'Elle, you look amazing. Isn't this place wonderful?'

'My erudite Sister is lost for words?' I joked.

'I know, I know. I'm just so happy. Let me show you around.' She took my arm, and I followed her throughout the two-storey building, that had been twelve months in the making, even though I'd already had several grand tours.

'Look at the beauty in this oak', Lucy marvelled, stroking the dining table. 'There will always be food available for our guests, and I can't wait to see it laden with glowing faces and gorgeous cake.'

'You and Cain have created something beautiful. I mean, besides Lottie!'

'Do you think so?' I nodded without hesitation.

'You're already booked up until Christmas, aren't you? As an events coordinator, I know that's no mean feat.'

'Thank you so much for helping with promotion.'

'Uploading a few posts was nothing. The hygge surrounds sold themselves.'

'You really should visit Copenhagen one day, Elle, you would love it.'

'Oh, no, no, these feet are heading back to the north east next week.'

'Elle.' My Brother-in-Law scooped me into a hug, a genuine embrace that surprised me every time. Except for Cain's love, I preferred when people kept their distance. I was so glad he was in Lucy's life. His arms rested around Lucy's shoulder, and she naturally sank into his embrace, a move I'd seen hundreds of times these past few weeks, but it always tinkled with my heart. They were absolutely perfect for each other.

I finished the rest of my drink and Jam easily took the glass out of my hand. I smiled my thanks, catching a sudden scent of his cologne, a designer brand I knew very well.

Well, well, well.

The party lasted well into the evening, and had now relocated to the garden. Lottie lay sleeping across Cain and Lucy. Sarah and Seb curled up alongside each other in a love seat. Jam sat next to a brunette I recognised as one of Lucy's former students who had been studying out here. Tallie, I think she was called. A few other guests lingered around tables, listening to a two-piece band play on the stage.   Country music, of course. There was no other kind around here.

I sat on a sofa, feet tucked under me, a glass of Tennessee bourbon in my hand, my phone in the other. I'd been on social media most of the evening, sharing photos of this inspiring creative place, and arranging dates for my return in just six short days.

As the photos uploaded I sipped the honeyed liquid and glanced around. Jam was staring at me and I smiled, raising my drink. He whispered something to Tallie and made his way to my sofa.

'Mind if I sit?' He asked. I shook my head and he sank down into the cushions. Then he reached over an arm for a quilted throw and spread it across us.

'Cold?' I asked.

'Aren't you?'

'I'm from Manchester. This is a heatwave.'

He had a lovely smile. But altogether too much hair either side of his face, the brown locks easily brushing his forearms. I never dated guys with more hair than me – who needed a fight for the bathroom?

'When do you go back to Boston?'

'Sunday. I promised Lucy I'd be here for the launch, but I have a new job, and civilisation, to return to.'

'You don't think we're civilised?'

'Well, of course, you're travelled. But Nashville could do with a few non-boot related stores.'

His laugh vibrated the cushion we sat on and I found myself scrutinising him. He looked different in this light. And my dates rarely filled out their suits quite so well as a musician filled out a vest.

Cain and Lucy disappeared with a still-sleeping Lottie, and one by one the guests began to drift away.

'What are you up to now that Cain's on a touring hiatus?' I asked Jam.

'In the fall I'm heading off to Thailand again.'

'You have a girl down there?' I sing-songed.

He shook his head. 'Several.'

'Pardon?'

'I teach music in a school when I visit. Your face, Elle.'

'For that you can buy me another free drink.' I held out my empty glass. After a brief hesitation he stood and mock bowed, heading to the kitchen.

I played with the pretty pink and green floral patchwork blanket across my lap. I didn't have to check the label to know this was home made. Cain's Mum had recently taken to quilting, and I suspected it was one of her projects. It was beautiful. Their guest house in West Cornwall was filled with country American interior designs, no doubt reflecting her pride in her family. I enjoyed chatting with Nancy, it was a shame they couldn't have stayed for the launch. But they'd be back once the summer season quietened down.

Jam returned with my drink, and with a huge bag of crisps; chips would always belong with fish on a plate.

'Hmm, good idea.' I delved into the packet for a handful, settling further into the sofa.

'What's your new job?' He asked.

'I, Elle Rawcliffe, will be the PR Executive for the cutest art gallery, promoting events for wealthy clients.'

'Wow. Congratulations. That sounds like a big deal.'

'It is; I fought hard for this position, interning every vacation until they realised how essential I was.' Suddenly his fingers reached for a strand of hair and tucked it behind my ear.

'I miss your pink hair.'

'It was pretty vulgar, though.'

'It was pretty.'

'As soon as I dyed my hair black I was taken more seriously. I intend to own my own gallery before I'm twenty-five.'

'That's ... ambitious.'

'The world doesn't hang around.'

He shook his head.

I reached for his chin with my face, turned him to me, and brought our lips together. For a brief moment I fell into his scent. Then he pulled away. A slight smirk on his face.

'No, Elle. This isn't right.'

'What?'

'You're leaving soon. So am I.'

'Exactly. Think of the possibilities.'

'Elle.'

'Jam.' I reached around for his neck, intending to pull him the short distance to me.

But he was resolute.

I sat up then.

Was I being rejected?

As Jam stood, his hands in his pockets, head hung low, I realised I was.

I hadn't ever been rejected by a man.

He certainly wasn't worth my attention.

I stood up and strolled into the house, sweeping my hair over my shoulder, knowing my purposeful stride always had an effect on anyone watching.

When I glanced over my shoulder, he was in conversation with the singer from tonight's act.

I couldn't believe it.

For the next few days I dived into being fun Auntie Elle, giving Lucy and Cain some much needed time together, before their new venture took on the life of its own that it was destined to do.

On the last night we were seated around the modest six seater table in their own dining room, just wrapping up the key lime pie.

'I can't believe you made that, Sis. You only ever operated a microwave.'

She smiled and stroked her daughter's hair.

'I'd still rather read than cook, but this is my absolute favourite American dessert, so I made sure I can make it well. For when the cravings strike again.'

'Be careful how you throw that word around.' I began. Then caught their expression.

'Oh my absolute world. You're pregnant again?'

Lucy nodded, patting her stomach. 'We just found out. The baby's due early spring.'

I rushed over to hug my darling Sister and Cain, congratulating them.

The next time I visited I'd be an Aunt twice over. I didn't look anywhere near old enough.

Cain drove me to the airport the next morning, for my ridiculous o'clock flight. We chatted about the lack of glitz in Tennessee, and he just laughed. Then I casually asked about Jam.

'Oh, he flew out to Indonesia for a few weeks, ahead of his Thai trip.'

'Oh.' To my recollection I had never caused a man to fly half way around the world to avoid me; his loss.

2

Jam

Elle had changed considerably in the years that she'd been studying.

The effervescent pink-haired screwball woman had morphed into a corporate, dynamite, raven-haired woman I would do well to avoid.

We had nothing in common. We were almost related by marriage, actually, such was my friendship and adoration for the big brother that had taken me under his wing, offered me the opportunity to do the only thing that ever mattered to me – drum. All across the States and Europe.

I loved Lucy like a Sister, so it was a safe bet that I should stay away from her actual Sister.

After the retreat's party, when we'd spent the evening under the blanket, beneath the stars, I thought I'd glimpsed a sense of the woman she could have been in my arms.

She needed more, I knew that. She had her mark to make, in a world I had no desire to be part of. The only time I'd ever worn a suit was to Cain and Lucy's wedding, which had been at his parents' guest house in Cornwall, overlooking the Atlantic Ocean, surrounded by love.

The place where I'd last seen Elle, and the scene of so many memories she'd evoked in me, since I'd had to pull her cramped body from the ocean when she had been about to embark on her US adventures. I associated her wild personality with the wild Atlantic, and that was my fault. She was no more a product of her environment than I was.

So I'd booked a trip to Bali to catch up with friends a few weeks earlier than planned, before I flew to south Thailand.

Elle didn't need me in her life.

I dove back into the Indian ocean as the sun set.

A few days battered by the surf ought to convince me of that.

To be continued... Summer 2020

It's me again...hello!

If you'd like to keep up to date with the happy ever afters of Jam and Elle, Lucy and Cain, I'm often found on the Twitters (when I'm not scribbling away in between gig reviews and the school run), and love to connect with my readers, so come and say hello: **@dgtlwriter**

I also blog at **size15stylist.co.uk**, about books, music and film...all of my favourite stories in once place!

Natter soon.

Printed in Great Britain
by Amazon